THE LAND DARKENED

Cannibal Country - Book 1

TONY URBAN
DREW STRICKLAND

PACKANACK
publishing

"Ye who hate the good, and love the evil; who pluck off their skin from them, and their flesh from off their bones;

Who also eat the flesh of my people, and flay their skin off them; and they break their bones, and chop them in pieces, as for the pot, and as flesh within the caldron."

— MICAH 3:2-3

CHAPTER ONE

I WAS THIRTEEN YEARS OLD WHEN THE WORLD ENDED...

"Now what the hell am I supposed to write?" Wyatt stared down at the moleskin journal, hoping more words would come. It was easy for him to make up stories. Gory thrillers about superheroes or zombies. Heroic tales where brave people saved the world. But that was fiction.

Reality was hard. Reality was pain and loss and hunger and hopelessness. So much had happened in the last five years, since the world changed forever, but what made his story worth writing about? Wyatt struggled to find any point.

His previous life, that of a teenager without a care in the world, seemed insignificant and naïve at best. Selfish at worst. Back then his biggest concern was hanging out with his buddies and trying to pick the lock to his parent's liquor cabinet with a safety pin. Or teaming up with Cliff Barbin to try to cajole the Ewing Twins into going to the quarry for make-out sessions.

Wyatt smiled at the thought. Five years wasn't that long in theory, but these five years were an entire lifetime that made everything that had come before seem like a fairy tale. Ever since he'd watched the news reports of bombs exploding and people dying by the millions in the cities, his old life had ceased to matter.

He pinched the pen hard between his fingers and stared at the almost blank page. Where should he even start? His point of view of the United States crumbling from Middle of Nowhere, Maine was hilariously detached from the reality, the terror, that the people who'd actually lived through it, or died in it, must have experienced. For him, the beginning of the apocalypse consisted of watching his mother go half-crazy with worry over her husband, Wyatt's father, missing in Boston. And that was a story he didn't want to relive.

"Screw it." He placed the pen inside the journal and closed it. The sound of the pages smacking together was like a firecracker in this silent world. He flinched at the noise, then smirked, embarrassed over being easily startled.

He shifted his weight and stretched his legs which had gone half-numb from straddling the tree branch for the last two hours. It gave a pained groan that reminded him of an old man trying to stand after sitting for too long. For a moment he wondered if the branch might snap. A few years ago he'd have believed the towering oak would stand a century or more. But now it was as brittle and bare as a skeleton and he knew it was as dead as almost everything else.

He'd been nervous, coming here and climbing the tree alone. But Trooper had seen deer tracks in the area a few weeks earlier and even the slightest chance of harvesting a deer was worth the risk. As he settled back into position, the tree gave another sound of protest and he took a long look at the ground twenty feet below. He didn't think the fall would kill him, not outright anyway, but it could lead to broken bones, if not worse.

That's just what we need, Wyatt thought. Two cripples in the family. Part of him hated that word. Cripple. But Seth threw it around often enough that it had lost most of its meaning.

While he waited to see whether he would fall, there came another sound, but this one from ground level. Wyatt looked past his own legs to the dirt forest floor underneath him. When he saw it, his breath caught in his throat.

A buck pushed its way through a long-dead hedge of laurel. Once free of it, the deer gave a full-body shake that sent up a puff of dust or dander, Wyatt couldn't be sure which. Maybe both. The exertion almost caused the animal to tumble over and its long legs teetered side to side before it stabilized itself.

The buck was anything but a prime specimen, however it was the first deer Wyatt had seen in going on a year. Its fur was patchy and missing in places, revealing gray flesh. One antler was snapped off, but the other was tall and thick - seven points, Wyatt counted - and he imagined it might have been a trophy in its day.

But Wyatt wasn't after a trophy. He was after food. It had been a full season since he'd eaten meat that wasn't from a can. And that long-ago meal was a groundhog that Trooper had shot so full of shotgun lead that Wyatt spent most of the dinner spitting out pellets and trying to avoid breaking a tooth. But even that glorified rat tasted divine against his tongue.

Venison... Damn... Just the thought had his mouth-watering.

He shrugged the rifle strap free and raised the barrel. As he placed the butt of the gun against his shoulder and peered through the scope, he kept his breaths long and calm. Just like Trooper had taught him. Breathe in. And out. In and out. Shoot on the exhale.

Wyatt saw it all happening through the sights like they'd transformed into a miniature, prescient TV. He shot the buck, dropping it in one clean shot. Then he descended the oak and dropped to the hard Earth. He considered gutting it right there, but he knew he couldn't let anything go to waste. Besides, it wasn't heavy at all - no more than seventy pounds. He could handle that. He slung the deer over his shoulders, its limp neck allowing the head to loll to and fro, bouncing against his back. And when he brought his kill home, his family feasted.

It would be amazing.

Wyatt curled his finger around the cold trigger of the Marlin rifle and squeezed. One pound. Two.

His heart thudded in his chest, the sound like thunder in his ears.

Three pounds of pull. Over half way there.

The buck's head snapped sideways, its dull eyes coming alert and aware. It stood, poised to flee, and Wyatt was sure it had smelled him.

And then he saw the second deer. This one had no antlers and was skinny and fat at the same time. Wyatt realized the doe was pregnant.

His finger froze on the trigger, unsure how to handle this development. The rational part of his brain knew the choice was easy. Shoot the buck. Bring home food. Be a hero. But as he stared at the pendulous midsection of the doe, he knew he couldn't do that because somehow, in a world where everything was already dead or most of the way there, these two deer had managed to create life.

What gave him the right to destroy that?

Hands trembling, he lowered the barrel of the rifle. "Get the hell out of here!"

The buck stared up at him with startled black eyes, as if it understood how close it had come to dying. And then both animals disappeared into the brittle brush.

"Don't come back because, if Trooper's here the next time instead of me, you won't be as lucky." Wyatt sighed and his stomach responded with a resentful, or pissed off, rumble. "And you shut up," he said.

He was done there.

CHAPTER TWO

BARBARA'S STOMACH MADE NO GROWLING NOISES. THERE'D been days when the food had grown truly scarce, about three years into this mess, that it seemed like her stomach talked more than she did. But it didn't anymore. She'd noticed that some time ago. It had gone silent as if it had resigned itself to perpetual hunger and want and had grown accustomed to its hollow, empty fate.

How long has it been since we had a good meal, she wondered? Good meal? Well, that was a bit of a stretch. Any meal was more truthful. On the fleeting occasions where she allowed herself to think about what used to make a good meal - like Thanksgiving with Turkey and so many sides it filled a dining room table that could seat twelve - she struggled to believe that such opulence, such gluttony, was ever a real thing. That life seemed as fanciful as the stories she'd read when she was even younger than her boys.

It used to be so easy. Want a hamburger? Steak? Even a whole damned chicken? You could get anything you desired by driving five minutes. Hell, you could order food via an app on your cell phone and have it brought to your house and didn't even have to tip the driver unless you were feeling generous. What would she give someone for real food now? What wouldn't she give, might be a better question. She didn't want to allow herself to consider how far she'd go for a meal that didn't consist of long-expired vegetables that carried the metallic flavor of the can that housed them.

She appreciated that Wyatt still went hunting every day even though she couldn't remember the last time he'd brought anything home. It wasn't his fault. The wildlife died off about the same time as the plants. It wasn't just the humans that saw their all you can eat buffets come to an end.

Now and then Trooper would show up with a squirrel or rabbit that had somehow managed to stay alive. Once he even brought them a rat. And when she saw him carrying that disgusting, disease-carrying creature, swinging it by its limp tail, she told herself she wouldn't dare take so much as a nibble. But she did, of course. The days of picking and choosing what you ate were long gone. There was a reason you never even saw dogs or cats anymore.

But Wyatt didn't even bring them rats. He brought nothing but disappointment day after day. She didn't blame him - at least that's what she told herself. But each day when he emerged from the gray dusk carrying nothing but an unused rifle, she couldn't help but feel let down and she loathed herself for that.

Wyatt was a good kid, even if he wasn't exactly a kid anymore. He'd grown up quick and done a fair job of filling the vacancy left in the house when his father never came home from that job interview down in Boston. He might not be a provider, but he was loyal and willing to do whatever she asked of him.

So, when she saw him emerging from the dusty, gunmetal gloom, empty-handed as usual, she put on her best fake happy face and unlocked the front door. She opened it and watched him come to her.

"I'm sor--"

She held up her hand, shushing him before he could finish. "Not another word about it. You try and that's all I can ask. And there's always next time." She studied his face, relieved to see he believed the lie.

"Thanks, Mom. I just wish it was easier, you know?"

She smiled, brushing his dark hair out of his eyes. I need to give him a haircut, she thought. He was starting to look like one of those boy band kids all the girls used to swoon over. And it wasn't just the hair either. He was handsome, or damn close.

"We were never promised easy. So we just have to muddle through and try to make things better."

"Or we could get it over with and die already."

Barbara slapped his mouth, her false smile replaced by pinched lips from which deep wrinkles trailed out like roads on a map. Smokers lines, her mother had always called them, usually when trying to get her to give up the nasty habit. But she hadn't.

"Listen to me, Wyatt. You can be sad. You can be depressed. You can be angry. But you can't quit. I won't stand for that. Do you understand me?"

Wyatt rubbed his mouth where her wedding band had left behind a pink welt and nodded. His eyes welled with tears. "I'm sorry, Mom."

"I'm sorry, too," she said and wrapped her arms around him. She couldn't recall more than a handful of times she'd spanked or slapped her boys when they were growing up, but every part of living was different now. And if it took a little smack to get him to stop feeling sorry for himself, she'd do it. It was her job to hold everyone together.

"Come. I've got a present for you." She turned and moved into the house.

"A present?"

"God Wyatt, I know they're not going to award me one of those World's Best Mom trophies but I didn't forget your birthday." She passed him a small bottle of tequila - the miniature type they overcharged for in hotels. She'd come across it a few months ago when they were scavenging houses in Rosemont. At the time she was tempted to drink it straight down but she wouldn't allow herself the pleasure. Besides, she preferred gin. She'd kept it as a backup, in case her own stash ran too low but it hadn't and now she could pass it on.

"Tequila?" Wyatt asked. "My mom's giving me tequila?" He glanced around the otherwise empty room as if expecting Allen Funt to pop out and announce that he was on Candid Camera. Not that her son would know who Allen Funt was.

"You're a man now, even if I'm loathed to admit it. And a man is entitled to a drink on his birthday."

Wyatt laughed. It was deep and rhythmic and reminded her of her husband. "Thank you. I guess."

"That's not all." She pulled a small strip of beef jerky from her pocket and handed it to him. She'd found that foraging too. Actually, five times as much, but this was all that remained. A dappled spattering of mold covered it, but she scraped that off and didn't see any point in sharing that nugget of information now.

"No, Mom. I can't. I don't deserve this." His expression was almost pained, and she wondered if she was too hard on him, put too much pressure on him.

"You do. And if you don't eat it this very moment, I'll throw it in the yard for the bugs."

Wyatt shook his head and bit a piece off. "You know you're kind of manipulative, right?"

"I'm your mother. That's what we do." She gave him a kiss on the cheek, the opposite side of where's she's slapped him moments earlier. "Happy birthday, Wyatt."

Hinges squeaked and both of them turned to watch as Seth rolled his wheelchair through the hallway and into the room. When he stopped, he rubbed his barely open eyes and spoke through a yawn. "Happy birthday, brother."

"Thanks. Were you hard at work on your afternoon nap?"

"Sure was. Rested up and ready to run a marathon."

"That's messed up," Wyatt said.

"Only if someone else says it. If I say it, it's funny."

"No one thinks you're funny, Seth. They only laugh at your jokes because you're handicapped."

"Wyatt!" Barb slapped him again, but playfully this time, and on the shoulder.

"It's okay, mom. I know I'm handicapped. But it could be worse, I could have the IQ of a troglodyte like Wyatt."

Wyatt wrapped his arm around Seth's neck and gave him a hard noogie that turned his straw-yellow hair into something resembling a bird's nest. Seth responded by rapping Wyatt in the groin with his fist. Both laughed through their shared pain.

Watching them play fight-filled Barb's heart with hope, with love. She needed that because both were in short supply these days. So even as they fought and cursed, she was content to let boys be boys until they tired themselves out.

When that happened, Seth pointed to the rifle which Wyatt had leaned beside the door. "You're really running this 'no meat Monday' thing into the ground."

Barbara knew he didn't mean it to bring Wyatt down, but Wyatt took everything to heart and his smile vanished. "Sorry."

"You better be sorry. I'd kick your ass if my legs worked." Seth wore a Cheshire cat grin as he shifted his torso as if trying to make his immobilized legs move and his perverse sense of humor worked because Wyatt barked out a laugh.

"Hunting might have been a bust, but mom gave me this."

Wyatt pulled the remainder of the jerky from his pocket. Seth's emerald eyes widened at the sight.

"No shit? The old lady's been holding out on us?" Seth swiveled his chair in her direction.

"It's for his birthday, Seth."

"Well mine's in three months and my wish is for a whole damned cow." Seth grabbed the jerky and stuffed it in his mouth. He closed his eyes and chewed, savoring the small piece of dried beef.

Barb shook her head. "Alright, Seth. You go ahead and wish in one hand and shit in the other and see which one fills up first."

Seth laughed so hard he choked on the jerky which made Wyatt and Barbara almost convulse. And she realized their lives weren't so bad after all.

CHAPTER THREE

Wyatt slipped out the front door, careful not to make any noise. Even if his mother told him he was a man, she remained reluctant for him to go out at night. Maybe it was just being a typical, overprotective mother. Or maybe it was the fact that the nights now were so black. It wasn't just the lack of streetlights. It was the lack of all light.

The days were bad, with their unrelentingly dreary, lead-colored skies, but at least you could see what was in front of your face. No chance of that at night unless you had a flashlight or lantern. Wyatt carried the latter.

He flicked on his lamp once off the porch and swung the beam in both directions. All clear. He aimed it at the front door of a brick ranch house which was two houses up and across the street from his own. A baseball bat propped open the door, and the sight never failed to make Wyatt grin. It was as if the inhabitant was not only inviting would-be intruders inside but also supplying them with a weapon. As well as Wyatt knew that home's owner, it wouldn't have shocked him if both were true.

He crossed the street and continued to the house, setting the bat aside as he opened the door.

"Trooper? You awake?"

The only response that came was a low, phlegmy rumble of a snore. That answered his question. Wyatt knew better than to go inside and startle him. Doing so wouldn't just piss off the man who had become a stand-in father figure, but was also apt to get him shot. To avoid both, Wyatt knocked on the flimsy metal storm door, sending hollow thunderclaps throughout the surrounding area.

"Trooper!" Wyatt was louder now, having given up on subtlety.

The snoring came to a quick, choking halt. "That you, Wyatt?"

Wyatt heard a hard, heavy sound of Trooper setting his pistol on the ceramic tabletop inside the kitchen.

"Yeah, it's me."

Inside, the legs of a chair scrabbled across the tile floor, noise then followed by footsteps. As they neared the door, the shape of the man came into view.

"Wyatt Morrill. How was your birthday, son?"

Wyatt considered the query. Aside from the bad start with the deer, it wasn't too awful. "I guess I can't complain."

"That's good. Cause I ain't up for listening if you wanted too."

The light hit Trooper's weathered face, which despite the illumination was nearly as black as the night. Deep crevices criss crossed his sable skin and the only bright spots were his white hair, teeth, and eyes. Those eyes narrowed, and the man raised his hand and pushed the lantern to the side.

"Get that outta my face. Now I won't be able to see right for half an hour you little basta'd."

Trooper could be a cantankerous, old fart and his Downeast accent got even thicker when he'd been drinking or was angry and it never failed to make Wyatt smile. "Sorry."

"Ayah. You sure are." He glanced back into the house. "Hold up a second, I got something for ya."

"You already gave me that journal."

"Well, I gotcha something else."

Wyatt watched Trooper disappear into the house, moving out of range of the lamp. With the man gone, Wyatt took the chance to be nosy and light up the dwelling. Trooper had been a constant in his life since even before the bombs went off, but the man had never allowed him inside his home.

What he saw was clutter. He wouldn't call Trooper a major league hoarder, but he was clearly Double A. Stacks of canned goods five feet high lined two of the walls. Rifles, shotguns, and knives covered the couch. What looked like a hundred-gallon jugs of water-filled a corner. And there must have been twenty cases of toilet paper.

Wyatt wondered if the man had always been this well-prepared or if such preparations and precautions had come as an aftereffect of the attacks. He only recalled snippets about Trooper from before. In addition to being his neighbor, the man was a retired state police officer. One who often chased Wyatt and the other neighborhood kids off his lawn.

Trooper re-emerged from the recesses of the house and Wyatt spun away the light. Neither of them acknowledged the snooping.

The old man held two cans of beer in one hand. "Thought this was appropriate considering the occasion."

He passed one to Wyatt, who accepted even though it shocked him. The thought of drinking the warm beer made him feel a little sick - or maybe that was the lingering buzz of the tequila - but he didn't want to be rude so he popped the top. Trooper did the same and then raised his own beverage for a toast.

"To my friend, Wyatt. Happy birthday."

Wyatt touched his can to Trooper's. "You know I'm underage, right? I feel like this might be a sting."

Trooper laughed, a joyful but raspy and unhealthy sound that didn't put Wyatt in a celebratory mood. "I'm retired going on twenty years. Even if I wasn't, I ain't never busted a boy for something as petty as a beer, long as he wasn't driving aft'ah."

Trooper took a long drink, so long Wyatt suspected his can was empty, or damn close, by the time he finished. Wyatt didn't want to be rude and took a sip of his own. It tasted like lukewarm piss and he fought not to grimace.

"I think everyone's trying to get me drunk," Wyatt said.

"What's that?"

"My mom, she gave me some tequila earlier."

Trooper limped toward a wicker chair on the porch then half-sat, half-fell into it. Wyatt heard joints pop and snap like someone stepping on rice cereal.

"Barbara squirreled away some tequila? She's crafty, that one. Keeping secrets from me." He flashed a wink, then tipped his square chin toward Wyatt's beer. "Don't got to ration that. I got plenty."

"How's that even possible? I'd have guessed you drank every beer from here to Bar Harbor by now." Wyatt flopped on the cushion in the chair across from his old friend. A small puff of dust flew in the air as he did. "Do you have a microbrewery in your basement or something?"

"I got my sources." Trooper chuckled. "You go hunting today? Have any luck at that spot I tipped you too?"

Wyatt considered lying outright, then thought better of it. Maybe it was Trooper's training as a cop, but Wyatt couldn't recall even a single time of getting one past him. But maybe half a lie would work. "I saw a buck. But he made me before I could get off a shot."

He could feel Trooper examining him. And he knew Trooper had seen through the untruth.

"Well, betta luck next time. I suppose."

"Yeah." Wyatt knew there wouldn't be a next time. After he'd descended the tree, he emptied his bladder onto the tree and surrounding brush, hoping the scent would send the buck and doe somewhere else. Somewhere away from people wanting to kill and eat them. Even though he believed, he knew, sparing them was the right thing to do, it also made him feel ashamed, and he needed to change the subject.

"I started writing in that journal you gave me." He didn't say it was only seven words.

Trooper's eyes lit up at the mention of the gift he'd given Wyatt three days earlier. "Did ya? That's good. How did that go?"

"Well, that didn't go so great either. I couldn't decide what to write about. Me not getting any food again, or that today was my birthday, and I spent most of it up a tree. Both seemed boring."

Trooper shook his head. "Journaling isn't just about what's happening outside." He waved his hand in the air like he was conducting an invisible orchestra. "The sky was gray. The trees were bare. My belly was empty. Ain't no one gives a happy crappy about any of that. It's all superficial. It don't matter a none of it." He poked Wyatt in the chest with a finger gone askew from arthritis. "Journaling's about what's happening in here."

Wyatt laughed. "Damn, Trooper, you're turning my world upside down tonight. You're the toughest guy I've ever known. You're not supposed to be this deep."

Trooper leaned forward in his chair, crinkling the empty beer can between his hands as he spoke. "Why? You think a strong man's not allowed to have feelings? I'd expect that kind of attitude from Seth, but not you. Thought you were betta than that."

Wyatt could see something akin to confused hurt in the man's muddy brown eyes and wasn't sure how to react. As he struggled to find the words to free him from the hole he'd dug, he wished he'd have stayed home. "I don't know. It's just... You've kil--" He stopped himself. No need to bring that up. "You always do what needs done. Even when it's hard. And it never seemed like it bothered you."

"I've done things to keep people safe. Don't mean it's easy." Trooper set the crushed can on a small table beside him. "When it gets easy, when you stop feeling, that's when it becomes a problem."

Trooper fell silent, staring into the distance. Wyatt sat with him for a while, not minding the quiet. He asked no more questions because he wasn't sure if he could handle the answers.

"If you ain't gonna drink that beer hand it ova."

Wyatt did.

CHAPTER FOUR

A CRACKING NOISE WOKE SETH FROM WHAT HAD BEEN AN especially deep and restful sleep. Earlier Wyatt had given him half a shot of tequila and while it wasn't the first alcohol he'd consumed in his fifteen years on the planet, he was still a featherweight As he sat upright in bed, his head felt on the verge of floating off his body and he wasn't sure there'd even been a noise at all until there came another.

It was definitely a crack, not a creak. A creak would mean someone was being careful. Maybe Wyatt creeping to the bathroom and trying not to wake the others. A crack, especially one this loud, not only meant someone else was around, but that they didn't give a shit if you knew. Hell, maybe they even wanted you to know.

Seth grabbed hold of his limp legs and pushed them over the side of the bed before reaching for his wheelchair and rolling it his way. With a grunt he lifted himself up and over, plopping down into the chair, a move that resulted in a second grunt. After he'd lost use of his legs, that move had taken him half a year to master and he thought, with a pang of sadness, that it now seemed as normal as taking a breath.

Once in his chair, he rotated it toward the bedroom door. Not that he could see it. It was beyond black and as he wheeled himself into the hallway, he had no idea what, or who, might lie ahead.

He hesitated, listening so carefully he would have heard a mosquito fart.

There was nothing. Maybe it was just the after-effects of a dream, coupled with the buzz from the booze. After all, if there'd actually been a crack, his mother and Wyatt would already be up and out of their rooms as they could move much quicker.

Even though he was well on his way to convincing himself this was a made-up danger, he'd gone to the trouble of getting into the chair and figured he may as well give the house a once over.

The front door was closed and the dead bolt still in place, no one had kicked it in. No broken glass littered the hardwood floor. He wheeled himself to the bay window that looked into the yard and saw more black and nothing.

"Note to self. Don't tell Wyatt about this or he'll make you stay sober for the rest of your life." Seth chuckled, an embarrassed, soft sound that barely slipped free of his lips.

A cool breeze caressed the back of his neck and he shivered. It reminded him of the cold hand of an old person suffering from poor circulation. That visual made him shiver again. He didn't fear ghosts - there was already so much to fear, who had the time for spirits - but at this hour, in this pitch blackness, the possibility was enough to raise goosebumps on his arms.

Time to return to bed and slip under the covers where he could warm up. Why did it have to get cold so damn fast now? It was only half way through August, which meant his near future held a good seven months of frigid temperatures. He wondered if he could spend the entire coming winter in bed and under blankets and figured it was worth a shot.

Another wisp of wind fluttered his hair. That's when it registered with Seth that there shouldn't be a breeze inside the house.

He slowly rotated his chair, not wanting to know what waited behind him. Like he was still a little kid and could make any poten-tial bad shit go away by not looking. By not seeing. Because, if your eyes didn't face the reality of the situation, you could live happily in a world of denial.

At least that was the logic back then. Now he knew better. Bad shit happened whether you saw it or not. But he could still hope it was nothing.

By the time Seth completed his 180-degree turn, that hope vanished. The kitchen door stood wide open. And beyond that he could see obsidian shadows skirting through the dark.

Those shadows were people.

Seth pumped his arms so fast he felt the muscles burn almost immediately as he wheeled himself through the living room and down the hallway which led to his mother and brother's rooms. As he faced the empty corridor, he didn't want to again look to the kitchen door, but he needed to. He needed to know if whoever he'd seen had abandoned the outdoors for his home. So he looked. And saw a man.

Then the man saw him.

They stared at each other for what seemed like an hour but was a second if that.

The man stepped forward and raised his hand. He was holding something that, by its size and the way the man gripped it, could only be a gun.

Seth screamed. "Wyatt!"

CHAPTER FIVE

WYATT HAD BEEN WHAT HIS FATHER CALLED "A GOOD SLEEPER" for most of his life. It was one of many traits he inherited from his mother. To the both of them, insomnia may as well have been an exotic, faraway foreign nation. It mattered not whether they'd downed caffeine-laden sodas or coffee or been wide awake ten minutes earlier. As soon as their heads hit the pillow, it was lights out and waking them was an almost Herculean task.

It changed a little after Seth ended up in the chair. As the older brother, Wyatt felt the need to be alert, to rush to Seth's aide if he fell getting into his chair or transferring onto the toilet. That happened a lot the first few months, but in time, Seth got stronger and adapted to the reality of his new life and Wyatt felt less and less need to be on call all hours of the day and night. And once that happened, he was back to being Rip Van Winkle's understudy.

It had been several years since Seth required his help, but a part of his brain remained tuned in 24/7 to the sound of his brother's pleading cries. It was the only thing that could bring him around in an instant. And when he heard Seth screaming his name, he was awake and on his feet before his eyes had fully opened.

"Wyatt!" Seth screamed again.

His startled body moved in slow motion as he stumbled toward his bedroom door. "I'm coming."

He fumbled with the knob, spinning it all the way on the second attempt and opening the door. Wyatt was wide awake now. The tone of Seth's plea and his own adrenaline ended that. That tone wasn't the sound of his brother slipping off the commode and cracking his face against the tub. It wasn't the sound of him shitting his bed because he couldn't move quick enough and not wanting their mother to find out. Wyatt knew those tones. This was different.

This was terror.

The cool air assaulted his bare chest when he stepped into the hallway and he fought back a full-body shiver. He dragged his fingertips across the wall as he moved through the dark, an old habit he'd picked up and never let go. He'd expected the blind trek to continue to the other side of the house, to Seth's room, but his journey came to a fast halt once the kitchen came into shadowy view.

Seth rocked forward and back in his chair, playing a sort of tug-of-war with a man that loomed in front of him. Except, it wasn't really tug-of-war. Seth had latched onto the man's wrist and, as they struggled, Wyatt realized the man was clutching the carving knife that usually held residence in the kitchen's butcher block.

"Wha--" Wyatt didn't even get the word out.

"Help me, damn it!" Seth's muscles strained as he tried to tilt the sharp end of the knife away from himself.

Still half in shock, Wyatt finally reacted. He'd never been in a fight that escalated beyond pushing and shoving and he wasn't sure what to do. Grabbing a weapon of his own didn't even cross his mind. Instead, he drove himself into the man's side in a move that made him think about tackling the quarterback during his one year of junior high football. Their two skinny bodies collided, and they tumbled to the ground in a flailing heap.

Wyatt scrambled to get on top, to get leverage over the man who stank of sweat and smoke, but the man was faster or more desperate or both and he had his hands around Wyatt's throat before he could react. His fingers dug into the flesh and Wyatt felt a sharp burst of pain and hot, oozing wetness as the man's ragged fingernails pierced his skin.

The man's thumbs found their way to Wyatt's windpipe and pushed inward with suffocating force. Wyatt swung his arms, slapping at the man's face and feeling his coarse beard. He grabbed onto that hair and yanked.

The man squawked a shocked "Yow!" but didn't let up on the pressure that was keeping him from taking a breath.

Then the pressure disappeared. The man's head snapped backward and a spray of blood that looked black in the darkness arced through the air. Wyatt looked to see what happened and found Seth clutching the meat tenderizer.

He had a moment to wonder why they still had that utensil, considering there was never any meat to tenderize when the man recovered and threw a fist toward Seth, knocking him backward and sideways in his chair. With the intruder's attention diverted, Wyatt hammered a punch into what he hoped was the man's kidney.

It worked, and the intruder stumbled to the floor. Wyatt dove onto him and, as their bodies pressed together, he could feel the almost feverish heat of the man's flesh against his own. Wyatt slammed his head downward, his forehead connecting with the man's nose which exploded with a geyser of blood.

He reared back to punch, to hit, to do anything he could to further immobilize the man who'd had the nerve to break into their house when three more intruders burst through the opened back door. Wyatt saw a foot fly at his face just before it connected with his jaw. He fell backward, slamming into the tile floor.

"Fucker!" Seth yelled. He swung the meat mallet at the man who'd send Wyatt to the ground but only landed a glancing blow. This new attacker was bigger than the first, tall and thick and from Wyatt's vantage point looked something like a giant.

The man grabbed Seth's wrist, squeezing down with nearly

crushing force and disarming him of the tool in one effortless motion. Seth grabbed for it but the big man held it out of reach and a grin that revealed rotting teeth spread across his ruddy face. "Uh-uh, kiddie. This is my toy now."

As Wyatt tried to regain his footing, bloody saliva seeped from his mouth and dripped onto the tile, forming a shallow pool in which he could see the outline of his own reflection. He made it to his knees when one of the other intruders, a gangly man with matted hair that hung halfway to his chest, bucked a booted foot into his ribs and he was down again.

The man who'd returned him to the floor grabbed a fistful of Wyatt's hair and yanked his head skyward, hyper-extending his neck. Wyatt caught a glint of metal and realized the man had the carving knife.

This is quite the pickle, he thought. His father used to say that when things weren't going well. Then Wyatt or Seth would respond with 'No big dill.' But this was a whole new level of not going well. This was the mack daddy of pickles and a very big dill.

The giant raised the hammer, ready to bring all its weight down on Seth's skull. At the same time the other man brought the knife close enough to Wyatt's throat that he could feel the cold radiating from it.

Getting murdered on his birthday hardly seemed fair, but Wyatt had almost accepted that fate when--

A thunderous boom sent his ears ringing. Wyatt watched the giant drop, hitting the floor with enough force to shake the room.

The man who'd been on the verge of cutting Wyatt's throat released him, but before the intruder could take a step there came another flash and boom and he joined Wyatt on the floor. Their faces were less than a dollar bill's length apart and Wyatt watched his eyes go dull and sightless as he died.

Wyatt clambered to his knees and found Trooper standing in the open kitchen doorway. The old man looked straight out of a western as he clutched a pistol in each hand, smoke wafting from each barrel.

Wyatt thought Jesus himself wouldn't have been a more welcome sight at that moment.

One attacker sprinted past Wyatt, away from his dead comrades and from their executioner. He didn't hesitate as he dove through the bay window and vanished from their view. Trooper followed and, when he reached the gaping cavity, raised one pistol and shot again. Wyatt heard a pained shriek and knew Trooper hadn't missed.

He'd nearly forgotten about everything other than the man who'd saved them from certain death when he heard Seth grunting. He turned toward the noise and found his brother on the floor, on top of the man with whom he'd been struggling when this mess kicked off. Only now Seth had the advantage.

He had a fistful of the man's scraggly, gray hair in each hand and slammed his face into the floor. Wyatt heard bones break.

The man's arms flailed as he tried to free himself. "We was just looking for food." The man's words came out clumsy and garbled, like someone speaking through a mouthful of partially chewed meat. Seth pulled his head back and smashed it down again. More wet crunching and popping noises, so thick and loud Wyatt felt his stomach tighten.

"Please don't." That plea was nearly unrecognizable - lees ont - but Wyatt got the gist of it.

Seth either didn't hear or didn't care. He lifted the man's skull a third time and pounded it into the tile yet again. A scream that Wyatt initially thought was a pained sound from the intruder followed that blow, but then he realized it had come from his brother. Seth's upper body shook, his face a mask of rage and fury. The man under him didn't move.

"Seth." Wyatt reached for his brother's shoulder, eased his hand onto him. He could feel him trembling.

Seth dropped the man's ruined skull and turned to Wyatt, tears in his eyes. The dead man's blood intermixed with Seth's tears creating a watercolor painting of carnage across the palate of his face.

Wyatt had seen nothing like that from anyone let alone his own brother and the brutality of the act scared him.

"You boys alright?" Trooper asked, limping toward the kitchen.

"Yeah," Seth said.

Wyatt wasn't able to get out any words.

"I'm gonna check the perimeter, make sure no one else is lurking around outside." He holstered one pistol. "Although, if there was, I imagine they high-tailed it outta here when the shooting started."

Trooper was half-way to the front door when Wyatt realized no one, no matter how good of a sleeper they were, could have slept through that madness.

As if their lives had turned into a bad B movie, on cue, Barbara screamed.

Wyatt sprinted toward the sound which took him past Trooper. Without a thought, he snatched a pistol from the holster at his side. The old man's hands clawed at him, trying to stop him from rushing headfirst and stupid into danger or maybe just to retrieve his gun, but Wyatt's youth and speed were too much and he blew past.

His bare feet pounded against the floorboards as he raced down the hallway, past his own bedroom, and to his mother's room. The door was two-thirds of the way closed and through the opening spilled whimpering and grunting sounds. Wyatt didn't hesitate and threw the door all the way open as he pushed through.

Barbara was on the bed, on her back. A string bean of a man was atop her, his narrow body positioned between her legs. The man's pants were around his ankles and his pale, bare ass shone like a beacon in the dark as it swayed and thrust.

Wyatt realized his mother was naked from the waist down and averted his eyes in shame. He saw her nightgown and a pair of ripped underwear on the floor beside the bed and forced himself to return his focus to the struggle taking place.

"Hold still you sow!" The man grunted as he tried to plant his pole.

Barbara bucked her hips, defiant. The man bounced up and halfway off her, now straddling her right leg.

"Do that again and I'll gut you. I done it before." He pressed a knife against her cheek, indenting her skin.

Wyatt had seen more than enough. "Get off her!"

Both the aspiring rapist and Barbara looked to Wyatt, and they appeared equally shocked. The man appeared to be about thirty with a long, droopy face that reminded Wyatt of the painting they based the Scream mask off for the movies.

"This your whore? Little old for you ain't she?" The man asked.

Wyatt raised the pistol. It felt heavy and slippery in his hands and he realized his palms were wet with sweat even though it was near freezing in the house. He tried to hold them steady, but they shook and he could only hope the bastard couldn't see that in the dark.

"Get off or I'll blow your brains out." The words felt as forced as if he were reciting Shakespearean dialogue in a high school class play.

"Shoot him," Barbara pleaded.

The man looked away from Wyatt just in time for Barbara's hand to connect with his face. Her fingernails raked across his cheeks, carving shallow channels through his doughy skin.

"Bitch!" He slammed the handle of the knife into her forehead, breaking open an oval, oozing wound and some of the fight left her.

Wyatt's index finger tightened. He had never shot Trooper's pistol before, but he suspected it was close to going off. But he hesitated. "Pay attention to me, asshole. Get out of this house right now and you can live. It's your call."

The man swiveled his head back to Wyatt, grinning a toothless and joyless smile that revealed milky white gums. "You ain't gonna pull that trigger. You ain't got the balls. So why don't you skidoot while this sow and me get on a good rut. She wants it too. I can smell it drippin outta her like parfum."

He licked his thin lips with a tongue that was thick and dry, then turned back toward a dazed Barbara. With one hand he pressed the blade of the knife against her face. With the other, he pushed her legs apart to give himself easy access.

Wyatt knew his mother was in no shape to carry on the fight. It was up to him to stop this. It was up to him to do what he couldn't do earlier that day and shoot. To kill. For his family.

I can scare him away, Wyatt thought. If he sees I'm serious, he'll tuck tail and run and then I don't have to live with murdering a man. Because he was the guy who couldn't even shoot a deer so how was he supposed to shoot a man? He raised the pistol, aiming just over the man's head. It seemed the coward's way out, but he believed it would work.

Wyatt pulled the trigger. The bullet blasted into the wall kicking out a spray of debris in its wake.

It worked. The man was scared. His body jerked. And so did his knife-wielding hand.

The scream that followed was a sound Wyatt knew he'd be forever unable to forget.

The blade of the knife sliced a four-inch long gash through Barbara's cheek but that wasn't the worst part. The worst was when Wyatt realized the tip of the knife had disappeared into her eye socket. The blade had bisected her left eye and a jelly-like fluid escaped. Blood mixed in creating a pink, viscous tide that ebbed down her ruined face.

She screamed again. It was a sound Wyatt imagined was audible miles away.

"Oh, Jesus." Wyatt tried to aim, this time actually at the man, but his hands were shaking so bad he thought he might blow a hole in his mother if he actually fired. Before he could do anything, another gun went off.

The attacker's head seemed to implode and explode at the same time sending blood and shattered bone and chunks of brain matter splattering against the bed and floor and walls all at once.

Wyatt turned and found Trooper standing in the doorway, his

remaining pistol raised. Of course, it was Trooper. Saving them again when he couldn't. When all he did was make things worse.

Wyatt ran to Barbara and grabbed the top sheet from the bed, trying to shake it free from the bloody detritus that had been a man's skull a few seconds earlier. "I'm so sorry, mom. I'm sorry." He raised the linen to her face, not sure if he wanted to use it to stop the bleeding or cover up the carnage so he didn't have to see what he'd done.

CHAPTER SIX

THE SCREAMS FROM BARBARA'S BATHROOM WEREN'T AS BAD AS the ones she'd made in her bed but they were damn close.

In his sixty-eight years on the planet, Trooper had witnessed and dealt with his share of pain. The worst, at least until now, had been Frank Hanzel, a fellow Maine State Police Trooper who caught a .338 magnum during a standoff with a moose poacher in Aroostook County.

The round had missed his kevlar vest and ripped apart the young officer's shoulder. Trooper used his hands to cover the wound and try to slow the bleeding, but by the time the paramedics arrived there was more of Frank's blood in the dirt than in his body. He survived, barely, but never regained full use of his arm and took medical retirement.

The man's agonized moans as Trooper kept pressure on the exploded remains of his arm came back to him now as he listened through the closed door.

She was alone in there. That was her call and while Trooper didn't like the thought of her trying to fix the damage to her face solo, he respected her wishes. Seth did too. Trooper sometimes thought Seth lazy, but he had common sense. Sense that Wyatt lacked.

As Barbara had stumbled into the master bathroom, Wyatt followed like an attention-seeking dog trying to win back its owner's affection. It didn't work.

"Get away from me! Go!" Barbara had screamed at her son.

Wyatt retreated, not saying a word. If he had a tail, it would have been between his legs. Then the door slammed and the three men were left alone with their shared helpless shame.

A mix between a cry and a groan seeped out of the bathroom. Trooper'd been staring out the window where the poor excuse for a new dawn was breaking. He heard the bedsprings creak and knew it was Wyatt.

"Don't." Trooper glanced back and saw the boy on his feet.

"She shouldn't be all by herself in there."

"She made her choice."

He turned to the closed door. Part of him wanted to know what the hell was going on inside that room as bad as Wyatt. He'd known Barb for going on fifteen years, since she moved to the neighborhood with a tot on her knee and another in her belly. She was a seamstress for one of the fancy, upscale boutiques in Portland so he knew the woman could handle a needle and thread but sewing up your own face...

Trooper was a prideful man, but he doubted he'd have the stones to do what she was doing. Just the thought of it, the cleaning, the stitching. Then doing whatever the hell she'd have to do with what remained of her eye. She was something else.

"She might have passed out," Wyatt said.

"You hear a thud?" Trooper asked.

Wyatt shrugged. "Guess not."

Another moment passed in silence.

"What if--"

"Wyatt, shut the hell up," Seth said. "Mom's tough. She'll be fine and doesn't need you up her ass."

Trooper's mouth curled into a grin. The Morrill's had always been decent boys. Not perfect, but what kids were? Wyatt was the more outgoing and affectionate of the two, always wanting to do what was right, be liked, and win your approval. Seth was more aloof, sometimes bordering on cocky, but despite those faults he got it. He was more savvy, more intuitive, and more prepared for the world even though he was the younger of the brothers.

Before Wyatt could complain about Seth chastising him, the bathroom door opened. Barbara stepped out, wearing an oversized gray T-shirt, stained with drops of blood that had dried to the color of Hershey's chocolate syrup. She stared at the men with a steely resolve that almost dared them to look away. Trooper did not.

The stitches were small and even and extended from below her mouth, through where her eye had been, and into her eyebrow. The tension of whatever string she'd used to close it had puckered the skin in spots and thin, watery plasma seeped from the wound.

From the day the Morrill's moved into the neighborhood, Trooper, himself a lifelong bachelor, thought she was a fine-looking woman, just a few notches short of beautiful. The bastard who mauled her face had robbed her of that, and the attack had certainly caused different kinds of wounds too, but she still impressed Trooper.

"You alright?" Trooper asked.

She gave a curt nod. "I suppose."

"Mom, I'm--"

"Save it." Barbara cut him off, her voice flat. "It's done now."

Wyatt stared at the floor. "Okay."

Barbara glanced around the room. Trooper and Wyatt had dragged the bodies out of the house and left Seth to clean up the gore. He'd done a fair enough job but a large spot of pink lingered on the eggshell paint of the bedroom wall where the would-be rapist's blood and brains had splattered.

"You take care of all of them?" Barbara asked.

"Ayuh. The bodies are outside. I'll burn them in the morning," Trooper said.

"I don't give a shit about their bodies. I want to know if you killed them."

"We did," Seth said.

Barbara looked at the boy and Trooper saw some of the brave facade she'd been wearing like a mask crack when she realized Seth, her youngest, had killed a man.

"That's good, Seth. Thank you."

Trooper thought Seth looked on the verge of making one of his ill-timed and usually bad jokes, but his common sense kicked in and he only shrugged his shoulders.

"Sure."

She turned her attention to Trooper, and he saw tears forming in her remaining eye, tears she quickly blinked away. "How can we be sure there aren't more of them in the neighborhood? Maybe hiding out in one of the abandoned houses?"

Trooper had considered this too. He'd planned to inspect the block once he knew the Morrill's were okay, check for kicked in doors or broken windows. Because he knew these days people traveled in packs.

"There could be, but I doubt it. We made quite a ruckus last night and laid the dead on the front lawn for anyone who cared to see. A sight like that is apt to give any cohorts not much want to come around."

"But it doesn't mean more won't come," Barbara said. "Especially if some got away. They could regroup and come back and next time they'd be better prepared."

"Winter is almost here, though," Wyatt said.

"So what?" Barbara asked.

Trooper knew the woman was hurting, physically and emotionally, but the frigid tone of voice she directed at Wyatt made him pity the boy. He'd have to live the rest of his days knowing his hesitation had caused his mother a horrific injury, and Trooper was getting the feeling that, should he ever forget, Barbara would be quick to remind him.

Wyatt dared turn his gaze from the floor to the others. "They'll never come up here in the winter. They'd wait until spring at the soonest."

Trooper nodded. "That's what I'd expect too. And you know damn well I can handle anything that comes my way."

Barbara shook her head. "No. There's nothing for us here anymore. Not even safety."

"That's not true," Wyatt said.

"Wyatt, when's the last time you shot a deer? Or anything for that matter?"

Wyatt didn't answer.

"Sure, we've got canned goods but even those are turning. The other week I had to throw out an entire case of beans because the cans were rusting. And do you remember how cold it got last winter?"

None of the men answered because they all knew. Trooper had stayed wrapped in three blankets for the near entirety of January and still felt frozen stiff.

"All we're doing here is delaying the inevitable."

"What are you saying, Mom?" Wyatt asked.

"We need to leave. And we're going today."

CHAPTER SEVEN

Barbara knelt on the floor before her closet and stared at the clothing, the shoes, the handbags, almost all of which she'd have to leave behind. Doing so didn't bother her. They were just things, after all. Material goods which had ceased to have any actual value. But the juxtaposition between her life before the attacks to her life now was sometimes so jarring she wondered if this was all some fever dream from which she would eventually wake.

She passed up the few designer items, a pair of Louboutin heels, a Givenchy handbag, she's saved up for months to purchase, instead being practical. She grabbed a few pairs of jeans, some heavy sweaters, gloves, and didn't bother folding any of it before cramming it into her oversized backpack. It was only half-full, but she needed to save room for supplies so she zipped it shut and left the room, and her old life, behind for good.

She found Wyatt in the kitchen where he used a spoon

to eat cold creamed corn straight from a can. His eyes were blood-shot, as if he was on the verge of crying.

"You're really doing it?" He asked.

"Of course." She grabbed the spoon from his hand and helped herself to a mouthful of the corn. It was tasteless, just like almost all the canned goods these days. Even the food which hadn't turned had lost its flavor. It all tasted the same. Like nothing. She handed the spoon back to her son who wouldn't look her in the eyes - or eye, as the case may be now. "It's too dangerous here. So we're going south like everyone else did three years ago."

"Everyone else is probably dead. That's why no one ever came back."

She'd considered this. It was certainly possible, maybe even likely, but this house, her home, was spoiled now. She couldn't stay here another day let alone another season.

"Maybe. Or maybe they found some place worth staying."

Wyatt shook his head. "Someone would have come back for us. The Jacoby's, the Russell's. They wouldn't all just leave us here alone if there was some safe haven waiting."

Barbara didn't have an answer for that and busied herself with transferring cans of food from the pantry to her backpack. She heard the legs of Wyatt's chair scrape across the floor and his footsteps as he moved to her.

"Where will we go?" He asked.

She turned to him and saw it wasn't just confusion on his face, but pain. She took his face in her hands. He hadn't shaved that morning and rough stubble pricked her palms and she had to remind herself yet again that this was a man, not a boy.

And he needed to be told the truth. "As far south as our feet will take us."

"What are you talking about?"

"Remember those French-Canadians that came through town about two years ago?"

Wyatt couldn't hold back a smirk. "Henri and Francois. Sort of hard to forget. What did they keep asking us about? Poutine?"

Barb surprised herself by still being able to laugh. "Yeah. That was it."

"What about them?"

"The big one, the one with the glasses--"

"Henri."

"Yeah. He was a scientist. He said the bombs and fallout might not have affected land south of the equator. Something about the air streams or currents or something." She tried to put on her most optimistic expression. "Wyatt, he said there might still be sunlight there. Plants and animals and life."

"He also said that it was only a theory. And his backup plan was to commandeer a submarine and live underwater for the rest of his life. Remember?"

Barbara shrugged. Truth be told she doubted there was some magical part of the planet where life went on as usual. But she also knew that staying here would only end in death and whether it was from starvation or bastards like the night prior meant no difference. Dead was dead.

"It's a chance. That's more than we have now, Wyatt. I know this is your home. That you think we are safe here. But it's a prison and you've been inside it for too long to know anything else. It's my fault for letting us stay so long. And I will not let you rot here."

She thought, from his expression, that she was getting through. "I want to do more than just survive. Don't you?"

"What about Seth? How is he going to make it all the way down there?"

"Rolling like the wind, brother." Both turned to find Seth sitting in his chair at the edge of the kitchen. He had a full pack on his lap. "I haven't been working on these guns for nothing." He flexed, revealing the lean, ropey muscles in his upper arms. "And when I need a break, you can push my crippled ass."

"How long have you been snooping?" Wyatt asked.

"Long enough to hear your dramatic theatrics. Man, you two could be on a soap opera." He pushed himself closer to them and intentionally bumped his chair into Wyatt's shin. "So you think I'm going to slow down the wagon train?"

Wyatt's face flushed crimson. "No... I... It's not..."

Seth rolled his eyes. "You're looking at it all wrong."

"How's that?"

"It's like that old joke. How fast do you have to run to outrun a moose?" He paused a beat. "Faster than the slowest guy!"

Seth cackled at his joke. Barbara didn't see the humor but was relieved the tension had been deflated. And that maybe they could get on with this.

"Actually, I think the wheelchair will be an asset," Barbara said. "It'll allow us to carry so much more. Food, jugs of water."

"Sounds like I'll be doubling as favorite son and pack mule. That works." Seth's grin faded, and he turned serious. "But you guys have to make me a promise. If things get bad, like, really bad and I'm slowing you down, you need to leave me behind."

Barbara inhaled sharply. Just the thought made her want to abandon this whole plan. "Seth!"

Seth held up his palm, silencing her. "I'm not going to be an anchor that gets my family killed. Those are my terms."

Barbara looked at her son, at both of them. "You can't ask that of me."

"Then I won't go."

Barbara knew trying to win an argument with Seth was pointless. He was as bull-headed as her husband. Maybe more. She swallowed hard. "Okay." She told herself it wouldn't come to it but knew that, if it did, she'd end up a liar.

Seth looked to his brother who only nodded. "Good, then we're on the same page. When does this road trip kick-off?"

"As soon as we convince one more to come along. And I'm going to need both of you to help."

CHAPTER EIGHT

"NOT GONNA HAPPEN," TROOPER SAID.

"You can't stay here, Trooper," Barbara said. "How long can you last all alone?"

Trooper slouched in his recliner, surrounded by supplies in the middle of his living room. The chair still faced the oversized television that hadn't worked in five years. He'd sometimes considered tossing it out, to make more room for canned food or beer, but never got around to it. Old habits, and all that.

He turned from the black screen to Barbara. "Your choice if you want to go. I'm not gonna stop you even though it's dangerous and most likely won't end well. But you're a grown woman capable of making up your own mind just like I'm a grown man capable of making up mine."

Barbara shook her head. "A stubborn old man."

"Tell me something I don't know," Trooper shot back. It wasn't an insult to him because it was true. He liked being stubborn. Stubborn kept him alive, so why should he change?

"You really expect us to leave you here?"

"That's the idea."

"After last night? Next time it could be twenty of them all against you."

"Maybe. And if they break into this house, they'll regret it for the rest of their lives, which I guarantee you are apt to be short."

He looked up at Barbara, his friend, as she paced through the maze of boxes and bottles that filled the room. Her stress was obvious now that the conversation wasn't going as she'd hoped.

"Then I'm staying with you," Wyatt said. Up until that moment, both he and Seth had let their mother do all the convincing.

Trooper's ears perked up to his voice. "Now don't--"

"No, I mean it. If you're staying then so am I." Wyatt looked to his mother and brother. "You do what you want but I'm not leaving Trooper behind."

"Goddammit, Wyatt." Trooper leaned forward in the chair and his spine popped. He didn't appreciate this guilt trip. None of this was his fault. People weren't supposed to base their decisions around him. Just thinking about it pissed him off.

He raised his voice as he stood. "Don't be a little shit, you hear me? I got a duffle bag of guns and ammunition by the door for you to take with. Now go with your family and leave me be." He cocked his chin at the arsenal he'd gathered for them.

Wyatt closed the distance between them by half. "I can't leave here knowing that I'd never see you again."

Trooper stepped up into Wyatt's personal space. "I'm an old man. I've lived more life than you and your brother combined and doubled. When my time's up, it's not gonna be any great loss."

He turned his gaze to the dusty mantle above the fireplace. There were a myriad of pictures from his life, his official Maine State Trooper portrait, a photo of him holding an 18-pound bass, but the one that mattered most was in the center.

It was a picture of him and Mother sitting on the porch of this same house and had been taken nearly a decade before diabetes put her in the ground. He dragged his fingers through a layer of dust he'd allowed to accumulate on the glass.

A hand touched him on the shoulder and Barbara's voice reached his ear. "We can't do this without you, Trooper."

Trooper blinked away wetness at his eyes. Damn dust. He'd let the housework go for too long. At least, that's what he tried to tell himself. He sighed, not with relief, but resigned.

"The house hasn't had a good cleaning in a long while." He turned to face Barbara. "And I hate cleaning. So I suppose now's a good time to leave. Let it be someone else's problem."

Wyatt smiled. "You're coming with us, then?"

Trooper did a poor mimic of Wyatt's younger voice. "You coming with us? Like I had a choice. Damn neighbors always up in my business. Don't know why I didn't buy myself a place out in the country."

Barbara surprised him with a hug. He awkwardly put his arm around her shoulder. He still wasn't happy about this turn of events but some of the annoyance was fading.

"It'll be damn dangerous."

"We know that," Barbara said.

Trooper suspected they had no idea the kind of hell they were walking into, but it was three against one and he wasn't about to let them do it alone. "Alright, then I guess we'll do this." He strode toward the front door.

"Don't you want to pack first, Trooper?" Wyatt asked. "We'll help.".

Trooper opened the door to a small closet, leaned inside, and emerged holding two bags and one small suitcase, all packed to the brim. He dropped them to the floor and unzipped them with something resembling a flourish. One of the large bags was stuffed with food, bandages, and assorted practical supplies like matches, rope, and tarps. The second was filled with guns. Lots of guns. The suitcase contained a few changes of clothing and two pair of boots. "I'm ready."

"You were packed?"

"These are my bug out bags. Always at the ready in case shit goes down and I need to hit the road in a hurry. Just never thought I'd be doing it with you fools."

He stepped outside took a deep breath as he surveyed the neighborhood he'd never see again. He didn't want to leave, but he had to admit, life had been on the boring side lately and he could use one last adventure. "Are you coming, or what?"

CHAPTER NINE

LEAVING WAS THE HARDEST ON WYATT. AS HE TRUDGED ALONG the street, it seemed every house he passed carried with it a memory. In the big pine tree outside Ricky DeHaven's house, he spotted the remnants of the treehouse Ricky's dad had built when they were all about nine years old. Now it was only a few weathered planks, but at the time it had been large enough for Wyatt and Ricky and three or four of their best friends to hang out, sleep out, or do whatever the hell they wanted to do. It was only 15 feet off the ground, but when they were nine, they felt like they were a mile high and everything below was little more than an ant colony.

Wyatt had no idea how many nights they'd spent in that tree-house staring up at the stars or playing cards or gawking at dirty magazines that seemed to show up by osmosis. And just being kids. It seemed like yesterday and forever ago at the same time.

Everything about the past seemed that way now. He could close his eyes and remember minutiae from his childhood like it happened five minutes ago. Like The Great Wallpaper Debate as they'd grown to call it. That happened when Wyatt was 11 and his parents were remodeling the house. His parents battled between gray-ish blue and blue-ish gray wallpaper for nearly a month before his mother won out. Wyatt smiled at the memory. But that smile faded quickly because their jokes about The Great Wallpaper Debate ended when his father never came home from Boston.

Everything changed then.

As they passed Thom's Burgers, Wyatt tried to push away the bad memories. Thom's was a throwback to the 1950s diner, white and chrome on the outside with red trim, checkerboard flooring inside. It had been the most popular restaurant in town and hands down the best place to get a hamburger, shake, and fries. The latter of which were cooked in lard instead of vegetable oil and had probably sent more than a few locals to early graves, but they were delicious and worth it.

Even better than the fries had been a date with Heather Rowling. He'd dropped two quarters into the jukebox and settled on "Can't Take My Eyes Off You" by Frankie Valli and The 4 Seasons before sidling up next to her. They'd just come from the movies, one of those sappy love stories where the guy was an asshole but the girl redeemed him. It all worked, and he got his first real kiss in the back corner booth. His mouth was cold from the ice cream, but that changed when their tongues met.

Now the plate-glass windows that opened to the inside were smashed. Random graffiti tags, mostly penises and swastikas, covered the walls. He wondered why people had to be so gross. As if it wasn't bad enough the world was ending, they had to make everything that had been nice ugly. It was like the attacks hadn't just destroyed the environment, but had poisoned people's minds too.

Wyatt realized he'd been lingering outside the diner too long and glanced ahead. His mother and Seth were fifty yards up the street but Trooper was only half that distance. Wyatt realized the man was waiting on him and resumed his trek.

When he caught up, the two walked side by side. Trooper's limp wasn't bad this morning, or maybe he was just doing a good job at hiding it. Either way, Wyatt thought determination might be as important, if not more, than physical fitness.

"I know it's tough." Trooper didn't look at him, just continued forward one step after another. "Leaving it all behind. All your memories. No shame in that."

Wyatt's throat was tight with emotion and he waited for it to pass before speaking. "I feel like I'm losing everything that makes me who I am."

Trooper nodded. "Ayuh. I get that. And in a way you are."

This wasn't the motivational speech Wyatt expected or needed and he blinked away tears that fought to burst free. He felt like such a baby. He was supposed to be the man of his family now, the one they could count on, yet he was ready to bawl over... What? Treehouses and root beer floats?

"What you got to focus on is that everything that is left for you, everything that matters, is forward. It's with them." He pointed to Barbara and Seth in front of them. "And me, too, I suppose."

Trooper paused, hyper-extending his back so his spine popped. Then he sighed with relief and resumed his pace, and his speech. "This place is just a place, Wyatt. Your memories aren't staying behind. They'll be with you no matter where you are. But it's time to make new ones now. And hopefully better ones."

Wyatt wiped at his eyes with the back of his hand and smiled. "You know, for a badass old man, you sure do know a lot about feelings."

Trooper nodded again. "My mom, she taught me well. That's why I'm bringing her with me." He tapped his chest above his heart and they walked on.

CHAPTER TEN

THEY'D BEEN WALKING FOR OVER A WEEK AND HADN'T SEEN A sign of life. No people, no animals, just the slowly decaying remnants of a dead world. The walk wasn't bad, Wyatt thought. It was boring, but not physically taxing. In a way, having something to do, even if it was just putting one foot in front of the other, took his mind off everything else. Like his mother's mangled face.

Her wound had turned bright red on the third day and Trooper insisted they break so he could clean it. She gritted her teeth while he scrubbed with near-boiling water and soap, then slathered half her face in ointment. Wyatt didn't want to watch but made himself. It was his penance.

Most of the redness had faded away on day five and by the sixth, it seemed to be healing. It would leave behind a horrible, disfiguring scar but at least it seemed like they'd avoided infection and whatever hell that might have brought with it.

The worst part of the journey was the cold. Even though they couldn't see the ocean from Interstate 95, the effects were all too clear as harsh winds whipped across the highway and cut into their bones. All four of them were bundled up like Eskimos, but the clothing and coats and hats seemed to have little effect against that wind and Wyatt could only hope that moving further inland would alleviate some of the frigid misery.

It seemed like the middle of the day when they paused for a small lunch of canned wax beans and water. Wyatt noticed Seth digging around in a pile of rubbish and watched as he picked up the remnants of a coffee maker. He examined the mostly destroyed appliance, then sniffed it.

They'd enjoyed coffee at the house frequently but none since hitting the road and Wyatt suddenly realized he longed for a cup. He moved to Seth's side.

"How's that going for you?" Wyatt asked.

"The best part of wakin' up," Seth said with a smile.

"Let me have a whiff. Maybe I can get a caffeine buzz by proxy." Wyatt took the coffee maker from him and raised it to his nose ready to breathe in that unmistakable, rich aroma. Instead, he retched.

Seth laughed like a hyena. "You are so easy."

"It's like week old ass." Wyatt threw the coffee maker to the ground. The stench from the rotten filter had settled on the back of his tongue and he spit, hoping to rid the smell and taste from his mouth.

Seth continued to laugh and Wyatt grudgingly joined in, although he wasn't quite as jolly.

"What's so funny?"

They turned and found Trooper and Barbara packed and ready to go.

"My brother's a dickhead," Wyatt said.

"And my brother's a dumbass," Seth added.

Trooper shook his head. "That's not funny at all. Sad's what it is. And here I am, almost seventy years old, and I'm babysitting a dumbass and a dickhead on a two thousand mile trip. Sad."

On day ten they abandoned 95 and headed inland, much to Wyatt's relief. A sign informed them that Chapinville, Massachusetts was ahead and, beyond that, Worchester. Wyatt's family had rarely left Maine - his father said everyone south of New Hampshire was a Mass-hole - but he was eager to get to a town. More specifically, he was eager to find a building in which to take shelter for the night. And a part of him, a part he didn't even want to admit to himself, thought that sooner or later they might find people. People living normal lives and doing normal things.

His excitement was for naught. The town of Chapinville had been razed by fire. The remnants of houses and businesses were little more than skeletons, scorched black by an inferno that looked to have taken place within the last month. It isn't even a ghost town, Wyatt thought. It's just destruction.

As they passed through the streets, their feet crunched against the charred cinders that were scattered everywhere, like hailstones from hell.

"What do you think happened? Lightening or something?" Wyatt asked.

Seth shook his head. "No way. This was arson. A firebug on steroids."

"How would you know?" Wyatt asked.

"Look at the foundations. The buildings weren't all butted against each other, some were almost half a block apart. A fire wouldn't spread like that on its own. Someone did this."

That brought conversation to a halt.

They were a third of the way through town when Wyatt saw the body. He'd seen dead people before, mostly suicides whose remains he discovered when they were scavenging abandoned, or what they thought were abandoned, houses. He'd found a dozen or so over the years. The majority died from gunshots. Pistols weren't bad but once Wyatt found the corpse of a woman who'd used a shotgun and the only part of her head that remained attached to her body was her lower jaw.

One man had been naked in his bathtub, which was stained a rusty brown from the blood that spilled from his slit wrists. Mixed in with the wetness were hunks of rotten skin that had become supersaturated and sloughed off. The two that really bothered him were an elderly man and woman who had hanged themselves from the rafters in their craftsman bungalow. They died holding hands, which might have been romantic, but their purple faces and bulging eyes and tongues robbed the scene of its sentimentality.

But this body was different because it was skewed on a piece of steel rebar and hung over a fire pit. Wyatt wasn't sure if it was a man or woman because the hair had been burned away and what little skin remained was beyond recognition, just a blackened husk. The mouth hung agape, revealing a maw with a third of its teeth missing. The arms, torso, and legs had been excised of their flesh and muscle, leaving behind nothing but bone and the occasional strip of sinew. The butchering ended at the feet, which were tied together by wire at the ankles.

The wheels on Seth's chair crunched through debris, getting closer.

"What is it?" Seth called out.

Wyatt spun around, positioning himself between his companions and the human barbecue, wanting to spare them that nightmare fuel. "It's nothing. Just a calf roasted and picked clean."

Wyatt strode toward his brother, grabbing the handles of his wheelchair and spinning him away before he could get too good of a look. That worked with Seth, but not Trooper who might be old but still had the eyesight, and experience, to know what lay ahead.

"Let's move on before it gets dark," Trooper said.

Wyatt nodded. He let his brother push himself and fell into step with Trooper, behind Seth and Barbara and waited until they were out of earshot.

"You think it was those bastards who broke into the house?" Wyatt asked. "They stunk like smoke."

Trooper shrugged his shoulders. "Possibly. I'd say the odds are pretty fair."

In a way that made Wyatt feel better. To think the monsters who had eaten a person were dead and rotting in his backyard. Any relief was short-lived.

"But even if they were, there'll be others capable of that and worse."

"That's not the kind of reassurance I was hoping for, Trooper." Wyatt tried to smile.

Trooper didn't. "Most important thing my job ever taught me was to never underestimate man's capacity for violence." Trooper watched him, examined him. Wyatt didn't respond.

"I think it best if we slept in shifts for the next while."

That was fine with Wyatt. All he cared about was getting as far away from this town as possible before dark, even if it meant sleeping in a field. He didn't want to be anywhere close to here when everything turned black.

CHAPTER ELEVEN

Just before full dark Trooper pointed to a copse of pine trees that lingered a quarter-mile off the highway. They were dead, just like almost everything else, but most of their amber-colored needles still clung to the branches and provided sufficient cover.

They had sat in the cold night, passing around a can of colorless, flavorless chicken and a bottle of water. They'd go to bed hungry, but they hadn't come across a single item of food since leaving Portland and needed to ration as much as possible because none of them knew when - or if - they might be able to restock.

That wasn't a concern to Wyatt who couldn't get the vision of the spit-roasted human being out of his mind. He felt that it was wrong to keep this from his mother and Seth. An unspoken lie. As he debated whether to tell them, Barbara spoke.

"You fellas know you're not being charged by the word, right?"

Wyatt glanced up, startled by her voice. "What?"

She gave a wan smile. "The conversation. I'd get more chatter out of a mocking bird than you three."

"Sorry." He tried to think of something to say, innocuous small talk to pass the time but came up empty. "Sorry," he said again.

Barbara grabbed her pack and laid it at the top of her sleeping bag for use as a pillow. "I'm so tired of hearing you say that word, Wyatt. Next time we pass by a library I'm going to steal you a dictionary."

Wyatt tried looking her in the eye, but he felt his gaze pull down instead. "I'll do better. I'm just tired."

"We all are." She laid down and covered her eye with her arm. "Good night, boys."

She was snoring within a minute.

"You're gonna have to come to terms with it," Trooper said.

"With what?"

"Her face." He said the words in a flat, unaffected matter, like he was stating something as clearly known as water is wet. "It's done. And you pussyfooting around it and not looking at her only makes it worse for her."

Wyatt wanted to respond, but again words failed him.

"I think it made her look badass," Seth said. "Like the supervillain in a Marvel movie or something. Kind of cool."

The notion that there was anything cool about their mother's missing eye and hacked up face made Wyatt's stomach tighten. He held the can of chicken but had no appetite.

"You gonna finish that or fondle it all night?" Seth asked.

Wyatt handed it to him. "Knock yourself out."

After swallowing the last bite, Seth unleashed a belch that echoed across the field. He tossed the can away from camp and flopped onto his side. "See you assholes in the a.m."

Trooper and Wyatt sat in silence for a good half hour before Wyatt spoke. "You want to take first shift?"

"Ayuh. I will."

"Be careful, okay?"

Trooper tapped the pistol on his hip. "Always am."

Wyatt laid back and closed his eyes without responding. He felt the weight of the darkness fall onto him and he was out.

ROUGH SHAKING WOKE HIM FROM A DREAMLESS SLEEP.

"Wyatt."

It was Trooper's voice, which made sense with how rudely he'd been awoken. Must be time for my turn on watch, he thought.

Before he opened his eyes, he heard the screaming. Any vestiges of sleep that clung to him vanished in a moment. He bolted upright, head snapping to and fro as he tried to figure out what was going on. Who was in pain. Who was, from the awful, shrieking wails, being slaughtered.

Trooper rested his hand on Wyatt's knee. "It's alright."

Wyatt's panic slipped from a ten to an eight. He realized Barbara and Seth and Trooper were all in camp and unharmed and he managed to steal a few breaths.

More screaming, to the east and close, prevented him from calming down further and he realized he wasn't alone in his unease. Barbara sat with her knees pulled to her chest, hugging them and holding a pistol at the same time. Seth didn't look scared, but his eyes were avid and alert. He held a shotgun. Trooper stood, pistol in hand and finger on the trigger.

"How long has it been going on?" Wyatt asked.

"A few minutes. I swear, you could sleep through a tornado," Seth said.

"I get it naturally." Wyatt scrambled to his feet, grabbing his pistol and moving to Barbara's side. He put his hand on her shoulder. "Right mom?"

She nodded but didn't smile. "Seth woke me so don't feel too bad."

He stayed at her side, wanting to be close, to be there for her this time if things went bad.

Another agonized howl ripped through the open field and into their camp. Wyatt realized it originated in the direction of the road and was glad Trooper had insisted they find cover for the night. He reached for a flashlight but, before he could flick it on, Trooper swatted his hand.

"Don't!"

"Someone's getting killed out there!"

"All we got is noise. Could be someone in trouble or it could be a trap."

"A trap?"

"Make a big ruckus, make it sound like someone's in trouble. Good way to draw out anyone else who might be in the area."

Wyatt felt his forearms break out in goosebumps. He hadn't even considered that. And if Trooper was right, he'd been a half-second away from giving away their location.

"Everyone sit down and stay alert. It's gonna be a long night," Trooper said.

The screams continued for hours. Even when they stopped, Wyatt could still hear them.

CHAPTER TWELVE

Seth tried to examine his reflection in the metal frame of his wheelchair. His hair bolted out at random angles like a cartoon character that had received a bad electrical shock. He spat into his palm, rubbed his hands together, then tried to mash his blond locks back into place. It was a poor substitute for hair gel, but it sufficed.

"Hell of a night, huh?" He cast a sideways glance at Wyatt who was busy rolling his sleeping bag into a perfect cylinder. It made Seth think of Hostess Swiss Rolls and that made his mostly empty stomach rumble to life. Shit, it was too early for that.

"Yeah," Wyatt, ever the chatterbox, said.

"Sounded like someone was being skinned alive."

"Enough," Barbara ordered through a yawn. "I don't want to think about that."

Geez, Seth thought, so touchy. He grabbed the road map Trooper had given him at the start of the trip, careful as he unfolded it as the creases were already threatening to split and they'd barely begun their long trek south. It got dark too fast the night prior, and he didn't have a chance to mark their day's journey, something he intended to remedy.

After pulling a red ballpoint pen from his pack, he traced the route they'd taken, then reviewed where they'd been. And then he looked to Mexico. Their progress seemed rather pathetic when compared to the big-picture view, so he tried to focus on the area ahead. The rest of Massachusetts, Connecticut, New York.

He didn't like what he saw, because the map also featured wavy lines that indicated the terrain and the territory looked anything but level. That was the worst thing about being in the chair during this trip, the hills. He did okay on the gradual ones, but anything too steep and he either needed someone to push his crippled ass up or hold on to him on the way down so he didn't go careening out of control like a kid whose sled hit an ice patch. Neither was fun.

Wyatt didn't complain about pushing him, but occasionally Trooper or his mom would trade-off. One more than twice his age, the other more than three times… It made him feel about as useful as a flat tire and he couldn't imagine hundreds of more miles being dragged along for the ride and letting the others do the hard work.

He began to refold the map, a skill that had taken him nearly half an hour the first time he tried, but which he now had down to a science, when he noticed a few small, neatly printed letters beside random towns. T.P. There had been one beside Kennebunk. Another in Lowell. The next was in a place called Kent in Connecticut, and then none until East Stroudsburg, Pennsylvania.

"Hey Trooper?" Seth asked.

Trooper was packed and pacing, ready to go. "What?"

Seth tapped the map with his index finger. "What's up with the initials you have written here. T.P. That some old girlfriend of yours?" He smirked. "A little jungle love, maybe?"

Trooper raised an eyebrow and stared for several seconds before answering. "Son, that stands for toilet paper. Reminding myself to stock up."

Well that was disappointing, Seth thought. He continued to refold the map. "You brought toilet paper?"

"You didn't?"

"Hell no. I've been wiping my ass with leaves."

Trooper nodded. "Now it all makes sense."

"What?"

"Why you stink." Trooper unzipped one of his bags, reached into it, and pulled out a roll. He tossed it to Seth who caught it. "There. Do us all a favor and use it."

Seth waited for Trooper to laugh, to let on that it was a joke. That didn't happen. He looked to Wyatt who was now packed and ready to move.

"Why didn't you tell me I smelled?" Seth asked.

Wyatt narrowed his eyes. "I didn't want to be the one to say anything..."

Seth was about to lob a comeback, to tell his brother that he didn't smell like freshly picked flowers either, but he saw the right corner of Wyatt's mouth tick upward as he held back a grin.

"You suck."

Wyatt gave up on suppressing the smile. "At least I don't stink."

Seth flipped him the bird, then scooted himself across the fallen pine needles to position himself in front of his chair. He checked to make sure the wheels were locked, then bent his knees and planted his feet. Mastering this move had taken him more than a year and caused countless bruises, scrapes, and gashes as he failed and crashed to the floor, but he'd eventually become proficient.

He knew he could ask Wyatt to lift him and Wyatt would have jumped to attention, but doing it himself made him feel more capable, and less like that flat tire. He grabbed the frame of the chair with his left hand and pushed off with his right, flopping himself into the seat.

He looked to see if the others had watched. If they'd been waiting to see if he fell or needed help or just to look upon him with pity, but they were busy going about their own business. And for some reason that made Seth feel like he wasn't so different after all.

CHAPTER THIRTEEN

THEY WERE A FEW MILES NORTH OF THE MASSACHUSETTS Connecticut border before they saw other living people. The day hadn't been different from any other, mile after mile of trudging along in silence under the gunmetal gray skies. They'd paused for a lunch that consisted of tea and stale crackers they'd found a few miles back inside an abandoned shack when Wyatt noticed Trooper's attention was focused on the road behind them.

He said nothing right off, but after a few minutes of watching the man stare in silence, his curiosity got the best of him. "What's so interesting?"

"Not sure yet. Maybe nothing. Maybe something."

"Way to be specific, Trooper," Seth said. "You're a riddle wrapped in a mystery wrapped in an enigma."

Trooper threw a side-eyed glance his way. "And you're a shithead."

Wyatt enjoyed seeing his brother get cut down and didn't bother holding back a laugh, but he too kept watching the road, even if he didn't know what he was looking for.

Barbara grabbed the pot and poured herself a half cup of tea.

"Anyone want to finish it off?" None of the men responded, so she filled her mug and set the empty pot aside. She dipped one of the crackers in the tea and let it saturate, but peer pressure was getting the best of her and she too kept looking behind them.

Seth sighed and scooted across the road until he reached Trooper's packs. He rummaged through them until he found what he wanted - binoculars.

"I swear, I'm the only one in this quartet with a brain."

Wyatt watched as Seth raised the binoculars to his eyes and peered through them. "Well?" Wyatt asked.

Seth lowered the glass. "Two people. A man and woman."

Wyatt thought he'd heard wrong. After weeks on the road, he'd almost given up finding other survivors. "Bullshit."

"Check for yourself." Seth extended the binoculars but when Wyatt reached for them he jerked them away at the last second.

Now Wyatt was sure his brother was pranking him and he didn't appreciate it. "Screw off." He grabbed his pack, ready to get a head start and put some distance between himself and Seth but he only took four steps before Trooper's voice stopped him cold.

"He's right."

Wyatt turned back to the others. He expected to find Trooper holding the binoculars but the old man had no visual aides. "How do you know?"

"I'm observant. Unlike the rest of you." He stood, sighing as his knee gave a firecracker pop. "They've been following us for two days now. This is the closest they've got."

Barbara scrambled to her feet, dropping the remains of her soggy cracker. She grabbed the binoculars and searched the road. "And you didn't say anything?"

Trooper twisted at the waist, stretched, and Wyatt noticed that while he did that he also unbuttoned the leather strap that secured his pistol to the holster at his side. "Saw no sense in causing a panic."

"They could have snuck into camp and slit our throats while we slept!" Barbara pushed Seth's chair nearer to him. "Get up."

He obeyed wordlessly and Wyatt saw from the look his mother's anxiety was catching.

"We ain't been in no danger," Trooper said. "Not yet anyway."

The foursome waited in place as the man and woman on the road grew near enough to see, then closer and closer. When they were forty yards away, the man called out.

"Hiya, strangers!"

He raised his arm in a wave and Trooper drew his pistol but kept the barrel pointed at the ground. Wyatt knew if the couple made one wrong move, it would be their last.

Wyatt thought standing there, silent, could be construed as not just rude but possibly threatening and the last thing he wanted was a reenactment of the Gunfight at the OK Corral over a misunderstanding.

"Hello," he risked.

The others looked at him like he was a traitor. "What? I just said 'hi.'"

"We don't know who they are." Barbara's hands were on the handles of Seth's wheelchair as if she were ready to sprint away, pushing him along for the ride, at the first sign of trouble. Wyatt couldn't imagine them getting far if shit did go down.

"Exactly," Wyatt said. "We don't know who they are. They could be good people, like us. And isn't that half the reason we left Maine? To find people? Something resembling civilization?"

The people were within ten yards now, close enough to begin to see details. The man looked to be in his mid-twenties and wore a tan, western-style duster that was too long and dragged on the ground as he walked. The woman traveling with him wasn't a woman at all. She was a girl, younger than both Morrill boys. Wyatt thought she looked no more than fourteen in the face but her distended belly, which bulged with a baby inside, made him think - or hope - she must be older.

"I'll be dipped in shit," the man said. "Just the other day I bet

June we wouldn't see any people until we got to Tennessee." He turned to her and grinned. "Never been so happy to be wrong."

The girl poked him in the ribs. "You owe me a foot rub."

"That I do."

They were just a few yards out and the man noticed Trooper's drawn gun. He lost his smile and quickly held his palms in the air. "Whoa, no need for that. I promise we ain't got nothing on us more dangerous than a rusty fork and so long as you got your tetanus shots you're safe."

"What do you want?" Trooper asked.

The two exchanged looks, then returned their focus forward. "I don't rightly know," the man said. "Nothing really. We was just happy to see people."

"Might be for the best if you keep looking somewhere else." Trooper still held his pistol at the ready. "We aren't interested in adding numbers to our party."

Wyatt knew sending them on their way was the smart thing to do, but the girl, June, looked on the verge of tears. He wasn't sure if it was fear or disappointment over being rejected, but her pitiful face, which was covered in girlish freckles that made him think of Pippi Longstocking, coupled with her wildly out-of-place pregnancy, made him feel like the world's biggest heel.

The man stared down at his feet. "Oh. Alright then."

Wyatt thought he might have been off on his age. His face was long and horsey, but had the plain, wide open innocence of a farm boy and Wyatt suspected he was no more than a year or two older than himself.

He risked a glance up, avoiding Trooper and shining his big, hazel eyes at the others, hoping to find a more receptive audience. "I understand that. But before we get on with the getting on, let me give you something. Just our way of saying 'thanks for not shooting us,' I guess."

He shrugged his pack off his shoulders and let it fall to the road. Then, with great caution he knelt beside it, keeping his eyes on

Trooper, and Trooper's gun, all the while. "I mean it, sir, we don't got no weapons."

As he unzipped the bag, Wyatt saw Trooper's finger slide onto the pistol's trigger and begin to squeeze. He must have two pounds on it already, Wyatt thought. If the guy tried anything, Trooper'd have a bullet in him before he could blink.

His hands dug through the bag and emerged with not a weapon, but a package of what looked like food. He raised it up, displaying it to the quartet. "See."

Trooper's finger left the trigger. "Toss it over."

The man did, lobbing it to Seth who snagged it with his left hand. "Good catch. You a southpaw?"

Seth nodded.

"My daddy was too."

Seth examined the pouch. "Mountain House biscuits and gravy. Freeze-dried."

"All you need's water." The man tried a smile and half-succeeded. "Now if you want to eat it alone, I understand and we'll move on."

The twosome stared in a way that made Wyatt think of the ASPCA commercials with the neglected and abused animals staring plaintively at the camera. How could they send these two off into the vast nothingness without at least giving them a chance?

"We've got a pot of water on the fire," Wyatt said. "Sit and eat with us and we'll see how it goes."

He saw Trooper stiffen, and he knew the man would chew him to pieces later when they were alone, but he also realized it was time he started acting like a man and that meant making decisions on his own.

THE MAN'S NAME WAS DEVAN AND THE GIRL, HIS SISTER, WAS

June. They'd been on the road for a month. They hoped to reach Tennessee before the girl gave birth.

"Our daddy and his second wife, they got a place just east of Clarksville. Little town called Adams," Devan said. "We never got along the best, but family's family, right?"

Devan did most of the talking, spilling a good portion of their life stories before the biscuits and gravy were consumed. Wyatt's group didn't share much more than their starting point in Portland and a few bits and pieces about the monotony of the road.

Trooper hadn't said a word until, "Are you gonna admit to tailing us?"

Devan's eyes grew so wide Wyatt half-expected them to tumble free of their sockets. "Oh, shit, sir, I'm sorry about that. It's just, with June's condition, I wanted to make sure you looked like good people before we introduced ourselves. I wasn't trying to be sneaky, I promise."

"Tell me, son, what convinced you were we good people?" Trooper asked, his face a mask void of emotion.

"It's gonna sound kind of silly," Devan said.

"Try us."

"Well, yesterday we saw you folks eating breakfast at the scenic overlook. Sitting at the picnic tables. Like you was just a regular family out camping for the weekend. And when you was done eating, we saw you." He pointed to Wyatt. "Gather up the garbage and put it in one of the trash cans."

Wyatt vaguely remembered that but didn't know why it had made any sort of impression, let alone convinced these people that he and his group weren't the types to roast people over open fires.

"And I thought," Devan said. "Bad people wouldn't do that. Put their trash in a bin. Not with everything all gone to shit. Only a good person does something like that. A person that thinks there might still be a reason to keep the world looking nice and pretty."

Devan half-turned to June and smiled. "That's when I knew I

could trust you. Trust you not to hurt my sister. And me too for that matter."

He laughed a nervous, rapid-fire rat-a-tat sound. "Like I said, silly."

Wyatt didn't think it was silly. Not at all. He realized that, even if they were hundreds and hundreds of miles from Mexico, this trip had already yielded rewards. For the first time since leaving his home, he felt like they'd made the right decision.

CHAPTER FOURTEEN

Trooper and Barbara both pushed shopping carts and brought up the rear of the newly expanded group. Devan, hadn't shut up for more than thirty seconds at a stretch and Trooper was already tired of the sound of his voice. He considered tearing apart a handkerchief and shoving the remnants into his ear canals, but knew plugging up one of his senses was a bad idea so he tried, with little success, to tune Devan out and hope that, sooner or later, he got tired of talking.

"The Finger Lakes region, that's where all the frou-frou people get together to drink wine and relax in the countryside, that was a jackpot," Devan said. "That's where we got all that freeze-dried stuff."

"And wine," June added with a giggle.

Devan blushed a shade Trooper thought was about the color of a good glass of pinot noir. "Yeah, that too."

"He drank so much one night he pissed all over hisself and then asked me when it started raining," June said.

"What can I say, it was tasty." Devan nodded toward Seth in his chair. This was a hilly area and Wyatt had been pushing for the last several miles. "Let me take a turn there, hoss."

Trooper could tell Wyatt was tired by the way he hunched his back over the handles.

"You don't have to."

"I know. I want to."

Wyatt let Devan slide into his place and arched his lower back.

Seth tilted his head backward and stared up at his new assistant. "So no one had been through and raided the place?"

"Nope. I guess they stuck more to the cities, Rochester and Syracuse and stuff. All those fancy lake houses were untouched. We stayed there for a couple weeks."

"He was drunk for a couple weeks is what he means." June giggled again.

"That too." Devan leaned toward June and smacked her on the butt with his palm. "But I wasn't the only one."

Barbara threw a glance at Trooper and raised her eyebrow. He was sad to see the expression highlighted her scars. It was ninety percent healed now, no oozing pus, no lingering scabs. But the wound had pulled tight as it healed and the side of her face was a jarring Halloween mask of angry purple tissue that had little malleability. He knew it could have been worse, but it was bad enough.

She slid close to him. "Think I ought to tell them she shouldn't be drinking while pregnant?"

"People got a right to make their own mistakes."

"Seems unfair to the baby inside her. It never had a choice."

Trooper shrugged. He thought the very idea of bringing a baby into this world was as dumb as dumb gets. Even if it didn't have a teenage rube for a mother, what chance would it have of surviving long enough to learn how to walk? He supposed the odds were about as good as himself making it to the age of 100.

"You're the mother in the group," Trooper said to Barbara. "You want to share some maternal advice, I'm not gonna protest."

Barbara considered it, but decided not to speak up. At least, not now.

Devan's voice, which he'd grown to equate to fingernails on a chalkboard, drowned out all other thought.

"The best part, aside from the wine, was what we found in a little, green A-frame. Bet ya can't guess what it was. Go ahead and try."

Trooper wished it had been a gag, but didn't tender that guess.

"Gold coins," Wyatt said. "A bag full of them."

"Nope. Try again."

"Bacon." Seth licked his lips at the thought.

"Nah." Devan looked back to the stragglers. "Barb. Trooper. You want to guess?"

Trooper chewed the inside of his cheek to prevent a rude comeback.

"That diamond necklace June's wearing," Barbara said. "I know that didn't come out of a gumball machine."

Everyone looked to the jewelry that decorated the teen, a necklace that would have looked more fitting on a Hollywood actress at an award show.

Devin grinned. "Nah. That was her gramma's."

Trooper's ears perked up and this time, no matter how hard he chewed his cheek, he couldn't remain quiet. "Your gramma's, you mean. You being siblings, that is."

Devan's aw shucks smile never faltered. "No, just hers. We got the same daddy but different ma's." He checked each member of the group. "I knew y'all wouldn't get it. Want me to tell you?"

I want you to shut your hick mouth, Trooper thought.

"Alright then, I'll tell you. It was a case, not just a box, a whole darn case, of Hostess cupcakes!"

"No way," Wyatt said.

"Yes, way! Here, take your brother."

They traded places and Devan slipped his backpack around to

his front and unzipped it. He extracted two plastic-wrapped cupcakes and handed one to Seth.

"Holy shit. I haven't had one of these in like three years. Mom, look." He held the cupcake up for everyone to see. Even from a few yards back Trooper noticed the signature looping white swirls on the top icing.

Devan pulled his arm back like a QB going deep and threw a cupcake to Barb then returned to his pack. "I was kinda a pig and ate a ton of 'em but we got five left. That's one for each of you and June."

Devan lobbed a cupcake Trooper's way and as much as he didn't want to like the man, just the sight of the pastry flooded his mouth with saliva. He felt the crinkle of the plastic in his hand and, even though the food inside was doubtlessly stale, couldn't wait to dig in.

June took a cupcake from her brother, then Devan handed the last one to Wyatt who looked from his gift to the man who'd given it to him.

"We can't eat these and leave you with nothing," Wyatt said. "Let's split it."

Devan shook his head. "No way, hoss. I'm sick of em if you want to know the truth. And it's my way of thanking you from saving me from listening to June talk about boy bands and make up for a few hundred miles."

Trooper unwrapped his cupcake and took a huge bite. The sugar rush was almost intoxicating and reminded him of days before this. Mornings at the station, sharing pastries with his fellow officers. Evening snacks with his mother, who was always trying out new recipes on him. It reminded him of home and for that, he was grateful.

He watched Wyatt chomp into his cupcake. Cream clung to his upper lip, entangled in the straggly mustache that had sprouted during the trip. June pointed and giggled. Even Trooper managed a smile. It was amazing what a little good food could do for a person's mood.

CHAPTER FIFTEEN

AFTER A DAY OF WALKING THE GROUP CAME UPON A SHELL GAS station that was in the midst of a long decline at the side of the road. Wyatt thought it looked as if it had been abandoned for decades and when he noticed the price of gas on the manual pumps was only $1.89 his suspicions were confirmed.

That didn't matter though. All any of them cared about was having a place to sit and get off their feet and the station was as good as anywhere for that purpose. An added bonus was the concrete floor which allowed them to build a small fire and cook up another pouch of Devan and June's freeze-dried food. The night's entrée was a chicken fajita bowl which Wyatt thought had more flavor than anything he'd eaten in years.

June leaned back and let out a soft moan, rubbing her belly.

"Eat too much?" Devan asked her.

"Naw. The baby's kicking at my guts like they're a soccer ball."

Wyatt noticed his mother perk up.

"How far along are you?" Barb asked.

June shrugged her shoulders. "Don't know, really. It's been since February that I had my flow though."

Barbara leaned in close to the girl and extended her hand toward June's midsection. June nodded and Barbara rested her palm on her stomach. She flinched a little and smiled.

"He or she's strong. That's for certain."

June almost glowed. "It's a boy. I just know it."

"Do you have a name picked out?"

Wyatt knew pregnancies were supposed to be miraculous events but talk of babies and menstrual cycles skeeved him out. He took another bite of his fajita and tried to ignore the feminine chit chat.

He was beginning to feel guilty for eating the siblings' food and reached into their supplies, grabbing a can of baked beans.

"I know these aren't refried beans, but it's as close as we've got." He lobbed the can to Devan who rolled it back and forth between his palms.

"You sure, hoss? If you want to ration your goods, we aren't gonna complain."

Wyatt nodded, but he could feel Trooper's stare. "We're sure."

"Alright," Devan said. "So a feast it is."

He popped the top and sat the can on the periphery of the fire so it could heat up. "But I'll forewarn y'all, you might not want to snuggle up next to me tonight after wolfing down beans and Mexican."

June pinched her nose. "He's not kidding. We should make him sleep outside so we don't all suffocate."

That drew laughter from Seth and Wyatt thought his mom even gave up a reluctant chuckle.

Trooper seemed to be the only one refusing to accept the good cheer and as much as Wyatt loved the man, he was growing weary of his grumpiness. This day had brought the most laughter, the most talk, and the most food they'd experienced in weeks on the road and Wyatt wasn't going to be made to feel guilty for enjoying himself.

"Let me ask you a question," Trooper said to Devan.

"Sure thing."

"I imagine you've known hunger, just like us. So why do you give your food away so freely?"

The high spirits took a nosedive and an uncomfortable silence lingered for a moment before Devan spoke up. "In all honesty, I guess I'm just hoping to make you guys like us."

Wyatt cocked his head. "Why wouldn't we like you?"

"Well, if you couldn't tell, I talk a lot when I get nervous. My daddy always said my mouth ran like a flapper on a duck's ass. That gets on a lot of folks' nerves and I suppose I hoped the food might make up for that and you'd let us stick around a good long while." He stared at Trooper, waiting to see if the old man would give him any type of positive affirmation.

Wyatt felt bad for him. He couldn't imagine what life on the road would be like if it was him and Seth out here all alone. And how hard it would be to fit into not just a group, but a family. No wonder he was nervous.

Trooper nodded. "Okay."

Devan gave a toothy, confused smile. "Is okay good or not?"

"It's okay. Don't press your luck." Trooper grabbed his bag and climbed to his feet. "Now I'm gonna sleep in the garage so I don't have to smell your gas all night."

That was as close as Trooper came to a joke and Wyatt couldn't hold back a laugh.

"Good call, Trooper," Devan said.

Trooper gave them a small wave as he faded from the light of the fire and moved into the garage bay.

"I think I'll join him," Barbara said. "No offense, Devan."

Devan grinned. "None taken, ma'am. And that's probably a wise choice."

Barb tousled Seth's hair and patted Wyatt's shoulder before she too left the room.

"Man, you're so lucky to have your mom," Devan said.

"What happened to yours?" Seth asked.

Wyatt thought that was a pretty personal question and shot him a look.

"It's okay," Devan said, reading Wyatt's expression. "She died about eight months ago. She'd been sick for a long time, coughing and hacking around. Got to the point where she was bringing up blood and losing weight. She was pretty much a skeleton at the end. I think maybe it was lung cancer but who really knows. No docs around anymore."

Devan wiped wetness from his eyes and June stared at the floor. Wyatt looked to where his mother had gone. He didn't want to think about life without her. "Damn. I'm sorry about that."

"That's life, right? No one said it was supposed to be easy." He sniffled a little and wiped at his face. "So whatcha heading south for?" Devon wrapped his shirt in his hand and pulled the can of beans away from the fire's edge. The side which had been closest was singed black and Wyatt caught the aroma of burned food. That was okay though.

Devan dumped some beans from the can into his palm then looked to June. She shook her head, so he passed it to Seth instead.

"Mom wants to go to South America."

"Why so far?" June asked.

"Supposed to be better. That's the theory, anyway. Something about the way the currents blew the nuclear fallout or whatever the hell it was that made everything up here..." He didn't know what to say.

"Turn to shit?" Devan volunteered.

Wyatt smiled. "Yeah. Pretty much."

Seth passed him the beans, and he took a mouthful, gasping a bit at the heat on his tongue.

"How about you, Seth? How'd you end up a cripple?"

Wyatt glanced at his brother, having an idea how this might go.

Seth leaned forward, pulling himself closer to the others, like any good story-teller. "You ever hear those stories about a crazy woman stealing a baby from the hospital and trying to pass it off as her own?"

June nodded. "That happened near where we was from."

"No it didn't," Devan said. "That's an Urban legend they told around town to scare people."

"Sort of," Seth said. "It became one anyway. Seems like it happened in every city, every hospital. But it got its start with me."

Wyatt watched their faces. Devan's was disbelieving but June's eyes were wide and awed.

"You serious?" She asked.

"Serious as a dead man." Seth stroked a few fine hairs which had sprouted on his chin and carried on. "I was a month or two old and had to keep going back to the hospital because I was jaundiced. It wasn't anything major, but they had to put me under a light, had little glasses on me so I didn't fry my retinas."

"Like a tanning booth!" June said.

"Pretty much. But instead of this light turning me into a Cheeto, it was to make me normal. Anyway, one time I was in for a treatment when mom went to get some Funions out of the vending machine and I guess the nurse on duty was out on a smoke break or something and I was chilling under the light all alone and this woman came into the room. They said she was wearing scrubs so she fit right in didn't look suspicious at all. And she grabbed me.

"She was halfway out the front door before anyone even knew I was gone and by the time they called for security, she had me in the passenger seat of her Mazda and was zooming away from the hospital like she was trying to win the Indy 500. That, of course, drew some attention so the police, they closed in on her right away and it was high-speed chase time."

By this point even Devan watched, rapt.

"The helicopters were flying overhead, news stations broke into the afternoon soaps to show it all going down live on TV. They said there were fourteen cop cars following. But she didn't care. She was on her way to the Canadian border and I was along for the ride."

"Holy shit!" Devan rubbed his palms together. "That's fucking amazing!"

"You're telling me," Seth said. "But she forgot one thing."

"What's that?" June asked.

"To fill up her tank."

"Oh, man!" Devan said.

"So she's running on E and I guess she knew her goose was about to be cooked so she decided to go the distraction route. She slowed down a bit, not a lot, I'm talking about going from eighty down to fifty. Then she leaned across the seat, pushed open the passenger door and shoved my one-month-old, yellow ass straight out of the car!"

"Oh my God!" June said.

"I bounced off the asphalt, did a few somersaults and cartwheels. The cop cars, they swerved all over the place so as not to run me over. A few of them crashed even. Eventually I stopped rolling and, well, I was a little worse for the wear." Seth slapped his thighs.

Wyatt felt like his head was going to blow off from holding back laughter but he didn't want to spoil his brother's fun.

"Are you shitting me?" Devan asked.

Seth shook his head. "God's honest truth."

"You poor thing!" June said. She grabbed Seth's hand and gave it a squeeze. Wyatt thought his cheeks flared in a blush.

"It's alright," Seth said. "My family got a hella sweet settlement from the hospital. And I got free wheelchairs for life."

"What happened to the woman who took you?" Devan asked.

Seth shrugged his shoulders. "No idea. They never caught her. She's probably living in Ottawa for all I know."

"That's fucked up," Devan said.

"Indeed." Seth nodded, sober. "Anyway, that's the story about how I ended up in the chair."

CHAPTER SIXTEEN

Seth came awake to a muffled, rustling noise. It took him a moment to remember where he was, then the leftover smell of smoke from the extinguished fire reminded him of their evening in the gas station.

It had taken him a while to fall asleep. He was excited over the new additions to their group and enjoyed having people closer his own age to talk to. The fact that June was the prettiest girl he'd seen in years factored into that too, of course. He didn't even mind that she might as well have been smuggling a watermelon under her shirt. He hoped that tomorrow he'd have more time to talk to her and to potentially show off and impress her with his wit and humor since the physical side of him was lacking.

He glanced around the small room and discovered he was alone. Wyatt's sleeping bag was empty. Devan and June's the same. They must have gone outside, Seth realized and felt a pang of disappointment. They were hanging out together, maybe even sharing a snack, and left him inside. Alone.

He knew his handicap made him a burden at times. There was

no spur-of-the-moment fun when you had to wait for him to climb into his chair and wheel himself around, but it still hurt.

"Fuckers," he muttered and rolled onto his side. He considered going to the effort of joining them in the night, if for no other reason than to tell them to screw off for leaving him out, for excluding him from whatever they were up to, but before he could get that far he saw movement in the garage.

Peering into the darkness was pointless, so he focused on listening instead. It was silent for a moment, then he heard whispers. Footsteps. And a crunch, like someone had stepped on a peanut shell.

"Hold still, pops."

Was that Devan's voice? He'd heard it so much throughout the day that he felt confident in the belief that it was.

"Devan?" Seth asked. "Wyatt? Are you guys in there?"

The noise coming from the garage stopped. Seth propped himself onto his elbows and army crawled toward the void.

He made it a fourth of the way there when June came into view. She sashayed to him, grinning.

"Sorry if we woke ya. We were trying to be discreet."

"What's going on?"

"We're having a surprise party."

June was close enough for him to smell the lavender body lotion she'd slathered herself in before going to sleep. She bent at the waist, bringing their faces only inches apart.

"A surprise party?" Seth felt his heartbeat quicken from being so close to the girl and wondered what she'd do if he leaned in and kissed her perfect, pink lips. But he didn't have time for that because Devan appeared behind her.

"Yeah," Devan said. "Surprise!" His arm arced down, and it was only when it was too late that Seth realized he was swinging a tire iron at his face. He felt a stinging pain as it connected with his cheek, and then all he saw were stars.

THROUGH THE FOG THAT FILLED HIS HEAD, SETH REALIZED HE was being dragged by the arms. He struggled but Devan's grip was a vise and he couldn't pull free.

It was a short trip and a few seconds later he was in the garage. He saw his mother on the floor, arms and feet bound together with Bungie cords.. Across from her Trooper sat propped against the garage door. He too was tied up and his mouth was covered in duct tape for good measure. Seth saw a stream of blood coming from the man's nose which was bent at a harsh, unnatural angle.

Devan dropped Seth's arms and rolled him onto his back. "We don't want to hurt anyone, okay? We just want your stuff and we'll be gone so don't do anything stupid." He reached for an extension cord.

"You don't gotta tie him up," June said. "I'll take care of him. You go get his brother."

"You sure?" Devan asked.

June nodded. "Sure as sugar." She stepped over Seth and then sat on his legs, straddling him.

"What are you doing?" Devon asked, his whisper rising slightly.

"I just want to have a little fun." June began to rub his chest with her hands.

Seth heard Devan leave the room but his attention was on the girl on top of him. The way she felt against him. The heat of her body transferring to his own. He wanted to fight back, to stop them from robbing his family - or worse - but he was a boy who'd never so much as kissed a girl before and he had no fight to give.

"I always wondered how it worked with cripples" June said. "Your legs don't work but what about everything else?"

She rocked back and forth on top of him, their crotches separated only by their clothing.

"Stop it." He wondered if the plea sounded as fake out loud as it did in his head. He could feel his mother's eyes on him, Trooper watching him. He was ashamed that he wasn't doing something to prevent this, but at the same time, he enjoyed it. This was what he dreamed about, albeit not in such a fucked up scenario. And no matter how embarrassed or ashamed he was, his body was in charge and he felt himself get hard against her undulating hips.

June giggled. "Oh wow, I guess some parts still work, huh?"

She reached down and rubbed him with her hand, through his jeans, then just as suddenly as it had began, it was over. Seth felt damp heat spread across his groin and let out a soft "Oof."

June leaned down, whispering in his ear. "You're welcome."

As she slid off him Seth turned his face away from his mother and Trooper, unable to meet their gaze. It was the best and worst moment of his life.

CHAPTER SEVENTEEN

Wyatt crouched behind a dented newspaper machine that hadn't peddled the daily news since the 1990s. The cramps were awful, but the smell was even worse. It had been eons since he'd eaten well but now he was paying the price. As hot, liquified diarrhea shot out of his body, he wondered if it was worth it.

Yeah, probably.

He ripped a fart so loud he looked to the gas station and watched, wondering if he'd woken the others. The thought of any of them stumbling outside, startled and scared only to find him squatting over a steaming pile of excrement terrified him.

Then he saw movement. "Oh, fuck me."

He tried to will his asshole shut, his bowels into submission, but knew the battle was only half-won as he scrambled to wipe himself clean.

Through his panic, he realized that he might be dealing with something even worse than getting caught beshitted. Because the person moving away from the gas station was pushing a shopping cart filled to the brim. And they were running.

Wyatt jerked up his jeans, not caring whether or not he still reeked. He grabbed the pistol he'd set aside before beginning his expulsion and rose to his feet. The person with the cart rapidly disappeared into the night and he realized they weren't worth chasing, at least not yet. All that mattered was figuring out what had gone down inside the garage.

He didn't make it a yard in their direction when he heard Devon's voice.

"Where ya been, hoss?"

Wyatt turned and found Devan behind him. The man had a grin on his face and a shotgun aimed and ready to fire. He took a step, his foot splashing into Wyatt's waste, and lost his smile.

"Aw, fuck." Devan stared down at his foot which was ankle deep in shit. "I liked these boots. Now they're all cocked up. I oughta shoot you just for that." He let the barrel of the shotgun drift over Wyatt, first his midsection, then his chest, then his head.

"What the hell are you doing?"

"What the fuck do you think?"

Wyatt supposed that was a dumb question. It was all too obvious what was going on. He'd been a fool, an idiot, the world's biggest moron. And now everyone he loved was going to pay the price. His gaze fell to the ground, and he almost wished Devan would shoot him and save him that shame.

"Aw, don't blame yourself, hoss. I've been perfecting this act for five years now. Shit, I'd have been damned offended if you'd caught on. No one ever does."

"So you've done this before?"

Devan rolled his eyes. "Not all of us have been holed up in Maine. We've been out here in the weeds having to stay alive. Doing what it takes to stay alive."

"But I really liked you." Wyatt knew that was a pathetic thing to say. That it made him sound weak, but it was the truth. He felt like he'd found a best friend in Devan and that hurt almost more than anything else.

Devan lowered the shotgun. "Look, Wyatt. I'm sorry. You're a good kid, but it's just the way the world is."

Wyatt shook his head, hoping it was enough of a distraction that Devan wouldn't notice as he flicked off the safety of his pistol. It worked. "It doesn't have to be. Just because everything else sucks doesn't mean you have to suck too. It's not too late to be a decent person."

"Yeah, it is," Devan said.

Maybe he's right, Wyatt thought.

He fired the pistol from his hip. The explosion as the gun went off sounded like a thunderclap, echoing over the flat land again and again and again.

Devan spun sideways, dropping the shotgun and falling to a knee. Wyatt raced to him, kicked the gun away, then kicked him in the face. Devan hit the ground hard.

Wyatt stood over him, holding the pistol with both hands. "I should blow your head off you fucking thief. Fucking liar." His voice cracked with fury.

Devan held his hand up. One of them was smeared red with blood but his face remained calm, smug even. "It's your rodeo."

No matter how much Wyatt tried to hold firm, his hands trembled. "Tell me why I should let you live?"

"I ain't gonna do that. A man's got to decide what kind of person he wants to be all on his own." He propped himself up on his elbows, wincing. "I'm unarmed. Hurt. And I might've stole from you but I didn't kill none of yours. They're all safe in the garage. Cause I'm no killer, hoss, and I don't think you are either."

"You have no idea what I am." Even Wyatt wasn't believing that bluff.

"That's right, I don't. But if you kill me then June's out there pregnant and all alone and what chance do you think she's got? You want to live with that?" He scooted himself back, putting a few more inches between himself and the gun Wyatt had trained on him. "Now I'm gonna stand up real slow and harmless-like. And I can either walk into the dark or you can shoot me down. I won't judge you either way."

He stood, hands still raised and backed away, step after step. Wyatt wanted to shoot him, needed to shoot him, even though doing so would solve nothing, but Devan knew him better than he knew himself. He removed his finger from the trigger.

"We left you enough food for a few days because we're not all bad. And you've got that little Ruger and the shotgun so you can fend for yourselves." Devan faded away, only an outline now. "I used to be a lot like you, Wyatt. But there's no place for good folks anymore. You change or you die."

With that he was gone.

CHAPTER EIGHTEEN

"I HEARD A GUNSHOT," TROOPER SAID AS WYATT PEELED THE tape from his mouth, the skin stretching, fine hairs ripping free from his face. When he'd heard the pistol, his first thought had been that Wyatt had been shot. That he was out there, lying in the parking lot bleeding to death or was dead already and they were trussed up like turkeys unable to do a damned thing about it. At least he wouldn't have to live with that.

Wyatt nodded. "I shot Devan."

Trooper sucked in a mouthful of air. Truth be told, he didn't think Wyatt had it in him. He was never so happy to be wrong. "You kill him?"

Wyatt's gaze shifted to the floor, and that was answer enough. Part of him was glad Wyatt wouldn't have to live with the guilt of taking another man's life, because no matter how wrong they'd done you, no matter what horrible acts they'd committed, there was always guilt.

On the other hand he wanted that hick dead. Dead for stealing. Dead for talking too much. And maybe most of all, dead for being able to fool them. Because even though he had reservations about

Devan and his sister, if she really was his sister, which Trooper doubted, he'd let his guard down enough to sleep soundly enough to be taken by surprise. And that pissed him off to no end.

"Motherfuckers!" Barbara screamed from the next room over. Wyatt had freed her first, and she immediately went to check their supplies.

"Don't sound good," Trooper said.

Wyatt shook his head.

Barbara stomped into the garage.

"How bad is it?" Trooper asked.

"They left our clothes. Took all the guns. All the bullets. All the food except for a case of wax beans." She kicked an empty oil drum and the hollow thud reverberated off the concrete block walls.

Trooper almost said 'Calm down' but he knew from decades of living with his mother that those words were apt to have the exact opposite effect. Besides, she had a right to anger. The way it sounded, anger might be about all they had left.

She wasn't done. "I can't fucking believe this! Is this how it is out here? Is this what we left our homes for? To be tied up and robbed by a couple kids?"

As annoyed as Trooper was with the night's developments, he knew just how much worse it could have been. Devan and June could have easily murdered them, but they didn't. Sure, they were in a bad spot now, but there were ways out of it. It was time to be the leader they all needed and try to put as good a spin on the situation as possible.

"Barbara, we're alive," Trooper said.

"Oh fuck off, Trooper!"

"Mom, please don't." Seth still sat on the floor. Trooper could see the anxiety on the boy's face.

"I don't want to hear it Seth. What do you think is going to happen to us now? Are we going to starve first or get picked off by more of these assholes? Make your prediction."

Trooper leaned against an old air pump. He watched Barbara

have her moment and debated on stepping into it again, but decided against it. In the corner, Wyatt was pressed so tight against the wall that he looked as if he wanted to melt into it and disappear. Trooper approached him and kept his voice to a low whisper.

"Have you seen your mother like this before?"

"Just once, when Dad... You know..."

Trooper nodded. He remembered that day. Her screams reached across the street from the Morrill house and into his own.

Before they left Maine, he knew something like this might happen. He almost assumed it would happen. And he'd made plans for how to fix it because that's what he did. Trooper prepared.

"Look, Barbara--"

"Trooper, I swear to God. Let me freak the fuck out for a few minutes, okay?"

"Let me tell you one thing first. Then if you want to freak the fuck out, I'll let you have at it."

She looked to him and he thought some of the boiling rage was already leaving her eyes. "What?"

"I know where we can get weapons and food." Trooper didn't enjoy being the center of attention, but now he was.

"You what?" Barbara asked.

He almost wished he'd have kept his old mouth shut. That he'd have just let Barbara go off the rails for a while and then hit the road, scrabbling together whatever they could find along the way. That would be hard, but the other option might be even worse.

"You still got that map, Seth?"

Seth nodded. "In my pack."

"Wyatt, get it."

Wyatt left the room and Trooper tried to avoid Barbara's curious stare until he returned. He took the map from him and squatted down beside Seth as he unfolded it. He was pleased with how well Seth had been keeping track of their progress. It would make what was to come easier, if that was possible.

"You've done good, boy. Real good."

Seth gave a contented smile.

Trooper pointed to the end of the line Seth had traced. "We're here." He dragged his finger southeast until it reached one of the T.P. markings. "And we need to go here."

"They even took your toilet paper, Trooper?" Seth asked.

Trooper couldn't hold back a chuckle at that. "No, son, I fibbed to you. T.P. doesn't stand for toilet paper. It means trading post."

Over the last five years he'd had to make friendships with the types of people he'd normally send to a jail cell. But desperate times and all that.

This was where they needed to go. He only hoped he wasn't taking his friends to their deaths.

CHAPTER NINETEEN

THREE DAYS OF WALKING, OF EATING NOTHING BUT A FEW spoonfuls of wax beans, of almost freezing through the night, and they still hadn't reached the mysterious trading post that Trooper assured them was out there. Somewhere.

Wyatt was beginning to wonder if the man had received bad info, that there wasn't actually anything to find. Or, even worse that his aged friend was losing his mind.

Stop that, he told himself. Trooper was razor-sharp and nothing had changed. He just had to keep believing. To have faith that something better waited ahead.

In his mind Wyatt was turning it into a mixture of the land of Oz mashed up with one of those towns that sit off the interstate that seem to only exist so you can fill up your gas tank and dine at any of twenty or so different restaurants. He pictured a smorgasbord of options from which they'd be able to choose, of foods to eat, of weapons to claim.

That's what the hopeful part of his mind conjured, anyway. The realistic part, the part he tried to lock away inside a soundproof box to protect himself from the nagging worry, knew they didn't have anything to trade. He doubted this world, which seemed more violent and selfish with each passing mile, took pity on those with nothing. That the people who ran the trading post had patience for beggars.

Trooper has a plan, he assured himself.

That wasn't much, but that was all he had.

They'd made camp as day transitioned to dusk, not that it was a dramatic change. Light gray to dark gray, quickly followed by pitch black. As Wyatt unrolled his sleeping bag, he thought the murky atmosphere mirrored his mood.

He blamed himself for the theft. For allowing Devan and June into their cadre. For trusting. It was another straw atop his back. First letting his mother be assaulted and mauled. Now putting them all at risk of starvation - or worse. He couldn't help but think how much better they'd all be if he was gone. Or better yet, had never existed.

"You okay, brother?"

Wyatt turned and found Seth sitting on the ground. He'd taken a break from arranging a pile of twigs and brush into a pyre and now stared at him.

"What? Yeah."

Seth snapped a small branch with his hands but didn't take his eyes off Wyatt. "I don't think you've said twenty words since the gas station."

Wyatt dug through his pack, avoiding his brother's prying gaze. "I didn't know you were counting my words. There's eight more for your tally."

"I worry about you."

This wasn't a conversation Wyatt wanted to have. He grabbed an empty plastic bottle from his pack and stood. "Well, don't."

"It wasn't your fault. We all got fooled. Even Trooper."

Wyatt understood that as the truth, but in his head, he'd forever be a thirteen-year-old boy. The one who'd helped his father lug his bags toward a taxi on the last morning they ever saw each other. 'Take care of your mom and Seth while I'm gone,' his father had said as he flopped into the back seat of the cab. 'I will.' Wyatt promised.

What a joke that was.

"I'm going to look for water."

He didn't wait for a response.

As he knelt beside a shallow creek and let the vaguely brown water fill the bottle, he heard a whimper. He flinched at the sound, the bottle almost slipping from his grip. After pushing it into the soft silt so it wouldn't float away, Wyatt drew his pistol and turned in the direction of the noise.

He heard it again.

It wasn't human. And that meant it could be food. The notion of returning to camp with a rabbit or hell, even a squirrel, to roast was better than finding a pot of gold. It would be his chance to make amends. And this time he wasn't going to fuck up.

He pushed through a thicket of dead mountain laurel, the dry branches clawing at his face and arms. He moved slow, trying not to snap them, trying to remain quiet. Between the brush and the rapidly coming dark it was almost impossible to see, and he worried that whatever was there would hear him or smell him or sense him and disappear into the shadows for good.

He crouched, kneeling on the soggy, rotting leaves and felt the moisture seep through his jeans and lick his skin. He'd regret that when it got cold, but if he handled this right, wet knees would be nothing more than a minor inconvenience because he'd sleep well with meat in his belly.

He reached forward and pushed aside a branch, easing it back far enough to gain a window through the bush. And there it was. A mass of tan fur thirty yards away. His mind immediately connected the color with a deer. One sprawled on the ground, resting before a long night of foraging.

Wyatt knew killing the deer with one bullet would be a challenge. An impossibility at this distance. He had to get closer.

He held his breath as he slipped through the last of the laurel and into the clearing ahead. Every footfall was slow, measured. He sought out leaves and mud upon which to step, careful to avoid any branches, anything dry, anything that might rustle or crack under his weight.

By the time he'd halved the abyss between himself and the animal he'd lost almost all light. What had been a mass of tan was now an outline. He knew he had to take his shot soon or it would be too dark, a waste of a bullet. But he needed to get a bit closer before he could trust himself to fire. Five more yards.

He only made it three when he mis stepped and his size tens came down on a broken tree limb. It popped, and he leveled the pistol, sure the deer would bounce to its feet and dash away. Only it didn't run.

Instead, the animal raised its head, swiveling it toward the disturbance. That's when Wyatt realized it wasn't a deer at all. It was a dog.

It whimpered again but didn't move from where it laid. As Wyatt got closer, he thought it looked like a German Shepherd, one mixed with something smaller, maybe a terrier. Its chest rose and fell rapid fire the closer Wyatt got, but still, it didn't flee.

It had been years since he'd seen a dog. The friendly, fearless animals had been some of the first animals picked off when fresh food supplies ran low. He could hardly believe any remained.

The dog wasn't running. It was sick or injured. It waited for Wyatt to put it out of its misery and provide for his family. Two birds, one stone.

But he wasn't ready to become that man. Not yet. He holstered the gun.

"I'm not gonna hurt you, buddy." He extended his hand. The dog sniffed, pressing its warm, dry nose into his palm, then gave a tentative lick. Its dry tongue felt like high grit sandpaper skimming his flesh.

"It's okay," he said. "You'll be okay."

Wyatt had no medical knowledge outside of prime time hospital dramas, but he didn't need a degree to know the dog was dying. A good forty percent of its fur was missing, allowing hard, dark skin to show through. Its body was riddled with scars and scabs. One area near the center of its back was ulcerated and oozed pus.

Despite all of that, when the dog felt his touch it panted happily and rolled onto its side to provide him easy access for a belly rub. As he scratched the dog's undercarriage, clouds of dust puffed from its fur and he watched fleas leap and bounce into the air. He saw the dog was a male, one that had been neutered, and realized it had been someone's pet.

"How'd you end up all alone," he wondered. But that train of thought came to a quick end when he caught sight of the dog's back right leg.

The appendage was two-thirds of the way to being torn off. The skin was mangled and ripped, hanging in loose tendrils. Through the gnarled mess of matted fur, dried blood, and pus he found something even worse. The flesh undulated and rippled and when the wound gaped open maggots rained from it.

"Oh shit."

He leaned in closer to inspect the injury. That was a mistake. The smell of infection and death and rot was worse than the sight. Wyatt felt his stomach tighten but aside from a half cup of beans he'd eaten nothing since the morning. He spat out a mouthful of saliva tinged with bile, then wiped his mouth with the back of his hand.

As he stared down at the dog, he knew what he needed to do.

CHAPTER TWENTY

TROOPER HEARD WYATT COMING BUT KNEW FROM THE SOUND of the boy's footfalls that something was off. He moved slower, but it also sounded as if he was dragging or carrying something as each step came down with more heft than usual.

"It's about time." Seth grabbed an empty pot, ready to accept water for boiling. "I was starting to think he got lost and we'd have to mount a search and rescue party."

Barbara stared into the fire, disinterested, or too tired to give much concern to her son's return.

Trooper made sure the shotgun was within reach, just in case, and held his breath. He didn't have to wait long.

Wyatt marched toward camp, his arms laden down with the scrawny husk of a medium-sized animal. It took Trooper a few seconds of staring before he realized it was a dog.

"Holy shit, dinner is served!" Seth shouted.

That finally brought Barbara out of her malaise and she turned toward the arriving party. "Wyatt?" She asked.

When Wyatt was within a few feet of the fire, he crouched down and eased the dog onto the ground. "It's not dead," Wyatt said.

Trooper leaned in for a better look, not that he needed to make a thorough examination. "It will be soon."

Wyatt was busy rummaging through his backpack and ignored the remark. Seth scooted closer to the animal but Barbara grabbed his wrist. "Don't! It could be rabid or have distemper."

Trooper grabbed the shotgun and rested it across his lap. "You want me to finish it?"

Wyatt spun toward him, eyes blazing with the reflection of the campfire. "Don't you dare. I'm going to help it."

Trooper fought off a sigh. They didn't need melodrama, didn't need a reason to bicker amongst themselves. This journey was hard enough without all that nonsense and he wanted to end it before it began. "It's beyond fixin, Wyatt. Anyone can see that. Hell, I can smell that."

Wyatt returned to his bag. "You shoot that dog, Trooper and so help me God I'll leave this camp, leave all of you, and never come back."

Damn fool, Trooper thought as he set aside the gun and stood. He circled the fire and settled in between Wyatt and the dog.

Its breathing was quick and shallow but, as he knelt beside it, that was the least of the critter's problems. Its back leg was near rotted off and infested with maggots and infection. He couldn't believe Wyatt thought it could be fixed. For a smart boy, he sure could be a moron at times.

Trooper turned to Wyatt and rested his hand on his shoulder. He felt Wyatt stiffen under his touch. "Wyatt, that animal's in pain. The merciful thing to do is to put it down."

Wyatt turned back to him and when he did, he held a buck knife.

"Jesus, Wyatt!" Barbara jumped to her feet and despite the situation being dire, Trooper was glad to see the woman had some spirit left in her.

"Come on, brother," Seth said. "You're making this worse than it needs to be."

Wyatt raised the knife, displaying it. "It's for the dog. His leg needs to come off."

Trooper shook his head. "You ain't got nothing to sedate it. Nothing for pain. That's tantamount to torture."

"If it doesn't die from the shock, it'll die from blood loss. Don't do this," Barbara said.

Wyatt looked at her, then Seth. He saved Trooper for last. "You just want to eat him. All of you."

Trooper didn't even consider lying. "You can stop its suffering and give us a decent meal. To me, that's an easy call."

"He's right. You know how much we need this, how hungry we've all been since Devan robbed us." Barbara reached for Wyatt but he pulled away. Trooper knew she'd gone too far in trying to guilt the boy. If anything, her words had solidified his resolve.

Wyatt moved to the fire and pushed the blade of the knife into the flames. "Stay back, all of you, and let me do this." He held the metal in the fire until it became discolored from the heat, then ignored the rest of them, all his attention on the dying animal.

"I'm really sorry, buddy. This is gonna hurt."

Trooper didn't watch what happened next, but he heard it and that was more than enough. He thought Wyatt was being foolish, was being dangerously naïve, but he realized something in the boy had changed. Wyatt didn't need or even want, their approval. He trusted himself. And Trooper thought that was the most important aspect of being a man. As much as he thought this was the wrong call, he admired Wyatt for standing up for himself, for doing what he believed was right, consequences be damned.

CHAPTER TWENTY-ONE

DISEASED FLESH SIZZLED AS THE KNIFE SLICED THROUGH IT. Maggots were bisected and dissected, bursting with yellow ooze. Although the dog howled in pain, it was too weak to put up a fight. Wyatt pinned its head to the ground with his left hand, but it never tried to bite. He kept cutting with his right hand and didn't stop until the knife broke free on the other side and the dog's rotten leg came loose.

Wyatt plunged the knife back into the fire as blood shot from the amputation site with alarming speed. The bottom half of Wyatt's shirt and the top half of his jeans were saturated in seconds. Oh shit, he thought. They were right. The dog's going to bleed out and all I did was make its last few minutes hell.

The dog wasn't struggling, so he used the hand that had restrained it to cover the wound and kept the knife in the flames until it was so hot the hilt throbbed in his palm. Then he pulled it from the fire and held the blistering steel to the wound.

Blood and infection and maggots boiled against the metal and the smell reminded him a bit of a time that he'd put hamburgers on the grill, then went to play video games and forgotten all about them.

When he remembered, almost an hour later, the burgers were the size of half-dollars and the color and consistency of hockey pucks. Despite the awfulness of the situation, the memory made him smile a bit. And gave him an idea.

While the wound cauterized, Wyatt grabbed the severed limb. He turned to the others who sat on their sleeping bags and ate beans. They weren't watching, but that didn't deter him.

"You all wanted meat for supper?" Wyatt asked.

They risked looking his way and, when they did, Wyatt tossed the leg to them. "Here you go. Dinner is served."

The leg skidded across the ground before colliding with Seth's useless legs. Barbara kicked it away, a look of horror on her face.

It was Trooper that picked up the limb. He sniffed it. "Spoiled," he said, then tossed it into the fire.

"Don't say I didn't offer," Wyatt said.

He looked down at the dog. Its eyes were closed, but it was still breathing. The wound, the makeshift surgical site, was charred black and mostly done bleeding. Wyatt didn't know whether it would survive an hour let alone the night but he knew he'd made the right decision either way. He used his fingers to pick the remaining maggots off the dog, dropping them into the fire after their removal, and waited.

CHAPTER TWENTY-TWO

WYATT STAYED AWAKE THE ENTIRE NIGHT, HIS HEAD IN THE dirt beside the dog, listening, maybe waiting even for its breathing to stop.

It didn't. Before the others came awake, the dog regained consciousness, first raising its head off the ground and sniffing the air, then sniffing Wyatt.

"Good morning, buddy. Glad you decided to wake up."

The Morrill's had never owned a dog, they'd been a cat family. But even though his experience with canines was limited, he thought the dog seemed better already. The vacant, barely there look in its eyes was replaced by an alert curiosity. It strained its neck to examine the joint to which its leg had once been attached, but which Wyatt had wrapped in gauze. He'd redressed the wound once through the night after it bled through, but this bandage remained clean. So far.

The dog sniffed, then took an exploratory lick.

"No, boy. Don't do that."

He stopped at the command surprising Wyatt. "You're a smart one, aren't you?"

The dog seemed to smile, mouth agape, tongue lolling. Wyatt ran his fingers through its fur, not caring about the stench or the bugs, although he knew he'd have to get him cleaned up if - when - his health improved.

"I see it lasted the night," Barbara said.

Wyatt hadn't realized she'd woken. He was still annoyed with her over the night prior. Over her willingness to give up on this living creature. "You sound disappointed."

Barbara clutched her hand to her chest. "Ouch. That hurt." She smiled.

Wyatt wanted to stay angry and sanctimonious, but her scarred face smiled so rarely these days he knew doing so would make him an asshole. And she didn't deserve that. "Sorry."

"No, I earned that." His mother crouched beside him and the dog. "I'm the one who's sorry. I was selfish last night."

"Because we're half-starved," Wyatt said.

"You're in the same state as the rest of us and you didn't want to kill it. You did the right thing."

Wyatt opened his mouth to speak but couldn't find the right words so he stayed quiet.

"I always wanted a dog, you know. But your father's allergies." She scratched the dog's head. "He's looking good."

"I thought so too but didn't want to get my hopes up."

"Hope's not a bad thing."

Wyatt realized she wasn't looking at the dog anymore. She was looking at him. And he looked back, really looked, for the first time since she'd been attacked. His eyes welled up with tears.

"Stop, Wyatt." She reached out to him and cupped his cheek in her palm. "Please don't let anything change who you are. Because you're the best of us."

Wyatt felt like anything but. For most of this trip, he'd felt like the anchor holding them back and making things worse. Even before they left Maine, he was always letting them down. And she'd felt the same way. He was certain of that.

He felt like he was supposed to say something profound, to spill his heart, but he knew if he opened his mouth he was more apt to sob than speak.

His mother drew him in close and embraced him. They stayed like that for a while.

"By God, is that mutt still alive?" Trooper said.

They broke apart at his voice.

"He is," Wyatt said.

"What a shame." Trooper stood over the dog, stared down at it. "I thought you were gonna be my supper." His accent came through. Supp'ah.

The dog's head snapped up, and it panted. Wyatt was sure now that it wasn't his imagination. The dog was happy.

"I think he likes that," Wyatt said.

"Likes what?"

"That name. Supper."

"Oh hell no. Wasn't nothing but a bad joke. You can't call that dog Supper," Trooper said.

The dog's tail thudded to and fro. Wyatt laughed and Barb joined in. "That settles it," Wyatt said.

Trooper shook his head but smiled. "All right then. I can see you're never gonna let me live this down. Supper it is."

The dog pushed with its front feet, raising its chest off the ground. Wyatt saw its remaining hind leg scratching for traction in the dirt and began to panic. He reached for it, ready to hold it immobile.

"Let it go," Trooper said. "Dog knows its body better than you."

"What if he falls? Or breaks open the wound?"

The dog - Supper - wasn't listening. His back leg flexed and, after a great deal of effort, he was on his feet.

He took a staggering step and Wyatt was certain he was going down. He gasped and lunged, but Supper steadied himself. He took another step. And another. Wyatt knew the dog wasn't out of the woods yet, there was the potential for infection, or worse, but he wasn't going to let himself think too far ahead. It was alive, and that was all that mattered.

CHAPTER TWENTY-THREE

SETH SAW THE MOUND BESIDE THE ROAD BEFORE ANYONE ELSE. He'd been staring ahead, making sure he had time to dodge potholes or debris while he pushed himself along. The last few days had brought them to roads that were on the flat side and he was glad to be able to move himself along most of the time.

The dog usually hobbled beside him although its hobble was already developing into an awkward limp. He was impressed with how fast the dog - he hated to think of it as Supper and hated Wyatt for deciding that was its name - was improving. They'd given it an entire can of wax beans which it gobbled up but the real treasure came when they passed by a discount grocery store.

All the human food was long gone but an entire rack of canned dog food remained untouched. Apparently, in the apocalypse, most folks only cared about themselves and stopped giving a shit about their pets. Real nice, Seth thought.

Supper ate one can. Then a second. Then a third. It stared longingly at the others but Trooper had insisted they stop at three and that any more might cause it to barf up when it had eaten. The day after it ate three more. And the next.

They also found some long-expired flea shampoo which Wyatt had used to clean up the dog. It made a dramatic improvement, both in the animal's smell and appearance and Seth also realized that he hadn't noticed any bugs on the dog lately. As Seth took in all of Supper's improvements, he felt damn guilty about wanting to eat him.

Supper loped ahead of him, veering toward the mystery lump. All Seth could make out was a dark color and something flapping in the wind. Maybe plastic or fabric of some kind.

"Hey, Supper. Don't run off." He wasn't sure why he was suddenly worried. They'd seen enough trash on this trip to fill Sebago Lake. There was no reason to believe whatever lied ahead was anything other than a garbage bag or chunk of a car or even some long-dead person's tattered wardrobe. But he had a feeling, an instinct, that it was something more than that. "Supper!"

The dog ignored him.

"He won't run off. He knows we got the food," Trooper said from behind.

Seth glanced back at the others. He didn't want to come off as a nervous ninny, but he was already attached to the dog. It was really the only good thing that had come of the trip - well, other than his ill-timed lap dance - and he didn't want to take any chances.

"There's something up ahead." Seth pointed to the mound which was now a hundred yards away. Supper was half-way there.

Wyatt had been lollygagging in the back, as he was prone to do, and jogged to catch up to him. He squinted and stared. "Looks like a tarp, maybe."

Seth thought that was as good a guess as any, but he picked up the pace even though the muscles in his shoulders and chest were already screaming for a reprieve. Wyatt matched him.

The dog was just feet from whatever was sprawled on the ground and Seth realized his heart was thudding, and not from kicking the chair into overdrive. He was scared.

That was stupid, he knew it. It's not like some person or some wild animal would be lying in wait along a random stretch of country road that probably hadn't seen travelers in two years. Nothing was that patient. So why was he so damn on edge?

"What is it?" Barbara called.

"Not sure," Wyatt said.

Supper was on the scene, almost dancing around whatever laid in the dirt. He alternated between poking his nose into it and scratching at it.

Whatever it was didn't react to that inspection and Seth's breaths came easier. He allowed himself to slow his pace, which also helped. Once they figured out what the damned thing was he was going to let Wyatt push him for a spell and not feel guilty.

It wasn't long before Seth understood what was cast aside like so much garbage. Only it wasn't a what but a who.

"Son of a bitch." Wyatt's words came out in a whisper.

"Devan," Seth said.

The man who had robbed them laid on his back. His long slicker was splayed out around him like a magical cloak, but if it had any special powers, they'd done him no good. Because Devan was dead.

Only he wasn't just dead. He was butchered.

Seth had seen the aftereffects of hunters breaking down deer. It was part of life in Maine. They'd hang the deer from a tree limb or sometimes even a basketball hoop above their garage door and start cutting. First, they'd disembowel it, dropping its gut pile in a steaming heap. Then, with a few slices in the right places they could peel away the skin easier than Seth could husk an ear of sweet corn at the annual Fourth of July picnic.

Once the skin was removed, they switched knives and started carving away the meat. They didn't stop until all that remained was the head, bones, and hooves.

That was all that remained of Devan, only swapping out hooves for hands and feet. It was like someone had tacked the ends of his extremities and his face onto a prop skeleton, the kind people sat in their yards on Halloween. Only the little bits of gristle, and the flies that feasted on those macabre bits that clung to the bones, made it obvious this was no decoration.

Barbara spilled out a startled yelp. "Oh my God!"

Supper jumped, startled by her exclamation. He stumbled to the side before recovering and hobbling away from the body and to Wyatt.

"Who could do something like this?" Barbara kept her distance from the carnage.

Seth caught his brother and Trooper exchange a look.

"Starving people get desperate," was all Trooper said.

Seth surveyed the area around the body. The ground was smashed and trampled, not by a single set of footprints, but many. He'd expected to see bad shit on the road. He even figured there was a decent chance he'd die. But this - people slaughtering other people for their meat - that was beyond anything even his vivid imagination had conjured.

"I wonder what happened to June," Seth said.

"I don't think I want to know." Barbara grabbed the handlebars to his chair and turned him away from Devan's corpse. "Come. I can't look at this anymore."

As she pushed him up the road Seth half-turned in the chair, still trying to grasp the reality of the situation and wondering what had come of the girl.

He didn't have to wait long.

THEY FOUND JUNE'S COAT LESS THAN A MILE SOUTHEAST. IT WAS sliced down the back and stained with blood. A football field past that they came across her flower print blouse which was in two pieces and soaked scarlet.

Her body was twenty feet away. She was in much the same condition as Devan, a skeleton with appendages. But it was clear she'd either put up more of a fight or had more fight brought to her.

Three of her fingernails had been ripped from her right hand. The soles of her feet were ragged and shredded from running shoeless. Her face, which Seth had found so pretty, was a swollen purple bruise and barely recognizable. The rest of her was gone.

No one said much and Seth wondered if they were in shock, or had already grown accustomed to the horror. He figured it was some of both. No one mentioned her empty midsection or the baby which had resided there either.

There was no sign of their food, weapons, or shopping cart. "Whoever did this got all our goods too," Trooper said.

Seth looked to him. "You think that's why they were attacked? For the supplies?"

"I'd say it's a good possibility." Trooper noticed a can half-buried in the dirt near the body and grabbed it. It was Moxie soda. "Real good possibility."

"I guess they did us a favor then." Seth regretted saying it out loud. Sometimes his mouth seemed to have no filter. The others were used to that, but he had a feeling this might have been too far.

"Seth!" Barbara's glare made him feel about five inches tall.

"He's right." Trooper said.

Now Barbara directed her laser stare Trooper's way. Seth was glad for the reprieve and considered thanking him, then thought better of it. Regardless, his mother's anger had no effect on the old man.

"Don't waste a good conniption over those two, Barb," Trooper said. "A man reaps what he sows. They found that out the hard way."

It sounded cruel, but it was true. Besides, the world was cruel. And Seth had a bad feeling that things would only get worse.

CHAPTER TWENTY-FOUR

WYATT SURVEYED THE AREA WITH SOMETHING AKIN TO AWE. He'd never seen anything like the trading post before, not in real life anyway. It reminded him of the old movies he used to watch on TV late at night. Shanty towns in the middle of nowhere run by outlaws or bikers. Places where the only law was to be stronger or meaner than everyone else and mayhem reigned.

Down an alley Wyatt had the unfortunate luck of spotting an older woman bent over at the waist and naked as the day she was born while a man with a wild mane of coal-colored hair pounded her from behind. Wyatt locked eyes with her thousand-yard stare and thought she must be sixty, maybe seventy. The skin around her toothless mouth collapsed inward and her face was a roadmap of wrinkles and age spots and strange growths.

The man screwing her grunted and spasmed. Then he yanked up his jeans and handed the woman a can of food before shoving her to the side and stomping away from her. She flopped onto the pavement, popping the top of the can and drinking its contents, not even bothering to dress herself.

When the man emerged from the alley, he caught Wyatt watching him. "The fuck you staring at, boy?"

Wyatt turned away.

"That's good. Maybe you're not as stupid as you look."

Further up the street, a trio of women in barely there outfits shared a blunt underneath the tattered awning of a one-time pharmacy. They watched Wyatt's group with hungry, desperate eyes.

One of them, a woman with dirty blonde hair that had matted into long dreadlocks, took a step toward the quartet. "Been a long time since I seen a dog," she said. "Can I pet it?"

Wyatt gave a brief nod and she staggered their way, crouching down beside Supper. She pushed her slender fingers through his fur, then buried her cheek in his side. Supper loved the attention, but Wyatt didn't.

From the windows and doorways, the few denizens stared with wide-eyed curiosity. Wyatt felt like he was an animal in a zoo and he didn't enjoy being on display.

"He got a name?" The woman's voice reminded Wyatt she was still there.

"Yeah. Supper."

She laughed, but it was a tired, joyless sound. "Don't keep him here too long or that's what he'll end up being." She looked up at Wyatt. Her eyes were so pale blue they were nearly transparent. As if the color had drained from her irises just like the life was draining from her body. It hurt to look at her.

"This ain't no place for a dog. No place for people neither," she said.

"We don't plan on staying," Trooper said as he pushed past her. The others were clearly expected to follow but Wyatt felt bad about pulling Supper away from the woman.

"How about you? You got a name too?" She asked.

"Wyatt."

She stopped petting the dog and pushed a hand toward Wyatt. He accepted, thinking it felt so fragile he might break the bones if he applied any pressure. "I'm Allie. And you're a pretty one. If you want to get to know me better alls it'll cost you is a smoke."

Wyatt released her palm and fought the urge to wipe his hand on his pants as he didn't want to come across rude. Still, the temptation was there. "Don't got any." He walked, but she followed.

"How about food?"

"None of that either. That's why we're here."

"You must got something in that shopping cart. Why else bother pushing it?"

"Clothes is all."

She laughed again. "Oh. I don't got much use for those if you couldn't tell." She did a clumsy pirouette that revealed her scantily clad figure. As much as Wyatt didn't want to, he appreciated the sight.

"Allie!" A man's voice shouted. Wyatt looked and saw him standing by the other two women. He was in his thirties, lean, and his narrow face was twisted in annoyance. His bald skull was shaved but covered with a tattoo that Wyatt guessed was supposed to be flames, but the work was so bad it was hard to be certain.

Allie forgot Wyatt existed and ran to the man. Wyatt watched him grab her wrist, saw her face contort in pain.

"None of our business," Trooper said. "Come on now."

Wyatt quickened his pace and caught up with them.

"What is this place," Seth asked.

"Post eleven." Trooper kept a steady pace, ignoring the lookie-loos.

"Remind me why we're here again?" Seth's head snapped side to side like a spectator at a tennis match.

"To trade. To restock."

Now Seth's attention went to Trooper and he asked the question Wyatt had been pondering since this idea was proposed. "How are we supposed to trade when we've got jack shit? You really think they're going to give us anything of value for my Portland Pirates sweatshirt?"

"We keep that info to ourselves," Trooper said.

Wyatt didn't like that answer. Not one bit. As the prying eyes watched them, he wished they'd have stayed on the road, where they were alone, or could pretend to be, anyway. They could have checked all the houses and lived off the occasional can of corn or packet of dry onion soup mix. That would have been better than strolling into this place.

"Look," Barbara whispered. They followed her gaze and saw a shopping cart turned onto its side in front of a squat, brick building. It had a red plastic cover across the handle that looked all too familiar. It was the Hannaford logo Wyatt saw nearly every day growing up in Maine.

"Is that ours?" Seth asked.

"If I was a betting man, I'd say so," Trooper said.

A broad, beast of a man with a mole the size of a walnut above his eye stepped out of a building and into what passed for the daylight. He tilted his head back as he drained the contents of a soda can. When it was empty, he crushed it in his oversized fist and chucked it sidearm into the street. It skidded past Wyatt and he knew immediately that it was Moxie brand cola.

Wyatt watched the man, a little too long, and Trooper jerked on his coat. "Not now. Keep moving."

Ahead, a group of eight men clad in leather jackets huddled in front of a clapboard building and guzzled beer and liquor. The men watched, silent at first but as Wyatt's group got nearer one of them, a gray-haired tub of lard with a beard down to his belly unleashed a shrill wolf-whistle through the gap where his front teeth had once been.

"Hey there, mama," the man yelled. "Come over here take a seat on my lap. We'll talk about the first thing that pops up!"

He and his cronies guffawed like that was the most original and amusing joke they'd ever heard. Wyatt didn't see the humor and shot a pissed off glare in their direction. Before he could do something even more stupid, Trooper stepped in front of him, blocking the view of the tough guys.

"Listen to me," Trooper said. "This is not a safe place, okay?"

"No shit," Seth piped in from behind.

Wyatt knew Trooper was right and that sending snark the way of the man who'd catcalled his mother would have been a dumb, maybe even a deadly mistake. He nodded. "So what is the plan?"

Trooper glanced around, checking their surroundings. "First, we acclimate. Far as they know, we're just passing through like any other party."

"Then what?" Wyatt asked.

"Then we rob these motherfuckers."

Wyatt had to fight to keep his mouth from falling open. "You're kidding?"

Trooper looked him in the eyes and he knew the man was dead serious. "We need to case the town, find its weak spots. I'll take Seth. You stay with your mother."

Wyatt nodded. "Alright."

"And don't piss anyone off." After that Trooper looked to Seth who held up his palms in a Who, Me? gesture.

"Are you sure about this Trooper?" Barbara asked.

"Hell no, I'm not. But do any of you have a better idea?"

No one said otherwise.

"That's what I figured. We'll meet up in a few hours."

Wyatt didn't think anything about this was a good idea, but it was Trooper's show now. He watched as he and Seth continued up the street, eventually heading to a storefront that had once advertised Men's Clothes and Hats.

Wyatt turned to his mother. "Do you think this is a mistake?"

"Do we have a choice?"

She was right. They were down to four cans of wax beans and had hundreds of miles to go before they neared their destination. Despite that, he struggled to see how in the hell this could end well.

CHAPTER TWENTY-FIVE

SETH FOLLOWED TROOPER INTO A BUILDING THAT SEEMED TO BE a cross between a grocery store and a boarding house. A half-dozen men and two women slept off hangovers on cots that lined one long wall. On the other side of the store, shelves contained a variety of canned goods, with the occasional box of dry pasta or rice mixed in.

A scrawny woman who Seth thought must be at least seventy-five stared at the shelves in a way that seemed all too familiar. He remembered family trips to the grocery store and having to navigate his chair around the old bittys who took ten minutes to decide whether they wanted their green beans whole or French cut. Seeing this woman do the same thing now elicited a snort of laughter.

The old bitty looked his way, as did a middle-aged man who stood behind a counter and read a paperback novel.

"Something amuse you?" The bitty asked.

Trooper glared down at Seth then looked to the woman. "Forgive the boy, ma'am. He's feeble not just of the body but of the mind."

She responded with a Hmpf then went back to staring at the canned goods.

Seth wasn't offended. In fact, he enjoyed play-acting and

wondered how far to take the role. He started by letting his jaw hang low and a thin string of saliva trickle from his mouth.

Trooper approached the man at the counter who dog-eared the page he'd been reading and set the book aside.

"Help you?" The man wore a pair of glasses that had only one lens.

"Possibly," Trooper said. "This your place?"

"It is."

"I'm traveling through with some friends and we'd like to stock up. What are you looking for in the way of trade?"

The man tilted his chin toward the food. "I take booze, cigarettes, chewing tobacco, and gold."

Seth wondered what good gold was in a world where there was so little to purchase.

"You have any firearms?" Trooper asked.

The man shook his head. "I do not. Guns are Big Josh's turf and his alone." His hand drifted to a ragged scar that curved from his temple to his jaw. "Learnt that lesson the hard way."

"Understandable." Trooper leaned in and flashed what Seth thought was the fakest smile he'd ever seen. "You wouldn't happen to know what Big Josh takes in trade, would you?"

The man leaned away, his eyes narrowing in suspicion. "How'd you find this place, anyway? Ain't exactly on the beaten path."

"We're from up north. Maine, to be exact. I used to do a fair amount of business at Post One."

For some reason, Seth thought the man seemed less nervous now, albeit by a marginal amount. "Yeah?"

"Yeah."

"Who'd you deal with?"

Seth felt like this was a test and hoped Trooper wasn't bluffing.

"Nathaniel," Trooper said and the man's eyes grew wide. "But he hasn't been up north in a long while. Heard he settled in Louisiana for the time being."

Whatever trepidation the man had been experiencing faded

away. He even managed a smile but when Seth saw his rotting, black and brown teeth, he wished he'd have remained less jovial. "That's right." The man extended his hand. "I'm Graham."

"Trooper. And this is Seth."

Seth reached toward the man but kept his wrist bent at an awkward angle and faked spastic, uncoordinated movements. After missing twice, Graham gave up on shaking and settled on a nod. He spoke slow and loud. "Nice. To. Meet. You."

Trooper looked down on him and shot him a look that said don't overdo it. That made Seth decide to skip the slurred speech he'd been saving up and remain wordless.

"Tell you what," Graham said. He moved from behind the counter and toward the food. "A friend of Nathaniel's is a friend of mine." He grabbed a can of refried beans and a can of mixed fruit off the shelf and handed them to Trooper. The latter was rusting around the base and Seth thought that his generosity had its bounds.

"Well thank you, Graham." Trooper dropped them into his bag. "Could you point me in Big Josh's direction?"

Graham did just that. Before they vacated the store, he pointed to the cots. "If you need a place to flop tonight, stop in. I usually charge but for your party, it's on the house."

When they left the store Seth whispered to Trooper. "Who's Nathaniel?"

"Fellow I used to know from my days on the State Police Force."

"A cop?"

"No. He operated on the other side of the law."

They headed up the street, toward an ornate limestone building which Graham had said was Big Josh's. Carved into the stone above the entry was "First National Bank". Seth wondered if Trooper really planned to rob the place and, if so, whether he saw any irony in the situation.

CHAPTER TWENTY-SIX

With Seth and Trooper gone, Wyatt felt even more exposed standing in the middle of the street. The wannabe Hell's Angel's who'd ogled Barbara seemed to have lost interest but there were dozens more who all eyed them up like they were fresh-caught shrimp on an all you can eat buffet.

"Let's get out of here," Barbara said.

That sounded like a brilliant idea.

He followed his mother toward a building where the front door hung agape and a painted sign above it declared "Ale and Licker - Cheap." It wasn't the kind of place Wyatt would have chosen but he supposed they had to start somewhere.

"Supper, come on, boy," Wyatt called.

The dog followed, close on his heels. He gave Wyatt a lick on the hand and Wyatt thought he'd have to look for a collar and leash first chance he had. The last thing he needed was someone thinking they'd get a hot meal off his dog.

From the exterior of the saloon, Wyatt had low expectations, but the inside managed to be even worse than he'd assumed. It had a dingy green and red and white color scheme with tacos and burritos painted on the walls. But its time as a Mexican restaurant was a past life.

Now, most of the windows were broken and bullet holes dotted the walls, floor, and ceiling. Eight or ten tables were scattered haphazardly through the main room, along with a random assortment of chairs of the folding and lawn variety. Worst of all, it reeked of piss and puke and from the scattering of puddles on the floor, it was easy to see why. He sidestepped the bodily fluids as they made their way to the bar.

On their side of it a man with straggly gray hair that clung to his bare upper body like ancient spaghetti nursed a beer and struggled not to fall off his stool. Barbara went to the other end of the bar and took a seat. Wyatt claimed the spot next to her. He patted his thigh and Supper huddled beside him.

A handful of drunks sat at tables, doing what drunks do. One couple in their twenties lounged next to a jukebox that hadn't played a tune in years and sucked face. Sprawled on the floor was a teenage boy who had clearly shit his pants. Charming place, Wyatt thought.

What he didn't see was food or guns and that was pretty much their only reason for being here. He was about to tell his mother that they should move on when a woman in her fifties approached from behind the bar. Her hair had been sheared into a buzz cut while her arms were as big around as milk jugs and covered in tattoos. Wyatt thought she looked strong enough to kick the ass of most men.

"Pick your poison." She leaned against the bar which looked as sticky as a bathroom floor and the idea of touching it made Wyatt queasy. When she leaned, her low cut tank top gave an obvious look at her ample breasts. Despite everything else, Wyatt had to admit it wasn't a bad distraction.

"Nothing. We're just waiting for someone." Barbara said.

"If you're not buying, you're just taking up space. Either order or get out." The woman stared Barbara down.

"What are the choices?" Barbara asked.

The woman turned around and showed the array of bottles that lined the shelves behind the bar.

"How about water?" Barbara asked.

The woman let out a throaty laugh. "Sure, but I don't know if you can afford it."

"How much?"

She shrugged. "Let me spend some time with your boy toy here and I'll give you a gallon."

"Spend some time?" Wyatt had an inkling what she meant, especially when the woman licked her lips.

Barbara narrowed her eyes and leaned across the bar. "That's my son."

The bartender shrugged. "Well then, how about you, sugartits?"

Wyatt watched with a mixture of disgust and bewilderment as his mother grabbed the strap on the bartender's tank top and jerked her over the bar. Before she had a chance to react Barbara kissed her roughly. The woman put her hand behind Barb's head, entwining her fingers in her hair, and kissed back.

"Mom!" Wyatt said and the two broke apart.

The woman laughed and slapped her thigh. "Hot damn!" She pulled a quart of water from under the bar and passed it over.

"That's it?" Barbara asked.

"You want more, take me upstairs."

"I think this'll do," Barbara said.

Thank God, Wyatt thought.

"Plus a round of vodka, on me, and I ain't takin' no for an answer." The woman slammed three shot glasses on the counter and poured until they verged on overflowing.

Wyatt reached for the glass, but the woman grabbed his wrist. He'd been right earlier, she was so strong it was almost scary.

"Where's your ID kid?"

Wyatt opened his mouth and fumbled for words. "I, uh, I'm--"

She unleashed a course laugh - HA! HA! HA! "I'm just fuckin with ya, handsome. Now down the hatch."

She took her own shot and threw it back before Wyatt had a chance to even pick up his glass. When he swallowed, the liquid burned like molten lava flowing down his throat. The only thing that kept him from barfing it back up was knowing it would hurt just as bad the second time around.

He shivered and shook his head, causing the bartender to laugh again. When Wyatt checked to see if his mother was experiencing similar distress, he instead discovered her unaffected and wondered what else he didn't know about the woman with whom he'd lived his entire life. On second thought, some things were better off unknown.

"You two need anything else, just holler for Doris." She tapped her chest. "I'm Doris."

"I assumed as much," Barbara said.

Wyatt watched the woman as she moved down the bar and took an empty mug from the drunk with the spaghetti-strand hair. She was rough around the edges, but he liked her. When she disappeared through some saloon doors and into a back room, Wyatt returned his attention to his mother who sat with a smirk on her face.

"Mom?"

Barbara turned to him. "Yes, honey?"

"What the hell was that?" he asked.

She smiled and took a sip of water, but never answered.

CHAPTER TWENTY-SEVEN

BEFORE TROOPER VISITED THE MAN THEY CALLED BIG JOSH HE parlayed the canned food he'd been given at the makeshift grocery store into four cans of beer. As far as plans went, this one barely registered half an ass, but it was all he had.

The windows on the bank had been boarded over with sheets of plywood on the inside, turning an already gloomy building into a cavern. Cases of food were stacked four feet high in random rows, creating something of a maze which Trooper navigated, pushing Seth, careful not to topple anything over.

Behind the half-wall which had one time separated the tellers from the customers, two men played a game of cards. One was a beanpole with a shock of red hair atop his pointy head. A cigarette hung on his lip like it was held in place with glue. The other man wasn't as tall but made up for it in girth. He rapped his knuckles on the wall.

"Hit me," he said.

Stretch tossed him a card.

Trooper doubted either man seemed big enough to be Big Josh but had little interest in watching two thugs play poker so he cleared his throat. Both looked to him and Seth, their faces clouded by boredom and annoyance.

"Sorry to interrupt your game, boys, but I was sent here to find Big Josh."

Stretch set his cards aside and stood. He looked tall sitting down but now he was basketball player height and Trooper noticed he'd taken on a stooped-over posture, probably because his head didn't clear most doorways.

"What's your business with him, gramps?"

"Looking to procure some firearms. Seems Big Josh is the man to see."

Stretch nodded. "Wait here."

He moved into a back room and Trooper waited. He noticed the other poker player sneak a peek at Stretch's cards and his eyes grow wide. Then he sorted through the deck and slipped free two cards, trading them for two of his own. Some things never change, Trooper thought. No honor among thieves.

Of course, he was about to become a thief too. Oftentimes, when he was on the job, he pondered the delicacy of the thin line that separated law-abiding from lawless. When you wore the badge, you told yourself there was only good and bad. White and black. You didn't want to see shades of gray because a middle ground, a world where you had to admit that good people could do terrible things when circumstances demanded it, that complicated matters. But the world was gray and so were its people. That was truer now than ever.

"Why'd you bring me along Troop?" Seth asked. Trooper had nearly forgotten the boy was there. "I'd think Wyatt would've been more helpful. You know, if shit goes down."

"I'm counting on shit not going down. Not yet, anyway." Trooper looked down at his young friend. "Look, I love your brother. He's a good kid. But sometimes he doesn't get it. He still thinks the world should make sense and when it doesn't, he gets flustered. I needed a level head and you're the best choice for that."

Seth nodded. "Cool. At least I'm useful for something."

Trooper knelt down to Seth's level. "You're useful for so many things. You're just as good as your brother, you're just as good as me. Fact that you're in a chair doesn't mean a damn thing, you got that?"

He watched Seth smile back at him, a Cheshire cat grin if he ever saw one. "I never knew you cared so much, Trooper."

Trooper licked his teeth and shook his head. The little bastard got him.

Hinges groaned as the door to the backroom swung open. Stretch stepped through first, ducking. Behind emerged a fireplug of a man who didn't top 5'5" but was wrapped in muscle. Trooper had seen the type many times before. Men who spent their waking hours pumping iron to compensate for what they lacked in height. His nickname - Big Josh - was most likely an inside joke to which he wasn't party.

Big Josh strutted toward them. He wore no shirt but had a holster and pistol on each hip. Trooper recognized the guns straight off because, until a short time ago, they'd been his. A large tattoo of a dragon filled Josh's chest and it wasn't half-bad. He stopped a few feet away from them and folded his arms across his broad chest.

"Whatcha looking for, old-timer?"

"You, apparently." Trooper extended a hand Josh's way, but the man didn't reciprocate. "I'm Trooper. This is my friend Seth."

Josh nodded. "Two more in your party, right? Another boy and a woman?"

"That's correct. We're traveling through from Maine. Ran into some bad luck and need to restock."

Josh pulled a chair away from a folding table, spun it backward and straddled it. "Sit."

Before Trooper did that, he turned to Seth who had the four cans of beer resting in his lap under a spare shirt. This was the tricky part.

Being careful to keep himself between Josh and the beverages, he popped the tops, then opened a small pouch of crushed pills. During the course of exploring abandoned houses over the last half-decade, he'd built up a stash of opioids and narcotics that would make most dealers salivate. He only used the pills on especially bad days, days when the knee he'd blown out chasing a perp through the woods in Piscataquis County, felt like it was as useless as a second dick.

Most of the potency had worn off over the years, but the night before he'd crushed up enough oxy, morphine, and codeine to send a small elephant to Never Never Land. Or so he hoped. The dissipating power of the drugs would, if his plan went as he expected, work to his benefit.

He emptied the white powder into three of the cans of beer, then gave them a little shake as he took them from Seth and turned back to Big Josh.

"For you and your colleagues." Trooper handed Josh a beer, then motioned for Stretch and the card cheat to join in. The cheat took one but Stretch shook his head.

"Don't drink," he said. "Sober since ought two."

"You're a stronger man than I," Trooper said as he took his spot at the table across from Josh. "Then this one's yours too." He pushed the unwanted can to Josh who only nodded.

"Not a bad offer," Josh said. He drank half of his first beer in a swallow. "I was in Maine once. Took one of those sightseeing boat tours out of Bar Harbor. Pretty place, I thought. Peaceful. Why'd you leave there for this shitheap?"

"Winter's are hard," Trooper said. "Doubted we could make it through another."

Josh nodded and finished the beer. "How long you been traveling?"

"Since the beginning of August."

Big Josh let loose a low whistle. "Hella long time on the road. You folks must be damned lucky. That or tough as fuck."

Trooper smirked. "Little of both if you ask me."

"How much further you going?"

Trooper was weary of the questions and wanted to get down to business, but knew playing along was the best option. "Far as our feet'll take us. The woman has it in her head that we'll get passed the equator and everything'll be sunshine and roses."

The man grabbed the second can of beer but didn't drink straight off. "I heard that one. Load of shit. Whole world's fucked. Better to settle in somewhere and ride it out to the end."

"Maybe," Trooper said. It wasn't like he hadn't thought that himself many times before. "Maybe."

"So it's guns you want?"

"It is."

"Alright then. I got in a Walther P22 and a box of ammo the other day. Yours if you want it."

Trooper thought that a shit deal but didn't say so. "I was hoping for something with a bit more stopping power. It's rough out there."

"Like I don't fucking know that." Big Josh started on the new can. The cheat nursed his. "If that's not suitable you can choose between a .38 special and a .32 acp. No negotiating. Take it or leave it."

"Now you're talking," Trooper said. It wasn't a bad offer really, but he hadn't risked their lives coming here for one gun. "I'll take the .38 if you'll toss in the .22 for this." He held up his own undrunk beer.

Big Josh considered it for a moment, then bobbed his head. "Hell, why not? You caught me in a good mood." He turned to Stretch, motioned to the back room. Stretch went to retrieve the guns.

"I'm curious," Trooper said. "What would it take to get one of those Desert Eagles?" He motioned to the guns on Josh's hips.

Big Josh grinned. "You want this?" He took one of the .44s from its holster and dropped the magazine before handing it to Trooper. "That broad you came into town with, send her over here for the night. I promise I won't beat her up too bad. Still leave you a hole to poke, although it'll be a bit looser than before I got at her." He cackled.

Trooper tilted his head toward Seth. "This boy is her son."

"Is he now?" Josh leaned forward. "Hell then, he can watch. I'll give him an education he'll never forget!" He smacked the table, rattling the cans, then turned to the card cheat who laughed on cue.

Trooper didn't laugh. He handed the pistol back to Josh. "We'll consider that."

Josh reinserted the magazine and returned the .44 to the empty holster. About that time Stretch returned with the two pistols and set them on the table. The .38 wasn't bad. It was the snub nose model and wouldn't be worth a shit at a distance but up close it would get the job done. The .22 was garbage. The barrel was covered in rust and the grip was duct-taped. Trooper thought it was as likely to explode upon pulling the trigger as it was to fire. But he kept his mouth shut because he had other, grander plans.

"Good dealing with you." Josh pushed the pistols, each with a single box of ammunition, across the table. "You think good about sending that broad over. Renting out some pussy for a gun like this is a hell of a deal if you ask me. And I bet the old gal'd enjoy a break from your limp noodle." He cackled again.

Trooper stood, shoving the .38 into his pocket and handing the .22 to Seth. "We'll get back to you on that."

"Good man," Josh said and finished off the second beer.

Trooper's face hardened as he spun Seth's chair away from the men. He'd walked in here with mild reservations about robbing them. Now he looked forward to it.

As they exited the building Seth peered up at him. "Trooper?"

"Yeah?"

"When we go through with this plan of yours, if things go south and we have to shoot our way out, will you let me kill that prick?"

Trooper liked the boy's spirit but not his eagerness. "Let's hope it doesn't come to that." As sweet as vengeance tasted, he wanted no part of a gun battle. But like the song said, you can't always get what you want.

CHAPTER TWENTY-EIGHT

Between the wretched odors inside the bar and the way the vodka was hitting, Wyatt needed some fresh air before he puked or passed out, or both. He left Barb and Supper at the bar and pushed out a side exit, sucking in big mouthfuls of air as soon as he was in the open.

As he gathered himself, he noticed the thugs who'd earlier harassed his mother huddled in a pack one building down. He could hear excited, animalistic sounds coming from them, noises that reminded him of monkeys at the zoo.

His curiosity got the better of him and he crept along the building, closing the distance until he could get a better look. When he did, he felt sick all over again.

Allie, the pretty blonde who'd been so enamored with Supper upon their arrival was encircled by the group. Her crop top shirt had been torn away revealing mosquito bite breasts and a torso so emaciated he could count her ribs.

"Give it back!" Allie reached toward one of the creeps and Wyatt saw him holding her shirt above his head, twirling it like a lasso.

"Go ahead, take it from me. I won't bite. Much!" He chomped his jaws for effect.

Allie looked beyond the men. Wyatt followed her gaze and saw the flame-headed man who'd yelled at her earlier. He lounged against the side of a building and smoked, paying no attention to the goings on.

"Come on, Pete!" She said to him. "This ain't what we talked about."

Rather than help, Pete turned away from her.

She tried to cover her naked chest with one hand and grab the shirt with the other. The effort was futile. The men whooped and hooted, like a cartload of chimpanzees. When she dove for the shirt, another of the group grabbed the waistband of her shorts and pulled her into him. He wrapped his bearish arms around her and ground his crotch against her ass.

"Just like that, babe. Keep fighting. T-Bone likes it rough."

"Let go!" She stomped her foot down on the man's toes.

The self-proclaimed T-Bone squawked a startled yelp and loosened his grip enough for Allie to slip away. Her freedom was short-lived as a teenager with a mohawk grabbed a fistful of her dreadlocks. With his other hand, he groped her groin.

Wyatt had seen enough.

"Eight against one," he said as he stepped into the open. "You sure are some real tough guys."

The gang looked his way, curious about the new arrival. The man who held Allie's shirt, an ugly son of a bitch with a nose that had been broken so many times it looked like a hunk of meat stapled to his face, spoke first. "None of your business, pretty boy!"

Wyatt knew that to be the truth. None of this had anything to do with him. Nothing to do with his family. Nothing to do with why they were here. But he wasn't going to sit by and watch as these cretins gang-raped the woman.

"Maybe I should make it my business." Wyatt hoped that didn't sound as cheesy out loud as it did in his head. He rested his hand on the grip of his pistol. He knew there were only four bullets. Not enough to get them all if they decided to bring the fight to him, but he hoped the insinuation would be enough.

"You even know how to shoot that?" T-Bone asked.

It was a test he needed to pass. Wyatt drew the gun and chambered a round, but kept the barrel pointed at the ground. Please, God, he thought, let them believe this bluff. "Seems like I do."

T-Bone and the nose exchanged a look but no words, like they were communicating telepathically. Then T-Bone turned to mohawk. "Let her go."

Mohawk did, but not before raking his hands across Allie's breasts, leaving behind angry, red trails against her alabaster flesh. She slipped away and ran not to Wyatt, who'd saved her, but to Pete. She latched onto his arm like he was a life preserver.

"We're just fuckin' around, kid," T-Bone said. "You should try it sometime if you can dig the stick out of your ass."

Wyatt holstered the pistol. "I think I'll pass."

"Your loss." T-Bone and the others shuffled back toward the street. The man with the meat nose dropped Allie's shirt on the ground, grinding his boot against it and mashing it into the mud. "Oops."

When they were gone Wyatt looked to Allie and Pete, the latter of whom looked pissed off rather than grateful. "Stupid prick," Pete said.

Wyatt held his palms up, confused.

Pete shook his head. "That little rooster show of yours cost us five cans of food."

"What are you talking about?"

Pete strode Wyatt's way and, when he reached him, shoved him in the chest. "How the fuck do you think we survive? It ain't on charm."

Wyatt looked at him, then to Allie who was digging through Pete's satchel. She pulled out another crop top and slipped it on. It made sense now. And he was the dumbass, as usual.

"Oh."

"Yeah. Oh." Pete spat in his general direction but missed. "Fuck off, kid. Go be a hero somewhere else."

Pete returned to Allie and grabbed her hand, spinning her away as they moved toward the main street. Before they slipped out of sight, Allie glanced back and wagged her fingers in a half-hearted wave.

Wyatt waved in return, even though she'd already looked away.

CHAPTER TWENTY-NINE

Night at the trading post was different from night on the road. Fiery torches lined the streets and cast their orange blaze onto the street and buildings. The other main difference was that it never became quiet. A constant flux of people loitered rather than slept. They drifted in and out of buildings and stores and bars like it was the middle of the day. Both of these circumstances complicated Trooper's plan which depended on darkness and privacy.

Nevertheless, he wasn't going to let that change anything.

The door to the Bank of Big Josh was ajar. Trooper looked to Wyatt who waited at his side, pistol in hand and ready to shoot should it come to that. Dear God, Trooper thought, don't let it come to that.

Ready? Trooper mouthed the word.

Wyatt nodded.

Trooper eased the door open, cringing as hinges groaned. He held his breath and kept pushing until there was a large enough gap to admit them.

He heard no voices, no movement. All was silent inside the bank. Trooper exhaled. He pointed to himself. Me first. That was the plan they'd set, but he wanted to make sure that Wyatt didn't charge ahead. On the chance that someone inside laid in wait to ambush them, he wanted to be first in the line of fire. This was his idea, after all. And the closer it got to coming to fruition the less he wanted to go through with it. But he wasn't a man to leave things half done, so he stepped forward and into the bank.

A few nearly burned out candles cast enough light through the room for Trooper to see that it was empty. He half-turned to Wyatt and motioned for him to join him inside.

They moved as softly and with as much care as possible, not exchanging a word. They'd already discussed what they would do and the order in which they'd do it a dozen times.

First, they moved ten cases of food into the doorway. With that finished Wyatt leaned out the door and did his best impression of a great horned owl. Trooper heard the front left wheel of the shopping cart squeak as it approached.

With the food taken care of, Trooper moved through the maze of boxes and toward the back room. Wyatt was close on his heels and he could hear the boy's breaths coming fast and nervous. He thought about telling him to quiet down but that would just make more unnecessary noise so he let it be. Besides, if a bit of panicked breathing gave them away they were already screwed.

The door to the back office was closed. Trooper spun the knob and opened it with as much care as his old hands could muster. But his caution appeared unneeded as rumbling snoring drifted through the doorway.

Thank God for small favors, he thought.

Inside the room, he spotted Big Josh sitting in a wheeled chair behind a metal desk. His head was tilted back at an angle that made Trooper's neck hurt just looking at it, and his mouth hung agape. He seemed to be the source of most of the noise, but the card cheat wasn't far behind. He appeared to have been laying on a stained, yellow couch when his upper body tumbled off, leaving him half reclining, half sprawled on the floor.

With the men momentarily out of commission, Trooper's eyes scanned the room for firearms and it didn't take long before he found what he needed. Setting in a magazine display rack were upwards of two dozen pistols and revolvers of varying calibers. Stacked against the same wall was a row of long guns, everything from .22 rifles to an AK 47.

As much as Trooper would have preferred to take the rifles, as they were both more accurate and more deadly, the handguns would be easier to transport and as time was of the essence, he settled.

Wyatt spread his pack open while Trooper filled it with guns and ammunition, only stopping when he worried the weight of the haul might split the bag at the seams. He nodded to Wyatt who zipped the bag closed.

As they slipped out of the room, Trooper lamented the fact that the .44s, his .44s, were still on that roid-raging asshole Big Josh's waist. He gave brief, but serious consideration to marching back into the office and taking them from the holsters, but he hadn't survived seven decades by being stupid and didn't see any purpose in changing course now.

They were halfway out the front door when a stair creaked.

"Son of a bitch," Trooper muttered.

"What are you doing back here?" Stretch asked.

Trooper turned toward the man who'd reached the bottom of the staircase. Damn the man for being a teetotaler. "Josh told us to come back tonight with the woman, remember?"

"Yeah." Stretch's eyes narrowed. "So where is she?"

Trooper pointed to the office. "In there. I might be kind enough to share but I'm not going to stick around and watch. That's not my scene."

Stretch paused halfway between Trooper and Wyatt and the office, and Trooper could practically see the gears turning inside his head. He hoped the man was dumb enough to fall for this. After thirty seconds that felt like an hour he came up with, "Can I?"

"Can you what, son?"

"Watch?"

Trooper sighed. That wasn't the best possible response, but it wasn't the worst. He felt Wyatt pulling at his coat and shook the boy off. They'd need to be quick now, but at least they had a chance.

"If you so choose," Trooper said.

Stretch grinned, revealing oversized, horsey teeth to pair with his long face. He moved toward the office and Trooper pushed Wyatt out the door and into the street.

It was only a moment before he heard Stretch scream. "Fucking cocksuckers!"

There was more shouting, more commotion, but Trooper didn't plan to stick around to listen in. He turned to Wyatt. "This is the part where we run."

And they did.

CHAPTER THIRTY

"ARE WE MOVING TOO FAST?" SETH ASKED. HE GLANCED SIDE TO side as he wheeled himself up the street. It seemed like every nosey bastard in this shitty excuse for a town had their eyes on him and his mother. "I feel like we're going too fast and look suspicious."

Barbara was at his side, pushing the shopping cart which teetered on overflowing with ten cases of canned goods hidden beneath a heap of clothing. "You're being paranoid. Most of them are drunk, anyway."

To prove the point, a man standing beneath a dead traffic light bent at the waist and projectile vomited all over the road. Seth made a quick turn to the left to avoid the splatter.

As he stared ahead Seth saw they were three blocks away from the edge of town. Three blocks away from freedom. He thought this scheme was ridiculous when Trooper proposed it but he was beginning to believe it might just work after all.

Then he heard the yelling.

"Fuck," Seth muttered.

"Yeah," Barbara said.

They ceased forward motion and turned to find out what had gone wrong and to what extent.

He saw Wyatt running. He saw Trooper trying to run, but it was the awkward, loping gait of a lame animal. And he saw a tall, gangly man standing outside the bank building, balled fists raised into the air like he was praising Jesus at a Sunday morning worship service.

"You cocksuckers get back here!" Stretch bellowed.

Nah, he's probably not the worship type, Seth thought. He glanced down at Supper. "You might want to hide."

The dog's ears perked up and Seth made a shooing motion with his hand. Supper trotted off the road and laid down under a tattered awning that read, Buster's Big & Tall Shoppe. "Huh." Seth said mostly to himself as he realized the dog was probably the smartest of all of them.

He tugged on his mother's coat. When she looked down on him he saw her face twisted in a grimace of worry and fear. "Well?"

"Well, what?" She asked.

"Are we going to join this fracas or stand here like two assholes who intended to buy our way into the peep show but left our wallets at home?"

That made her smile, a little. "I vote we stand here."

"I vote we join in."

"Then we've reached a stalemate."

"I'm your parent. My vote counts double."

"I don't think that works anymore." He slid the shotgun, which had been covered by a blanket in his lap, free.

"So just like that, you overrule me?"

"Come on, mom," Seth said. "You don't want to miss all the fun, do you?"

Barbara reached behind her back and pulled out the piece of crap .22. "No, I suppose not."

CHAPTER THIRTY-ONE

Wyatt felt his ear catch fire before he heard the gunshot. Once the report of the gun shattered the silence he realized that his ear was not, in fact, on fire, but that he'd just been shot.

His free hand, the hand not gripping the duffle bag full of guns, went to the side of his head and came away hot and sticky and covered with blood that looked rusty orange in the light of the torches.

"You okay?" Trooper shouted.

They'd both stopped running. "It just grazed me."

Another gunshot rang out and Wyatt heard it explode into a building nearby. A woman with a beer gut barked out a scream and took off in the opposite direction. He looked to Trooper who'd caught up to him. "Now what?

"We can't outrun bullets," Trooper said as he gripped the .38. "So I say we start shooting back."

They looked to the bank where Big Josh and the card cheat had joined Stretch on the crumbling remains of the sidewalk. Josh had a .44 in each hand but swayed side to side, like a greenhorn mariner trying to remain afoot during high seas. He fired and the bullet whizzed off course before hitting a woman Wyatt thought looked familiar. As she fell in a heap, he realized it was one of the girls who'd been standing on the corner with Allie when they arrived in town. One of the men he'd later seen harassing Allie, the one with the destroyed nose, knelt beside her and shook her limp and lifeless body.

"Marge?" He said. "You go and die on me?"

Marge didn't answer because she was dead.

Josh shot again, but that bullet bounced off the street, ricocheting wild and harmless. About that time the cheat fired off the bolt-action rifle he held in a death grip. That round too went astray, slamming through a window of an abandoned storefront.

"Give me that you drunk ass." Stretch grabbed the rifle from the cheat who appeared grateful to be relieved of it. He contented himself with clutching one of the granite columns near the bank's entrance and tried to keep the building from collapsing.

"Fuckers think you can steal from Big Josh?" Big Josh yelled.

"By God," Trooper said. "How I do loathe a man who refers to himself in the third person."

Trooper aimed and squeezed the trigger on the .38. The bullet didn't quite hit its target, which had been center mass, but it did clip Josh's left shoulder and caused him to drop one of the guns as he howled in surprise.

Wyatt realized he was standing there with his proverbial thumb up his ass and got around to taking a shot of his own. That one zipped by Stretch as he was busy aiming the rifle, distracting the tall man.

The momentary distraction cost him his life because a half-second later Trooper sent a bullet through his throat. Blood shot out like water from a drinking fountain, so hot it steamed in the cool, night air. He dropped the gun and fell to his knees, grabbing at his neck, but bled out within moments of hitting the concrete.

Although only recently awoken from his opioid-induced stupor, Josh must have realized standing in the open wasn't the best of plans and he took refuge in the bank's doorway. Wyatt shot and chunks of limestone blew out, leaving behind an irregular hole, but Josh was unharmed.

Big Josh responded with a shot of his own. It came close enough to Trooper that the old man dove to the street, landing in an awkward and, from the look on his face, pained heap. Wyatt was about to run to him when--

"Fucking fuckers think you can come into our place and kill our whores? Steal our shit?"

Wyatt sought out the voice and found the thug with the malformed nose marching his way. His shirt was stained with the dead woman's blood and, in his hand, he held a machete.

"What kind of dumbass brings a knife to a gunfight?"

Wyatt knew the voice of course, but even if he didn't such a wiseass, cocky comment could only come from one person. He turned and saw Seth in his chair, the butt of the shotgun pressed against his shoulder. The thug with the disgusting nose turned too. Just in time to catch a spray of buckshot in the face. The nose was the least of his worries now.

Although the plan wasn't going as smoothly as they'd intended, Wyatt was relieved and optimistic about their chances. For a moment.

"Get off the street!" Trooper shouted.

Wyatt almost asked him why. After all, they had the upper hand.

But they didn't.

Wyatt looked toward Trooper and saw the rest of the thugs from the alley coming their way. And three of them had guns.

Mohawk took a shot at Wyatt who felt the wind of the round blow past him.

Barbara fired the .22, but the round went astray and Wyatt saw the grip of the gun dissolve in her hands. About that time a shot came from Big Josh's direction and sparked off Seth's wheelchair frame.

Then T-Bone raised a rifle and aimed but Wyatt knew the score. There was a time to stand and fight and a time to run. He just had to figure out which this was.

CHAPTER THIRTY-TWO

"THAT BOY OF YOURS BETTER HURRY THE HELL UP SUGARTITS, because I'm closing this door in T-Minus five seconds."

Barbara put on her best pleading look as she stared at Doris who filled the doorway to the bar. In one hand she held an aluminum baseball bat, in the other a bottle of cheap whiskey. The barkeep looked into the street where gunshots went off like firecrackers on the Fourth of July.

"She a friend of yours?" Trooper asked. He was bent at the waist, a hand on each knee, and sucking in big mouthfuls of air as he recuperated from his mad dash.

Barb shrugged her shoulders. "We recently became acquainted."

She wanted to tell Doris to wait, to not lock Wyatt out there in the open with the bastards who were trying to kill him, when Wyatt made the potential plea a moot point.

"Took your sweet time didn't ya, handsome?" Doris smacked him on the ass as he scooted past her and into the bar. Then she slammed the door closed and switched three deadbolts to keep it that way.

Wyatt had been carrying Supper, only setting the dog down once they were safely inside. It took a brief glance at her son for Barbara to see the blood. She gasped at the sight of the head wound, already imagining the worst. When he got close enough, she grabbed his shirt and pulled him to her.

"You're hurt. Let me see."

Wyatt fended her off with his forearm. "I'm fine. The bullet just grazed my ear." He turned his head, displaying a channel that had been carved along the helix.

"They shot you?" The question came out in a startled bark. The realization that her oldest had come within two inches of getting shot in the skull made her head swim. "You could've been killed!"

He took hold of her shoulders. "But I wasn't. So don't freak out."

Don't freak out, she thought. He said that like he was five minutes passed curfew on a Friday night. He was almost killed. How was she supposed to not freak out? As she pondered that question, their reunion was interrupted by a foreign voice.

"Lookie who tucked tail and ran when the shit hit the fan." Barbara saw Pete and Allie sitting side by side in a corner booth. Both looked half-sloshed. Pete glared at Wyatt with amused, glassy eyes. "Not such a hero now, are you, kid?"

She watched as Wyatt saw them. He ignored the man's putdowns, his eyes locked on the waifish woman at Pete's side. Barb knew the look on Wyatt's face and she didn't like it. Not one bit. This felt almost as dangerous as the gunfight. Maybe worse.

"Fuckeroo, this is the most excitement I've seen since a forty-eight-hour layover in Jakarta." Doris bellied up to the bar and grabbed a fistful of shot glasses. "Who's joining me?"

"I will!" Seth was already wheeling himself in her direction.

"Jesus, Seth." Barbara chased after him but he beat her there. Doris already had a shot waiting for him. She knew the proper thing would be to tell her young son that there was no way in hell he was drinking that hooch, but the more she considered it, there wasn't anything proper about this situation. Or the world in general. So what good was putting on airs?

Seth grabbed his glass and downed it in a gulp. That was

followed less than two seconds later by a retching cough that brought half of it back up his gullet and onto his shirt. "The fuck is that?" Seth asked. "Lighter fluid?

"Pardon me, kid. Jim Beam's a little outta my budget."

"I'll take one of those." Trooper took a glass and made short work of it.

Barb swallowed her drink, enjoying the fiery heat that slipped down her gullet and settled into her chest. She needed that.

"Any of you yay-hoos got a plan to get out of this?" Doris asked.

Barbara looked to the men in her life. Their blank faces were answer enough.

"Didn't think so." Doris poured more shots. "Maybe this'll spark some creativity."

A few of them managed to get a drink down, but Barbara had just brought her glass to her lips when a volley of bullets punctured the walls of the pub. One of them shattered a bottle of liquor that had been residing on the shelf with the rest of the stock. Damn shame, Barb thought as she saw the spoiled contents rain to the floor.

"Shit!" Allie yelled.

Pete clutched his upper arm while scarlet blood oozed between his fingers. His face was contorted in pain and the woman at his side stared at the rest of them, pleading.

Wyatt grabbed a dirty rag from the bar and his undrunk shot before going to them. He handed the rag to Allie and Barbara noticed their fingers touch as she took it.

Pete removed his hand from the wound to reach for the shot glass. Blood ran out like water from a faucet. "Gimme that, hero. I need a fucking drink."

Instead, Wyatt held it out of reach. "It's not for that."

"Then what's it for?"

Wyatt grabbed Pete's arm a few inches below the hole. "Hold still."

He poured the alcohol over the wound. Pete yowled like a cat who'd just had its tail stepped on by a five hundred pound man. He thrashed, but Wyatt held firm, his attention now on Allie. "Take that rag and tie it tight so he doesn't lose too much blood."

Wyatt let go of the man and, for a second, Barb thought she was going to see her son get sucker-punched in the jaw, but Pete stopped himself and Wyatt returned to the group.

"Goddamn it!" Doris muttered.

Now what, Barb thought. Then she saw Doris examining a patron who Barb hadn't even realized was there until just now. She recognized him from her earlier visit, the gray-haired man who struggled to stay on his barstool. Now he was leaning over a table like he was taking a nap or sleeping off a bender.

"They killed Mute Sam," Doris said.

"Are you sure he's dead?" Trooper asked.

Doris grabbed a fistful of his spaghetti-like hair and lifted his head. Blood ran from his mouth and a bullet hole marred his bare chest. "Yeah. I'm sure."

She released the dead man's hair and his upper body hit the table with a floor-shaking thud. "That was damned uncalled for. And now I'm pissed." Doris stomped into the back room, out of sight.

Barbara thought the woman was hiding and, as several more bullets came through the walls, realized that wasn't a bad idea. She looked to Wyatt who was busying himself reloading his pistol, then to Seth who managed to grab one of the undrunk shots and made it disappear. She made a mental note to scold the boy later. If there was a later.

Trooper finished reloading the .38 and grabbed another gun from the duffle bag Wyatt had carried inside. He checked its magazine, saw it was loaded, and extended it to Barbara. "Want this?"

She shook her head. She knew how to handle a firearm and could plink a soda can off a stump from time to time, but she knew that pistol would be better in his trained hands than hers. "You keep that one. Give me the revolver."

He did. Then he checked Seth's shotgun, which was filled to capacity minus one shell.

"Are we going to shoot our way out?" Seth asked and Barbara thought his voice sounded giddy. And drunk.

"I'd rather not waste all the ammunition we only just acquired." Trooper drew back the slide on the pistol, chambering a round.

"Then what? We wait for them to come in and get us?" Seth said.

It was a fair question. Barbara knew they were outnumbered and likely outgunned. There seemed to be no good options and, for the hundredth time since leaving Maine, she cursed herself for taking her boys from their home. Because the paradise she'd promised them seemed more impossible with each passing day.

A gunshot and another bullet punched through the wall. That one shattered a framed picture of a dog with a cigar in its mouth

"Fuck waiting," Doris said. Everyone in the room turned to the woman and found her holding what Barbara first took to be a lime, but she hadn't seen fresh fruit in almost five years so that couldn't be right.

"Is that--" Barbara didn't get to finish the sentence.

"A grenade," Trooper said.

"M67. I've been saving it for a special occasion and I'm pretty sure this qualifies."

She moved toward the doorway, not even flinching as more bullets tore through the walls. Barbara didn't know where this woman had acquired her set of brass balls but wished she had half her courage. As it was, she was just glad someone seemed to have a plan to get them out of this mess.

"I worked too hard for this shithole to let those assholes shoot it up." Doris unlocked the deadbolts and reached for the doorknob, but Trooper put his hand over hers before she could turn it.

"Let me," he said. Barbara wanted to tell him no, to let Doris who they didn't know, be the one to risk her life, but she knew Trooper wasn't that kind of man.

Doris looked him up and down. "You were a cop, right?"

"Maine State Police."

"I could tell. You got the posture of one. And I know you boys got egos the size of Jupiter's moons so don't get offended now, but there's no way in hell I'm gonna let you have the fun of blowing those ugly fucks to bits."

"Are you sure about this?" Barbara asked. "I mean, this place is your home. We'd understand if you want to stay impartial.

"I didn't know you cared so much, sugartits." Doris used the hand that wasn't holding the grenade to push some sweat out of her eyes. "But you're right, this is my home. At least, it was before Big Josh and his cronies showed up a couple years back. Now it's a prison and we do as told. And I'm too old for that shit."

She turned the knob halfway, then looked to the others who were grouped together just a few feet from her. "I'll lob this. After it goes boom, I expect you folks to go out guns blazing, and finish off whoever's left, alright?"

Everyone nodded.

And Doris opened the door.

CHAPTER THIRTY-THREE

Wyatt half-expected Doris to get blasted the moment she threw open the door. That would have upset him not only because she was helping them, but because he'd grown rather fond of her.

She didn't get shot. Instead, she chucked out the grenade like she was a gold medal shot putter, then slithered back inside behind the relative safety of the door frame.

Someone outside did shoot and a bullet flew through the doorway before embedding itself in one of the tables. Then, Wyatt heard someone yell, "Hairy mother-humping balls!" Then, the detonation of the grenade had his ears ringing and he couldn't tell whether anyone else chimed in.

He imagined there was plenty of screaming and moaning and maybe even some crying. Part of him, a part he tried to pretend didn't exist, wished he could hear their sounds. After all, they had tried to kill him and his family. But, he supposed being momentarily deaf might be for the best.

Trooper was first out the door and, despite his ringing ears, Wyatt felt muffled gunfire. He realized he shouldn't be watching Trooper and should join the fray and then did just that.

He spied a few men upright, but not many. Most were on the ground, in pieces. T-Bone had been ripped in two at the waist, his bottom half a good yard away from the rest of him with just a few ragged ropes of intestines connecting the dots. The card cheat had both his legs blown off and bled out facing skyward. Wyatt wondered if he'd seen the light before expiring, but doubted it. Several of the men he'd seen taunting Allie were in similar, wretched condition and out of the game.

Mohawk stood, dazed and staring at the stump that had once been his right arm like he'd been the victim of a sinister magician's prank. He spotted Wyatt and examined him with wide, confused eyes. "I lost my fuckin arm, man," he said.

Wyatt nodded. "I see."

"Will you let me know if you find it?"

Wyatt wasn't sure how to answer that one. He had better things to do, after all.

As he surveyed the carnage, a machete-wielding man charged him from the side. By the time Wyatt noticed the would-be attacker in his peripheral vision the man was barely a yard away. Wyatt moved to raise his gun but, before he could get off a round, the man's head disintegrated in a kaleidoscope of red blood, gray brain matter, and white bone.

As the man fell, Wyatt saw Trooper standing, pistol raised, smoke wafting from the barrel. Before Wyatt could even nod his head in thanks, Trooper turned and sent a slug into the chest of a rotund, bearded man who'd been aiming a rifle in their direction.

Wyatt heard Seth's wheels crunch over the detritus on the ground behind him and realized his ears had mostly stopped ringing. Then he realized he could hear the plaintive wails of the few who had been injured by the grenade but hadn't yet bled to death. It was an abominable sound and he cursed himself for missing it earlier.

"Shit, brother, old Troop just saved your ass twice in under a minute. Maybe you should stop daydreaming and join the party."

Wyatt turned to him and shrugged his shoulders. "Guess I got caught up in the moment."

Barbara put her hand on Wyatt's shoulder and gave it a firm, reassuring squeeze. "Are any of the bad guys left?"

Wyatt wasn't sure. There were a couple of men alive but no one was shooting at them anymore. Somehow, it seemed... safe.

Trooper rolled over a lifeless body. At first, Wyatt thought he was making sure the guy was deceased, but when the old man leaned in close and took a good look at the dead fellow's face, Wyatt understood what he was really doing. Trooper was identifying the dead.

"Trooper?"

His friend looked to him. "I haven't found Josh yet. This isn't over until--"

A gunshot severed the sentence.

Wyatt saw it. The orange fire of the torches glinted off the bullet as it sliced through the air. If Trooper had been an inch taller, it would have taken the top of his head off, but he wasn't, and it didn't. Instead, it slammed into a building.

Trooper jumped back from the body he'd been examining, stumbling as his foot hit a divot in the pavement. His knee, his bad knee, twisted awkwardly to the side, bending at an angle Wyatt was certain human knees were not supposed to bend.

The man didn't make a sound but Wyatt saw his lips seize and eyes squint and he knew Trooper was in pain of the severe variety. He dashed toward Trooper, wanting to assist him, to help him off the street, but didn't make three steps before there came another gunshot. And that one hit its mark.

Trooper toppled sideways. He managed to partially raise his left arm and broke the fall with his elbow. And break his arm in the process. Wyatt heard the crunching of the bone breaking and it reminded him of cracking hard-boiled eggs before peeling off the shell. Then Trooper was on the ground.

"Wyatt!"

The feminine voice snapped his attention away from Trooper. He thought it was his mother and he tried to find her, worrying that she'd been shot too, but before he could find Barbara he was tackled to the ground.

He landed hard, the force knocking the gun out of his hand and sending it skittering out of reach. He grabbed for the knife at his belt.

Another shot. He didn't see that one, but he heard it go by and realized it would have hit him if he'd still been upright. As he tried to make sense of that, clumps of hair fell into his face.

The person who'd taken him to the ground wasn't an attacker at all. It was Allie and now she looked down on him with half a smile on her face.

"You can thank me later," she said.

Another bullet hit the road beside them, sending shrapnel in the form of concrete and shards of lead their way. Wyatt felt hot pain as some of it embedded itself in his upper arm. "I will. But for now, let's find some cover."

They scrambled to their feet, sprinting to the sidewalk and kneeling behind a cement bench. It was only then that Wyatt realized he was squeezing her hand. "Sorry," he said.

He threw it free like a man who'd just found out his piece of prized fudge was actually dog shit, then felt bad for being so rough.

"I didn't mind." Allie wasn't looking at him, which was for the best because he wasn't only embarrassed about the hand-holding, he was damn scared too and he was certain his face was as easy to read as a grade school primer.

Allie pointed across the street, toward a storefront where a picture window was half-shattered, leaving behind the remnants of a sign reading Priscilla's Sewing and Alte--

"He's in there," Allie said.

"Josh?"

Allie nodded.

Wyatt had no clue what to do. His gun was in the street and

retrieving it would be a suicide mission. Trooper was down and motionless. Wyatt didn't want to believe it but he knew there was a fair chance the man was dead.

That thought, even without knowing whether it held a semblance of truth, was almost too much for Wyatt to handle. He didn't know how they'd go on without Trooper to lead them. How he'd go on. In the last five years the old man, cantankerous and crotchety as he could be, had grown into Wyatt's best friend and surrogate father. He'd taught him everything he knew about being a man, but he still had so much to learn.

What if it was all over?

He wanted to cry but refused to give in, partly due to the fact that Allie was beside him, and also because a man across the street was trying to kill them. But even more so because he knew Trooper would want him to push past his pain and get on with what really mattered. He needed to protect his family.

"What are you doing?" Allie pulled at his arm as he stood.

"What needs to be done." Wyatt shook free of her grasp. "You stay here."

She stared up at him, her pale eyes plaintive. He wondered if he'd ever see them again as he left her.

Wyatt ran crouched over. A bullet zipped past him. Another ricocheted off the road near his feet. He ducked behind a wooden post holding up a metal awning. It was a third as wide as he was and offered a scant amount of protection, but it was better than nothing.

He took a moment to survey the scene. The door to the bar hung ajar and through it he could see Seth and his mother. Their eyes met. Barbara's were wet with tears and he saw her gaze shifting between himself and Trooper's still motionless body in the street.

He considered telling her It'll be okay but didn't want to lie. Supper sat at Seth's feet and Wyatt was relieved the see the dog had stayed inside where it was relatively safe.

A shrill wolf-whistle echoed through the near vicinity. Wyatt sought out the noise and found its source across the street, two buildings up from the store where Big Josh had set up his shooting gallery.

Graham, the man from the hostel slash grocery store, was plastered against the wall. He held a gun so long Wyatt thought it looked like something from Revolutionary War times. His mouth moved in silence and Wyatt realized he was mouthing something to him. But between the dim light and the distance he couldn't quite make it out.

Again his mouth moved. Slower, more deliberate, like he was speaking to an old person who was hard of hearing.

Hoover who.

That made no sense. Even though Wyatt had near perfect eyesight, he squinted and tried to pay close attention.

Cover you. I'll cover you.

The lightbulb went off and Wyatt cursed himself for not catching on sooner. He nodded, then held up three fingers. Graham was quicker on the uptake and knew the deal straight away.

Wyatt dropped one finger. Then the second.

On the third, Graham ran toward the window from which Big Josh had been shooting. He leveled the rifle and shot. The remaining glass burst in a glittering cascade that looked like raining fire as the light of the torches glinted off the falling glass.

Wyatt was too busy sprinting into the street to enjoy the spectacle. He snatched his pistol in mid-stride. Graham shot again, this time through the black abyss of the sewing storefront.

Graham got off one more shot before Wyatt was at his side. All was still inside the store but Wyatt had a feeling that wouldn't last long and he didn't want to waste whatever time they might have on their side.

"Are you willing to go in there with me?" Wyatt asked him.

The man gave a curt, no-nonsense nod. "Hell yes, I am. About time he got his just deserts."

Wyatt returned a nod of his own. "You want the front or back?"

"I'll take the back."

Graham disappeared down the narrow alley while Wyatt headed

down the sidewalk. Within seconds he reached the gaping hole that provided easy access to the store and, pistol raised, he stepped in front of that void.

He wasn't sure whether he expected to shoot or be shot, but neither happened. He saw no sign of Josh. Pushing aside a shard of broken glass, Wyatt climbed through the window and dropped inside.

It was darker in there. The scant light of the torches that lined the street did nothing to illuminate the murky chasm of the store and he realized that Josh could be anywhere, lining up the perfect shot, and Wyatt would be dead before he knew what hit him.

His heartbeat thudded in his ears and the noise drowned out everything else as he tried to concentrate and be less of a sitting duck. He scanned the store, straining to see and that's when he saw the silhouette.

Wyatt shot. His aim was true and the person toppled backward. He ran to him, ready to finally rise to the occasion and finish off Josh, only to find--

A dress form laying on its side. A black ring marred its pink, plastic flesh. He would have laughed if he wasn't so damned scared.

As he looked into that corner of the store he saw a dozen more mannequins and forms - the torsos of women in a variety of shapes and sizes.

"What did she ever do to you?"

Wyatt watched Graham emerge from the rear of the store. "Guess I was a little trigger happy."

"Glad you didn't shoot me."

"Me too."

The brief moment of relief was short-lived.

"You didn't find Josh?" Wyatt asked.

Graham signaled negative. "Back door was wide open. If I had to guess, I'd say he tucked tail and ran about the time I--"

There was no sense finishing the sentence as a nearby gunshot made it invalid.

CHAPTER THIRTY-FOUR

EVERYONE INSIDE THE BAR WAS SO BUSY STARING ACROSS THE street that they didn't hear Big Josh enter until he'd already fired one of his pistols. Doris, whose back had been turned, was the recipient of the bullet.

The shot blasted through the back of her head and burst through the front of her face, sending bits and pieces of teeth spraying from her destroyed mouth like she'd spat out a wad of chiclets. She was dead before she hit the floor.

Barbara was so in shock over seeing such an up-close and personal view of violent death that she didn't even bother turning around until Big Josh spoke.

"Never did like that one. Big, butch, bitch," Josh said.

Barb had almost forgotten she still held the .38 in her hand, but as surprise turned to anger, she shifted her finger to the trigger.

"Uh, uh, uh," Josh said. "Don't do anything rash now or I'll blow the head off your little crip son."

It's a bluff, she thought, but as she finished her 180-degree turn, she saw Josh standing behind Seth. He had the barrel of one of the .44s pressed downward against the top of Seth's skull and the other pistol was pointed toward herself, Allie, and Pete, all of whom had been spectators in the peanut gallery, waiting to see how the show ended, and unaware that the big finale was coming to them.

"You don't have to do this." What a cliche, Barb thought as the words spilled from her mouth. What's next? Please? Take me instead? Men like Big Josh didn't negotiate, especially after they'd been robbed.

"I do whatever the fuck I want, lady. And your cyclops-looking face isn't going to win me over so save your breath." He cocked his head toward the shopping cart in which they'd stashed the stolen food. "Fill that with old Dori's booze. She ain't got much use for it now."

Barb slipped behind the bar. Allie joined her. Pete sat worthless in a chair, still holding his wounded arm like he was afraid it was going to run off on him.

Josh looked to the man. "You throw in with these assholes, Pete?"

Pete shook his head almost violently from side to side. "Shit no. Me and Allie was just tying one on and enjoying a quiet evening when these fucking thieves busted in."

Josh looked him up and down, then nodded. "Good. I didn't take you for the Brutus type."

"Brutus?" Pete asked.

Barb fought not to roll her eyes as she carried an armload of liquor to the cart.

"As in et tu Brute." Josh grabbed a chair, spun it backwards and took a seat behind Seth. Now he had the pistol pressed against the rear of the boy's head.

"Sorry." Pete rubbed his bald, tattooed skull with his free hand. "I don't follow."

"Brutus was Julius Caesar's best friend. But he turned on him and participated in Caesar's assassination." Barb deposited bottles into the cart and turned to the bar to fetch more.

"Thank God," Josh said. "Someone else in this place with some culture. It's about damned time. What's your name, anyway?"

"Barbara Morrill."

Josh tipped his index finger her way. "Open one of those bottles and pour us both a shot."

Barb did as told. Not because she expected compliance would curry any favor with the man, but to buy time until a better idea came along. She handed Josh a glass. He accepted it but didn't drink it down immediately.

"That colored friend of yours, I'm pretty certain he drugged me earlier today."

Barb swallowed her booze, then refilled the glass. She had a nice buzz going and figured why the hell not.

"That's okay though," Josh said. "I ended him." He downed his shot and motioned to Barb for another. She obliged. "He won't be getting one over on me again."

The warm haze of the booze made Trooper's death something she could handle, at least until it wore off. But she suspected, if Big Josh had his way, there wouldn't be time for the latter to occur.

Barb swallowed her second shot then went to the bar for more bottles. As she did, she caught movement out the front window. Her vision was bleary from the booze but she was able to make out Wyatt and the man from the boarding house, or mini-mart, or whatever the hell it was. She quickly looked away so as not to alert Josh to their presence.

Behind the bar, Allie was busy shaking from head to toe and struggled to stack liquor bottles in her arms. She dropped one and it exploded against the wood floor.

"Clumsy slut!" Josh stood so fast the chair toppled over and that made Allie jump, and the remainder of her haul also fell.

Barb realized that Josh had temporarily removed the barrel of the gun from Seth's head. And she saw Seth's hands fiddling with the shotgun that still rested in his lap. She tried to stare him down, to send telepathic mother-son vibes that screamed Don't do anything stupid but it didn't seem to be working.

Her body was rigid as steel as she waited for Big Josh to start shooting, or for Seth to get caught, or for Allie to have a nervous breakdown, or for Wyatt and the man from the store to burst inside and save the day, but none of that happened.

Because somehow, in the brief chaos of the bottles falling, Josh had been shot. A crimson stain spread across the lower half of his shirt. He stared down at it, mesmerized by its growing presence. Then he looked up, eyes scanning the people before him, his face as confused as that of a second-grader who'd just been asked to recite the square root of 113.

"Which of you fuckers shot me?" The words came out lazy and slurred and followed by a thin dribble of blood and spit.

"I did." Trooper stood in the rear doorway, pistol raised. And without another word, he shot again.

That one punched a throughway in Josh's neck. The man took a staggering step to the left, then to the right, then back. Barbara thought he looked like a drunk at a wedding reception trying unsuccessfully to keep up with the electric slide.

His arm twitched as he tried to bring up one of the .44s and shoot back, but he was already halfway gone. Barb watched as Trooper aimed and shot one final time. That bullet tore through the center of his chest and Big Josh fell backward. He collapsed on one of the tables, then slid off and dropped to the floor as his body went limp.

"When did you get here, Troop?" Seth asked.

Trooper shook his head. "I've been outside that door for the last two minutes."

"Guess we were distracted," Seth said.

Trooper limped to Josh's body and poked at his head with his foot, checking for signs of life. There were none. "Ain't a one of you with a lick of situational awareness. Damned disgrace."

Barb ran to Trooper and threw her arms around him. He patted her back in a somewhat awkward manner as he was still holding the gun. "I thought he killed you."

He shook her off and she realized his left arm hung limp at his side. There was blood and it was bent in a way that made her feel woozy.

"He made a go at it."

Wyatt and Graham came through the front door and Barb watched her son's face brighten as he saw the dead man on the floor.

"It's over," Wyatt said.

Trooper nodded.

Despite having all odds against them, they'd come out victorious. A little worse for the wear, but alive. Barb thought that called for a drink.

CHAPTER THIRTY-FIVE

"Hey, can I ask you something?"

Wyatt spun around on the barstool where he'd been waiting for the throbbing in his ear to subside. Allie stood a short distance away and he noticed that her white crop top was stained with both blood, from bandaging up Pete, and dirt from tackling him to the ground and saving his life. Her face had also been scuffed in the fall and a red brush burn resided on her cheek, making it look like she'd been half-way through applying blush and given up.

"Yeah. Sure," he said.

Allie pointed to the empty stool beside him. "Can I sit there?"

Wyatt shrugged his shoulders. "Yeah." He tried to think of something to add, something clever or amusing but failed.

The woman sat, then reached for an undrunk shot that had been idling on the bar. She sipped it as she stole glances at him.

"Your ear hurt?"

"Not really." That was a lie. It felt like... well, like he'd been shot. Or like someone had sawed his ear in two with a butter knife. The pain spread to the side of his head and created a headache from hell.

But he wasn't about to admit any semblance of weakness to the prettiest woman he'd seen in years.

"Looks like it would." Another sip. Her delicate fingers curled around the glass and Wyatt noticed that her nails were pristine. It wasn't the type of thing he usually observed, but the cleanliness stood out and also made him self conscious of his own ragged fingernails which he cut occasionally, but more often chewed into submission.

It had been four or five hours since the gunfight. For the first few wondered if any of the leftovers from Big Josh's gang might show up bent on vengeance. None did though, leaving him to assume that they'd killed the lot of them or that any stragglers decided it wasn't a fight worth having. That's how it seemed to be with bullies. They were cruel and violent when they thought you were weak. If you could prove you weren't, they scattered.

Trooper had been shot in the outer flank of his thigh but it was a mostly superficial wound that Barb stitched closed after disinfecting it with high proof liquor. Trooper drank what was leftover. His left arm was broken too, but it seemed to be a simple fracture. They constructed a makeshift splint to immobilize it.

After tending to Trooper, his mother had also used her sewing skills to tend to Pete who was so drunk he was sprawled on the floor parroting a poor rendition of Willie Nelson's You Were Always on My Mind. He passed out soon after, a relief to Wyatt and, Wyatt imagined, anyone else who could hear.

Once the adrenaline wore off they regathered their newly obtained supplies and reclaimed their stolen shopping cart. They offered to dig a grave for Doris and Mute Sam but Graham and a few of the others from the trading post promised to take care of it.

Big Josh and his minions were tossed into a pile at the east end of town where all the buildings were abandoned. Wyatt didn't know if they'd be left to rot or burned and didn't care.

He was eager to move on. For their trek to recommence. Seth and their mother had claimed Doris's backroom to catch a few winks but Trooper stayed awake for a while before he too succumbed to sleep leaving Wyatt the lone member of their party to sit and wait and wonder what lied ahead.

Allie had been asleep too until just now. He wasn't sure if he appreciated the chance to converse with her or whether he'd have preferred to remain alone with his thoughts.

"You don't say much do you?" A final sip and the shot glass was empty.

"I guess not."

"Why is that?"

He tried to think of a good reason before answering, but that only prolonged the awkward quiet and he decided to wing it. "I'm not sure. Seems like most of the time, when I do talk, I say the wrong thing. You ever hear that saying, 'Better to stay silent and be thought a fool than to open your mouth and remove all doubt'?"

The woman laughed. It wasn't the tired, lifeless noise she'd made when he met her the day prior. This time there seemed to be genuine humor, maybe even happiness, along with it. "No. I never heard that, but I like it."

She reached for a bottle of liquor and refilled the shot glass, then tilted the bottle to him. Wyatt shook his head.

"No thanks."

"I don't know many men that turn down an open bar." She threw a glance toward Pete who was now snoring face down, his rumbles ricocheting off the dirty floor. "How old are you, anyway?"

"Eighteen. You?"

"Twenty-five. Before the attacks, sometimes it seemed like all I could think about was turning twenty-one because then I'd be a real adult and could get into the clubs and drink and dance and party all night long like they do in movies. They made it look so damn fun." She held her glass but didn't drink. "Never even got the chance because, when I finally turned twenty-one, it was already all over."

He considered adding a personal anecdote of his own, something in the same vein. Maybe telling her how much he'd looked forward to driving. But then he realized it would only serve to heighten their age difference. Eighteen and twenty-five didn't seem bad but thirteen and twenty... Yeah, he wasn't going to mention that.

"Where were you from?" He asked.

"South Jersey. Place called Cape May. You ever hear of it?"

"I haven't."

"It's a touristy place. Not too far from Atlantic City. Has light-houses and boat tours and the beach. I guess that stuff's interesting when you don't grow up around it but when you do..."

Growing up in Maine - Vacationland - Wyatt could understand. He looked toward the front window where small vestiges of light were beginning to appear. It would be time to move on soon and he knew he should wake the others. But when he moved to slip off his barstool Allie set down her undrunk shot and grabbed his wrist.

"You know you never did thank me."

"I didn't?"

She shook her head and her dreadlocks sashayed side to side. "Nope. But that's okay. You don't have to. You can do something else instead." She smiled, revealing somewhat crooked but white teeth and something about her imperfect grin made him appreciate her even more.

"What's that?" He asked.

Her smile faltered, just a tad, and a worry line made its appearance on her brow. He suddenly regretted asking.

"Take us with you," Allie said. "Please."

Wyatt swallowed hard. He knew his burgeoning crush on the woman was futile. She was older, more experienced, and worst of all, already in a relationship with another man. And even aside from that, the last time he'd welcomed two people into their midst it ended badly, teaching him a lesson he wasn't anxious to relive.

Something in his expression must have tipped Allie that good news wasn't coming and her powder blue eyes lost their joy. "Don't say anything now. Just think about it. That's all I'm asking, okay? Just think about it."

"I will." But he already knew the answer would be no.

CHAPTER THIRTY-SIX

"Are you sure that bullet didn't hit you in the brain after all?" Seth stared at his big brother, wondering how he could be so stupid. Wasn't wisdom supposed to come with age?

"I didn't say we should. Or even that I wanted to. I'm just passing along the request." Wyatt half-sneered at him. "Besides, she saved my ass while you hid out in the bar and got drunk."

Seth burped out a chuckle. That was true and he had no shame. "Not my fault I got all the brains in the family. Charm too for that matter."

Their mother and Trooper had been silent throughout the brief discussion and Seth checked their faces to try to get a read on where they stood, not that he had much doubt.

Only they didn't look like their minds were set and that shocked him so much he almost fell out of his chair. They were just weeks removed from being tied up and robbed by two strangers who seemed a hell of a lot friendlier than some tattooed pimp wannabe and his low rent girlfriend.

"Excuse me, family. Have you all lost your freaking minds? How is this even an option?"

"Seth, we have to consider the situation," Trooper said. "We have a long way to go and I've got a broken arm. It'll be a long time before I can push you, or even push one of the shopping carts."

Seth huffed. "I can push myself."

Trooper knelt down to Seth's level. It always annoyed him when people did that, made him feel like a child being talked down to. "Most of the time, yes. But we have to get across the Appalachians and no matter where we do it, it's going to be long and steep. Two extra people could be an asset."

"Or they could kill us for our stuff."

Barb finished off the can of fruit cocktail they'd shared for breakfast and set it aside. "If they wanted to kill us, they had plenty of opportunities already."

He couldn't believe his ears. It was as if sometime between when he'd passed out the night before and when he woke up this morning everyone he knew had undergone a lobotomy. But he could see the writing on the wall and knew stomping his feet in protest would only serve to make them take him even less seriously.

He turned his attention away from them and to Supper who had flopped onto his side on the dusty floor and rested. Seth snapped his fingers and the dog sprung to action and came to his side. He scratched under his chin and stared into his big, chocolate-colored eyes and shook his head.

"Fine then. But I'm putting it on the record that this dog is smarter than the three of you combined."

Before they set out Trooper laid out the rules.

"Neither of you will carry a weapon. Not a gun, not a knife. Not even the can opener. All you got are the clothes on your back and if we catch you with anything more than that, you're on your own."

Allie nodded, eager and submissive. Pete shrugged his shoulders.

"What if we get attacked? We won't even be able to fend for ourselves."

Seth was about to pipe in, to remind the man that he was oh so helpful when shit hit the fan the night prior, when Wyatt cut him off.

"We'll deal with that if it happens. But until then, you have to agree. And if you don't, you can stay here. That's the deal."

"We agree," Allie said. "We'll do whatever you say."

Seth imagined she had a lot of experience doing what men said. She didn't seem bad at all really, but he didn't like the way Wyatt looked at her. He'd seen that look before, for a whole year actually, when Wyatt was twelve and pining over Nikki Latshaw who everyone knew was the prettiest girl in the neighborhood. She was all he could talk about even though the girl never, so far as Seth knew, talked to him.

The fact that Wyatt was falling for the woman was as clear as the sky used to be and Seth was scared. Part because Allie already had a guy, one who looked and acted like a piece of shit and pieces of shit didn't appreciate someone else making moves on their girl. But also, maybe more so, because he didn't want Wyatt to have anyone else taking his attention. Because that meant less for him. And being the youngest of them and a cripple to boot was already more isolating than he could handle sometimes. He didn't need more piled on.

At least he had the dog.

Except, at the moment, the dog was nestled at Allie's feet while she gave him the world's best belly rub.

Fuckers, Seth thought. All of them sucked.

CHAPTER THIRTY-SEVEN

They were a little more than halfway through their first day together when they broke for lunch. There hadn't been much time for talking until then, not that Wyatt minded. Everyone seemed to be on eggshells, still trying to get a feel for one another and find their place in the expanded group.

Trooper had built a small fire upon which they boiled water for chicken noodle soup. It was the kind with stars and pea-sized bits of dehydrated chicken that Wyatt remembered as the go-to food he'd eaten while recovering from a cold or the flu when he was a kid. That soup, and jello, always seemed to make everything better.

"What was life like in Maine, anyway?" Allie asked.

Wyatt glanced around the group to see if anyone else wanted to answer. No one did, so he stepped up. "Cold."

"Were there other people there?"

"Not really," Wyatt said. He had no interest in telling them about the men who'd broken into their house. Who'd maimed his mother while he watched. He wanted to change the subject. "What about you, Pete? Where were you from?"

They'd been passing the soup around the loose circle and Pete accepted it from Allie. "All over."

"Well that's specific," Seth said.

Pete narrowed his eyes as he stirred the soup. "My parents were both in the Air Force. We moved around a lot. Longest I stayed in one place was fourteen months in Okinawa. Kadena Air Force Base."

Wyatt wouldn't have expected that. He knew the old saying about judging a book by its cover, but he was guilty of doing just that. If asked to guess, he would have said Pete probably grew up on the streets, or maybe an orphanage. That he had no family or support system. That he was probably in and out of prison all his life. He felt a bit like an asshole for jumping to such conclusions.

"Have any of you actually been south?" Pete asked as he blew on his spoon to cool the scalding hot broth.

"You talking about ever or?" Trooper asked.

Pete shook his head. "Recently. As in the last year or two."

None of them had of course.

"Have you?" Wyatt asked. He saw Pete glance Allie's way before looking to him.

"Made it as far as Kentucky the summer before last."

They waited for him to go on. He seemed to sense their anticipation and let the silence linger.

"Well, spit it out," Trooper said.

Pete took a bite of the now cooled and edible soup before continuing. "I won't lie to you. It's bad down there."

"Bad how," Seth asked. "I imagine you never bothered to crack open a dictionary, but there are a plethora of words available for you to use and a good portion of them would be more helpful than bad."

Wyatt saw their mother shoot Seth a look that would have made him shrivel, but Seth only grinned.

Pete didn't seem to find the humor in it and remained closed-mouthed.

It was Allie that broke the silence. "Cannibals," she said. "There are tribes of them. Like the Indians used to be. They fight with each other and eat anyone who enters their territory."

"Bullshit," Seth said.

Wyatt didn't understand why his brother could be so dismissive of the idea when they'd seen the aftermath of what happened to Devan and June.

Allie shook her head. "It's not. Most of them are further west, like Arizona and New Mexico, but some of them come more this way."

"You actually saw tribes of cannibal Indians in Kentucky?" Wyatt asked.

"It's Native Americans, Wyatt," Seth said. "Have some class. And I don't think she's actually discussing their ethnicity. Just implying they act like them. The stereotypical, Hollywood version, anyway."

"He's right." Allie's gaze drifted to the ground. "And, no. We didn't see them. But we met a guy who told us all about them. Said he was heading south with his wife when they got attacked in Arkansas. He told us they cut his wife open and ate her heart while it was still beating."

"And he just stood around and enjoyed the show?" Seth said. "Hell of a guy. I'd certainly trust him."

"It's the truth," Pete said. His voice teetered on anger. "That man had been scalped. And it's not like they show in the movies where there's just a little bit of hair missing. Like his barber got carried away with the clippers."

Pete used his index finger to draw an invisible line a few inches above his eyebrows. "They cut him here." He dragged his finger around the back of his head, behind his ears, then around the other side. "All the way to here. Then they ripped his scalp off."

Wyatt caught Seth stared at him, still wearing his grin. Maybe Seth wasn't buying what they were selling but Wyatt was. He'd seen the charred body in New England. He'd seen the butchered remains of Devan and June. He had no doubt that similar things, and worse things, were happening elsewhere.

"That's horrible," Barbara said. She'd been holding a canteen of coffee between her knees and set it aside.

Pete nodded. "It was. His skull was all scabby and black and half-infected. And the flies, shit, I can still remember those flies dive-bombing him and eating the skin that was rotting. And the guy acted like he didn't even notice. I suppose he was used to it."

Allie shivered and Pete rested his hand on her thigh. Wyatt looked away.

"If it's so fucking dangerous down there, why did you want to come with us?" Seth asked.

Pete didn't answer. Neither did Allie, at first, but after a moment she spoke up. "Life was hard at the trading post. Always people drifting in and out who acted nice but most of the time weren't." She looked to Wyatt, then Barbara. "We're hoping it's like you said. That maybe there's something better down there. Once you get past the cannibals, I mean."

"That's far from a certainty," Trooper said.

Allie gave a weak smile. "I know but it's something. It's hope."

Wyatt understood what she meant. What good was living if all hope was gone?

CHAPTER THIRTY-EIGHT

AFTER MORE THAN TWO MONTHS OF TRAVELING LITTLE HAD changed aside from their geographic location. Crossing the Appalachians wasn't easy, but it wasn't as bad as Wyatt had expected. Pete and Allie both took their turns pushing Seth which helped tremendously. Once they were out of Pennsylvania they continued southwest through Ohio, Indiana, and Illinois where the land grew flat and monotonous, but was easy to traverse.

Trooper's arm was mostly healed and out of the sling, but Wyatt wouldn't allow him to lift anything heavier than a fork. Their gunshot wounds were healed and hadn't become infected. The food was holding out and there had been no need to put their guns to use. All things considered, life was good.

Only Wyatt didn't feel good. The main issue was boredom. It seemed like they'd exhausted every life story, mined every possible anecdote, and played every road trip game they could imagine. If he heard another recitation of I spy with my little eye he'd be apt to shoot whoever said it. As each day blended into the next, he craved something new. Something, anything, that could break up the mind-numbing, soul-crushing sameness that had come to dominate his life.

It didn't help that his infatuation with Allie had grown by leaps and bounds, while Pete's whiny, selfish personality made him want to puke. Having to watch them be a happy, affectionate couple day in, day out was a special kind of torture. He tried to put aside his feelings for the girl, but it was still a work in progress.

On the less depressing side, contrary to Pete's earlier assertions that the land was riddled with cannibals, they had seen none. It wasn't only bereft of cannibals but humans as a whole.

They hadn't encountered a single person since leaving the trading post. Occasionally they'd stroll by a house or building and Wyatt would get the feeling they were being watched. And there were random signs of life. Footprints, freshly discarded trash, even some laundry hanging in a wash line to dry in western Missouri, but their eyes saw no people.

Not until they reached Arkansas.

THEY USUALLY HAD GOOD LUCK FINDING AN EMPTY HOUSE TO crash in for the night, but they happened to be on a long stretch of desolate highway when darkness fell and the best they could do was an industrial, brick building which looked to have been victim to an earthquake or tornado. Only two of the four walls remained upright, but a copse of dead maples stood guard against one of the open sides and would serve as a nice wind-break. It wasn't perfect, but it would do.

Their progress had been slower lately as the days grew shorter. The added hours of dark brought with them more time to be cold and a fire was no longer a luxury but a necessity to survive the night.

Trooper had a nice blaze going and Pete had gathered enough scrap wood to last the night. After a dinner consisting of canned peas, canned beets, and some hot chocolate it was time to turn in.

Seth had volunteered to take the first watch, but Wyatt hadn't yet drifted off. He stared across the flames to where Allie and Pete laid together, his arms around her waist. The flickering orange light of the fire danced across her face and Wyatt thought that would be the perfect sight to fall asleep to when--

Branches snapped and popped as something - someone - broke through the trees. Wyatt was first to his feet, followed by Trooper who was shockingly spry all things considered. Each of them drew the pistols holstered on their belts. Seth took hold of his shotgun, one hand on the barrel, one on the stock. Barbara held the .38 revolver she kept at her side through the nights.

Only Allie and Pete were unarmed. Wyatt wondered if it was time to break that rule but had no time to say it out loud before two figures sprinted into the makeshift campsite.

"You dumbo goons!" The man in the lead said. "What the Sam hell do you think you're doing?" He was scrawny with an unkempt beard that hung halfway down his chest. That, coupled with a blue slicker he wore made Wyatt think he looked like a ship's captain.

The man who was second in line was equally thin, but balding with only a horseshoe of gray hair atop his head. One of his eyes was clouded over with a cataract and both of his top front teeth were missing.

Wyatt wasn't sure who the Captain's question was directed at, or even if it was a question at all, but he raised the pistol, nonetheless.

Trooper had done the same and Wyatt thought his old friend was going to shoot if the man got any closer. But instead of approaching them, Captain went to the fire. He kicked at it, frantic, smothering it with dirt and chunks of bricks and anything else close enough to douse the flames. The second man joined in and did the same. Soon enough the fire was diminished to red-hot embers.

"What the hell do you thi--" Trooper began.

"No time to ask. Hide you ninny. Hide or die," Captain whispered.

"What is going--" Barbara's question was cut short when the balding man grabbed her and wrapped his hand around her mouth.

Wyatt's finger was on the trigger and he was ready to shoot, but the man holding his mother only shook his head and held the index finger of his free hand to his lips in the unspoken sign for quiet.

"They're coming!" Captain ran to a pile of fallen bricks and camouflaged himself on the ground behind it.

And then Wyatt heard it too. The noise was loud and only getting louder. Footsteps. Broken branches. It sounded like a stampede of horses galloping through the trees.

The two men who had invaded their camp were the least of their worries. Wyatt knew that now and so did Trooper.

"Everyone find cover," Trooper said. He grabbed Seth's wheelchair and the two vanished behind a portion of the wall.

The man who'd been keeping Barb quiet dragged her out of the building and away from the coming sounds. Then Pete and Allie hid behind a heaping section of collapsed roof and shingles.

Wyatt grabbed hold of the leash he'd found for Supper back in Indiana and pulled the dog with him until they were out of the building and into a thicket of dry brush. He pushed a path into it, the dead branches scratching at his face and arms, but he had to get his dog, and himself, out of sight. Out of view from whatever, or whoever, was coming.

As he settled in, he turned back to the building and saw a new man had arrived. He looked older than the others. His hair, more white than gray, was pulled into a ponytail. He scanned the area with wide, desperate eyes.

"River? Georgie?" The man asked. But no one answered. He turned, took a step away from where the fire had been and toward the back of the building, but didn't make it any further.

A pack of people, ten, maybe fifteen, broke from the trees and sprinted at the man. They looked wild and filthy. They clutched bats, axes, and chunks of metal. Anything that could do damage. Anything that could kill.

The man never had a chance.

One of the pack swung a baseball bat and struck his shoulder. He yelped as he fell backwards, landing hard on his ass. Another swung what looked like a tire iron and landed a glancing blow that ripped open the man's cheek, a hole so deep it revealed his decaying teeth.

A woman swung a bat and connected with the man's ribs. Wyatt heard the sound of his bones breaking even over his bellowing screams.

Then another figure stepped into the group. He was tall with broad shoulders and a wooly mane of red hair. The others seemed to part, to allow him better access. This new arrival gripped a double-bladed axe with which he reared back, then swung down.

The old man's screams came to an immediate halt as the axe landed just a few inches from his neck, nearly cleaving his upper body in two.

Blood was shot from the wound in wild arcs. More poured from the man's mouth and he gagged as he choked on it. A few moments later he went limp and the red-haired killer ripped the weapon free of the body, which fell sideways in a slow-motion tumble before landing in the dirt and weeds.

Wyatt had to remind himself to breathe.

"Where are the other two?" Red, the man who'd dealt the fatal blow, asked.

"Can't be far," one of the others said. "And look at all this shit." He motioned to the shopping carts of supplies. "There were more here."

Red nodded. "Get the body out of here and prep it."

Four people grabbed the lifeless body and carried it in the direction from which they'd come. Wyatt watched as the man's head dangled loose, flopping with each step of the people carrying him.

Then Wyatt turned his attention back to the man with the axe, to the one he thought of as Red. He dug through their carts, pulling out random canned goods and weapons. He seemed to have little interest in the firearms but fondled the knives with an unnerving amount of care.

The remaining others began to search the building and Wyatt

knew it was only a matter of seconds before some, or all of them were discovered.

He clutched the pistol, raised it carefully, trying not to break any branches and give away his location too soon. He was lining up his shot, aiming at Red, when--

Captain dashed from his hiding place and in the direction of the remaining killers. "You poon licking pinheads think you can kill West and get away with it?"

All the attackers turned toward him, weapons raised.

"Looney ding dongs all dressed up like dime-store villains. You ain't so tough. Psycho man-eating goons'll all rot in hell!"

He continued screaming, but the words dissolved into the unrecognizable mutterings of a crazy person. And Wyatt assumed that he likely was.

"Get him," Red screamed.

Captain spun on his heels and dashed toward the rear of the building. Toward the hiding spots of Wyatt and the others. The possibly crazy man pushed through the brush, less than a foot from Wyatt and Supper. He saw them and flashed a manic grin.

"Whatta ya waiting for, bonehead? Run!"

Wyatt was tired of running. As Captain disappeared into the night, he returned his attention to the coming mob. They were within fifteen feet, and easy pickings.

He shot and a man with a hatchet in one hand and a hammer in the other fell. Red and the others froze in place and looked to their fallen comrade.

Wyatt shot again. That round dropped a man who'd been carrying a spear fashioned from a rebar rod. It took him a moment to realize he'd just killed two people. That he'd joined the ranks of Trooper and Seth as a man who was capable of taking a life if the situation called for it. That didn't make him feel good. But it was too late to go back.

Then Trooper joined in. A woman with a baseball bat went down. Then a young man, maybe even a teenager, with a pipe.

Wyatt heard Seth's shotgun go off and the man with the tire iron squealed in pain and grabbed his midsection. Blood seeped through his hands.

"Clear out!" Red said as he turned and ran. The others followed.

Wyatt tried one last shot, but the bullet went astray. Trooper had better luck and felled another of their party. In seconds, the rest were gone.

Wyatt's heart pounded in his chest. He'd been longing for excitement, but not like this.

CHAPTER THIRTY-NINE

Trooper pushed Seth free from their hiding place. Wyatt and Supper were next out. Then Allie and Pete. Barbara and the man who'd hidden her emerged last.

"Everyone okay?" Trooper asked and they all nodded. He returned one of the Desert Eagle's to its holster. "Good."

Not that anything about this situation was good. A handful of dead bodies lay scattered around the floor. Several more of the killers had escaped and were likely pissed off. And they now had an additional new face clinging to the group.

He looked to the man, with his blank eye and haggard face. "What the hell did you bring down on us?"

The newcomer shook his head. "It's not like that, friend. See, they spotted your fire... We spotted it, I suppose. We came running through because we were being chased and--" The man stopped talking and dug his index finger into his ear, scratching. He smiled revealing a mouth filled with broken and rotten teeth.

"We shouldn't stay here. We can't stay here, see. They'll be back. They'll be looking for me. And now you too. River don't want to be here when they come back. Do you?"

The man, River, was frantic and obviously at least two thirds crazy. His presence made Trooper uncomfortable, like sharing a room with a skunk, but he was right.

"Who were they?" Trooper asked.

"Let's go and River will tell you all about it." He extracted his finger from his ear and examined the wax that had wedged itself under his long, ragged nail. Then he stuck his finger into his mouth and sucked away like it was the world's sweetest lollipop.

Trooper watched as he wandered out of the building, in a different direction than the killers.

"That dude's two fucking beers shy of a sixpack," Seth said.

Trooper thought the boy crass, but correct. "I would not disagree. But he's right. We can't stay here."

THE GROUP MOVED AS FAST AS THEY COULD AWAY FROM THE road and through the trees. Trooper was in the lead, trying to catch up to the newcomer who was surprisingly fleet of foot. He took a quick glance behind him, making sure everyone was there.

They were. Barb, Pete, and Allie were grouped together a few yards back. Wyatt pushed his brother and the two, plus the dog, brought up the rear.

Satisfied that all were accounted for, Trooper turned his attention forward and he saw River half a football field away, resting against a tree. A break seemed like a good idea as his own lungs were burning from the sudden exercise, made even worse as he hadn't been granted a minute of sleep.

After another thirty seconds, Trooper arrived at the tree and found River holding his dick in his hand as a weak stream of urine trickled out.

"Good, you made it. Let's go." River tucked himself back into his pants, not minding the fact that he was still leaking.

He moved to resume his run but Trooper grabbed a handful of

his filthy shirt and held tight. "Hold on. We're not going a step further until you explain some shit."

River bounced on his feet, head snapping side to side, up and down. He was spooked, and he probably had good reason to be.

"Not safe here," River said.

Trooper stared him down as the others caught up.

"What's going on, Trooper?" Wyatt asked.

"It's not a good place. Those monsters--"

Trooper pulled him closer, their faces only a few inches apart. River's noxious body odor was like soft cheese gone rancid mixed with chicken manure. Trooper regretted getting so close but he wasn't about to show weakness.

"If you don't start talking sense, it's not them you have to worry about. I'll kill you myself."

The man stopped bouncing, stopped his furtive glances. His eyes were locked onto Trooper's, understanding that he meant it.

"Alright, what do you want to know?"

"Who the hell are you?"

"My friends call me River."

"River?" Seth asked.

River smiled. It wasn't a pretty sight. "Cause I'm always runnin'."

"So, River. What the fuck was all that?"

"Cannibals, man. You guys are takin' a tour straight through cannibal country."

Pete ran his hand over his bald head. "I fucking knew it. We never should have gone with these idiots."

"You shut the hell up." Trooper was ready to smack the guy if he didn't close his yap. Pete obeyed.

"They caught me a few days ago. Me and those other fellers. But see, I got away. We all did. Well, until now." River locked eyes with Seth and pointed to him. "This one, he's no good. He'll get us all killed. You should leave him behind."

"You keep comments like that to yourself." Trooper shoved River against a tree, sending out another puff of toxic b.o. "We were doing just fine before you showed up with a gang of maneaters on your heels. We don't need that kind of trouble you stupid piss ant."

He let the man go and River dropped to the ground giggling. Trooper waved his hand to the others. It was time to go.

"You can't just leave. You need me," River said as he rocked back and forth.

"We need you just about as much as we need those killers to circle back around for you."

River shook his head violently from side to side. "Not just me now. They'll want you too. It's personal."

Trooper left him there. The others followed close behind. River alternated between laughing and sobbing, but Trooper cared not at all. This man had brought hell to them and he deserved whatever fate was coming.

They were fifty feet away when River composed himself enough to speak again. "I know where they hunt. I can keep you safe."

Trooper's pace slowed but didn't stop. He had a low opinion of River, but he had a low opinion of most people. If there was a chance what the man said was true, it would be stupid to leave him behind. Still, he wasn't ready to give in just yet.

"Maybe we should bring him," Barbara said.

Trooper turned back to her. "Have you smelled him?"

"He has a certain... musk."

"Musk my ass. Dumb bastard smells like he went skinny dipping in raw sewage.."

She looked to the man rocking back and forth on the ground. Trooper thought he seemed like a two-year-old throwing a temper tantrum.

"Still though, it seems cruel to leave him alone. With those savages around. And he did hide me from them," Barbara said.

Although he wouldn't have admitted it to her, the idea of River getting caught and eaten wouldn't have cost him the slightest amount of duress. But, as he surveyed the rest of the group, he could tell from their faces they fell more on her side than his. The only other hard case looked to be Pete and that was enough to sway Trooper's gut.

"Alright. But he isn't sleeping within twenty feet of me. Hell, maybe fifty."

Barb's face warmed and that made him feel a bit better about giving in.

"Go back and tell him to come along," Trooper told Wyatt who did just that. They watched as River bounced to his feet like he had springs in his shoes and raced toward them, quickly outpacing the younger and fitter Wyatt.

"You won't regret bringing River along," he said when he caught up with the rest of them. "I'm a good man to have around in a pinch. You'll see."

Wyatt rejoined them and they continued walking.

"Hey," Seth said to River. "If they're cannibals, then why are you still alive? Why didn't they just eat you?"

River shrugged. "Maybe they were full."

"What about the other guy?"

"West?"

"I guess. The one they killed back there. How come they didn't eat him?"

River laughed again. "When a hunter shoots a deer, does he grab his fork and dig in straight off? Not where I come from. The cannibals man, they aren't mutants. They like their meat cooked just like everyone else."

Trooper heard the disgusted groans from the rest of the group.

"I like steak rare," Seth added.

It was time to change the subject. "Alright, River, so you say you know things."

River nodded, grinning like a hyena. A mangy, old hyena. "I do."

"Then I want you to show us the safest way to the border."

"The border? Like, south? Like Mexico?" He said it with a bad accent - Meh-he-co.

"That's right. All the way down."

River shook his head. "That's a bad idea my dark friend. Real bad." He laughed, sounding more maniacal than ever. "You guys are crazier than me."

"Why's that?" Wyatt asked.

"Only way to get there is to go through their territory. Even River ain't that crazy!"

The way River said it made Trooper believe him. The man was insane, but he was convincing. Despite that, they had a plan to stick to and they'd come much too far to turn back.

CHAPTER FORTY

THEY WALKED THROUGH THE NIGHT, NOT BREAKING UNTIL THE
sky made its half-hearted transition from black to gray.

They'd made the decision to sleep during the day and travel at
night primarily because they could avoid building a fire in the dark.
A fire that could again give away their location. During the day two
of them would stay awake while the others slept, trading off every
few hours. It would be easier to see coming danger - cannibals -
during the day. In theory.

But before any of them went to sleep, it was time to eat. They
scrabbled together a small fire and boiled cans of potatoes and stewed
tomatoes which they combined into a poor excuse for a soup.

As he ate his gruel, Wyatt watched Supper scarf down dry dog
food and thought it didn't look much worse. Then his mind drifted
and he wondered what people tasted like. The punchline to an old
joke came to mind. Chicken. But somehow he doubted that. He
couldn't imagine people tasted like any normal animal. I hope I never
find out, he thought with a shiver.

At least he could stop worrying about being cooked and eaten
alive. Despite his faults, River had managed to dispel that worry.

Cannibals treated humans like livestock. Somehow, that wasn't a comforting thought.

"So, what's the kid's story?" River flopped down next to Wyatt.

Wyatt lifted an eyebrow. "My brother?"

"Brother, sure. The crippled boy who's gonna get you all killed."

"I'm right here, asshole," Seth said from less than ten feet away. Supper laid across his legs and basked in being petted.

"Never said you wasn't," River gave a wide, ugly smile.

Wyatt silently thanked his mother for always being on top of him about brushing his teeth when he was a kid. Even now, in the apocalypse, he brushed daily and made sure to floss as often as he remembered. He'd never end up like River in the dental hygiene department.

"Aren't you tired of talking?" Wyatt asked.

"Oh, come on, we're pretty safe for right now. Talking's good for the soul." River drank the remnants of his soup. "You know, my friends, they gave me shit for talking too much. But I was always right. I know when it's safe and when it's not."

"Good for you," Wyatt said.

"You didn't believe it was true, did ya?"

"That you know what you're talking about?"

"No, about the cannibals. You thought it was a story people told, like the boogeyman."

Wyatt shrugged. He really didn't want to speak to anyone, especially River whose lips never stopped.

"Eh, can't say that I blame ya. I didn't believe it either when we left Oregon. I was probably the same as you."

"I really doubt that."

"Oh yeah? I had a family, friends. We was trying to get somewhere safe, too. And people warned us,. Don't go south because there's maneaters down there. We didn't listen though. But we found out. The hard way. Like a fairy tale come true. Except whatever the opposite of a fairy tale is called."

"A nightmare," Pete said from across the fire. Then he yawned and his tired, bloodshot eyes drooped.

"No, well, yes," River said, ever specific. "That's not the word I wanted though. I meant like a story that's a warning. What do they call those?"

"An Urban legend?" Allie offered.

River shook his head. "No, not that neither."

Make it stop, Wyatt thought. I just need some quiet.

"A cautionary tale," Barbara said.

"That's it!" River clapped his hands three times. "That's it. The one-eyed lady got it."

Wyatt watched his mother, afraid her feelings might have been hurt, but she only shook her head and laid down to rest.

River cleared his throat and spit out a large wad of phlegm. "But the other story. The one about safety. The free land, or whatever people wanna call it. That's the real fairy tale. Ain't no such thing exists."

"How would you know?" Seth asked.

"Cause I been everywhere. Ain't no place safe. Just some places less dangerous than others. Lots of places are crazy, while others downright insane."

"That part I believe. You definitely seem like an expert on crazy," Seth said.

"Fine, don't believe me. What do I care? I'm just travelin' with ya. Helpin' ya find the border. Believe what you want."

River looked around, trying to find someone else to annoy for a while. He walked up to Pete and Wyatt watched Pete's face contort in disgust. That made him happy, for a moment.

As he surveyed their surroundings for anything that could signal danger, he realized there was nothing to see. It was mile after mile of flat, tan emptiness void of life, void of humanity. They were in a dead land.

Maybe cannibal country was a good description of where they

were. A place that chewed up and spat out everything that had once been alive.

WYATT VOLUNTEERED TO TAKE FIRST WATCH, MOSTLY BECAUSE he was still too wired from the previous night's events to even consider sleeping. He'd expected Trooper or his mother to join him, but was shocked, in a good way, when Allie raised her hand like a fourth-grader needing permission to speak. She asked if she could be the second on duty, ignoring a half-confused, half-pissed off stare from Pete. Wyatt saw no reason to turn her down.

River was first out. He scraped a small divot into the dirt and bedded down in it like an animal. Even Supper had better manners. The others didn't last long and soon it was Wyatt and Allie surrounded by a handful of sleeping, snoring companions.

"What made you want to take first watch," Wyatt asked.

"No particular reason." She hunched over and petted Supper who laid at their feet.

"Pete didn't look too happy."

She sighed. "He'll have to get over it. Besides, he's probably just worried he'll have to pair up with River."

That made Wyatt laugh, a little too hard. He glanced around to make sure he hadn't woken anyone, but they were all dead to the world.

"Pete can be an asshole, but he means well."

Wyatt shrugged. "I'll take your word for it."

Allie looked up from the dog, brushing away the dreadlocks that had fallen in her face. "You're thinking about something. Lost inside your own head. Have been all morning. I can see it in your eyes."

"What do you mean?"

"Something's wrong. And I mean, not just in the, we could be killed by cannibals any minute, wrong. It's something else."

Wyatt shrugged. He didn't realize he was so easy to read. "I guess, some days, I just struggle to find the point."

"Point of what?"

"Going on." He stared into the wasteland. "Back in Maine, in my home, I could sit in my bedroom and pretend that things were going to get better, eventually. That the sun would shine again and the people would return and things would go back to normal. Now I see how stupid I was."

He paused, not sure whether to go on but saying out loud what he'd been thinking for so long felt good. Felt cathartic. "Out here though, it's like every day something new and terrible comes along to show me that nothing's ever going to be good again. That I'm just putting in time. I should have never left home." His voice trailed off.

Wyatt could feel Allie's eyes on him but wouldn't meet them.

"About two years after it all went down, I was living in Virginia, the southwestern part of the state, with four friends I'd met along the way. I'd guess it was a lot like your set up in Maine. Peaceful. Isolated. Safe. Until it wasn't."

He risked a glance her way but now it was Allie who wouldn't look at him.

"One night a guy broke into our place. He said he was out scavenging and didn't know anyone was living there and that sounded believable enough. That's how we got by too, after all. We told him he could crash there for the night and have breakfast with us in the morning. Because, you know, we hadn't been shown how cruel people had become yet. We thought everyone was chill and harmonious like we were."

"I woke up to my friend Janey screaming. Not just screaming, it was that ear-piercing shriek that, as soon as you hear it, you know someone's dying. And she was. That bastard had gutted her with a bread knife, the kind with the scalloped edges. And he just stood over her and watched as she tried to push her guts back inside herself. And he was smiling."

She wiped wetness from her eyes but didn't break down. "He'd already killed the others. I don't know why he was saving me for last. If he even had a reason. Or maybe it was just the luck of the draw. He saw me watching him and I froze. He could've killed me. I was in too much shock to put up much of a fight. But he didn't. He just turned his back to me, walked to the door, and walked right on out of the house."

"I wanted to bury them, but it was winter and the ground was hard, so I ended up just leaving them there. I still feel bad about that."

"Shit," Wyatt said. Her story made him feel like an ass, like he had no reason for his own personal pity party.

"So I get it, Wyatt. Life's hard. Always has been, even before this mess. But you have to look forward, not back."

He thought that sounded like something out of a self-help book, or like something one of the motivational speakers that came into his school for assemblies would say, but didn't tell her that. She was just trying to be supportive, after all.

"I'm glad you left Maine," Allie said.

"Why?"

"If you never left home, you would have never met me. I'd still be stuck in that Godforsaken trading post, doing who knows what just to get by. But, because of you, we're here. You saved me, Wyatt."

He gave a wan smile. "I took you out of a shitty situation and put you into a shittier one. You're welcome."

She grabbed his chin and locked eyes with him. "I'm not joking around. I'd rather die out here being a decent person, than muddle through life where maybe I'm safe, but I can't look at my own reflection in the mirror because I hate myself so damned much. You understand?"

Wyatt nodded. Her hand drifted down the side of his face and he could feel the warmth it left in its wake.

The two of them spent the next few hours sitting side by side, chatting about the people they used to be, and taking turns petting Supper. Maybe things weren't so bad after all.

CHAPTER FORTY-ONE

In northern Texas, they came across a small town that would have fit in perfectly in New England. Aside from the store which once sold cowboy hats and saddles. The other businesses were a mix of specialty shops and antique stores which, to Wyatt's surprise, hadn't been vandalized and pillaged over the last half-decade.

But, the more he thought about it, the more he realized that fancy clothes and old furniture weren't of much use in the apocalypse.

"Oh my God." Allie stared through the plate-glass window of a vintage clothing store, eyes as wide as a kid in front of a candy shop.

Wyatt laughed, but Pete grabbed her hand and pulled her away.

"We don't have time for that shit," Pete said.

"Why not?" she asked.

Wyatt thought it a fair question. Dawn had just broken and it was almost time to hunker down for the day and get some rest.

"There's fucking cannibals somewhere out there and you want to look at old clothes? Sometimes I think you left your brain back at the trading post. If you ever had one."

Wyatt could tell by the look on Allie's face that she was on the verge of tears. Only her pride kept her from crying.

"This town is as good a place as any to sleep. Maybe better seeing as how it's out of the way enough to be in near pristine condition." Wyatt looked to Pete. "Besides, you don't get many opportunities to stand around and be bored while you watch your girlfriend shop these days. Think of it like nostalgia."

Allie looked over Pete's shoulder and smiled at Wyatt. For about the thousandth time on their journey, he wondered why she was with an asshole like Pete.

Pete dropped Allie's hand and waved to Wyatt. "She's all yours, kid. Go find a purse for her to carry your balls."

Wyatt ignored the putdown and strode past Pete. He extended his elbow and Allie took it as the two continued into the store.

The lock on the door was broken, but the hinges groaned in protest as Wyatt opened it. It had been closed for a long while. Supper followed them inside and Wyatt grinned as the dog passed under a sign that read, Service animals only. Pets not allowed!

"Look at all this." Allie glanced around the building in awe.

Wyatt was less impressed. There were tons of clothes, but it looked like the kind of stuff they wore on black-and-white TV show reruns. The kind of outfits that would have been tossed in the dumpster at Goodwill.

"I never knew there was a market for antique clothes," Wyatt said.

"Vintage."

"What?"

"You called them antiques. Clothes like these are vintage. There's a difference," Allie said as she fingered through the items on the racks.

"My mistake. Guess I missed out on the wild and crazy vintage clothes shopping part of my life."

Allie looked over at him with a raised eyebrow. "I imagine you missed out on a lot of things."

Wyatt shrugged. "No big deal."

"Maybe. But there's some big milestones around your age."

Wyatt felt his cheeks flush and turned away from her, both in the hope she didn't notice and also to try to change the subject. "Well then, teach me about vintage clothing. What am I missing?"

She grabbed his hand and pulled him close to her. He felt his heartbeat quicken and hoped his palms weren't sweating.

"Okay, look at this." Allie pulled a pink dress with a floral print off a rack.

"An old dress? What makes it special?"

Allison laughed. "No, not a dress. It's a housecoat."

Wyatt had no idea what she was talking about and she obviously saw it on his face.

"A woman would wear it around the house while she cleaned, made dinner, watched her soaps."

"Sounds a little sexist to me. I mean, they didn't have a special outfit for men to do that stuff did they?"

She smirked. "That's because men didn't help around the house then. Or now, for that matter."

He held his free hand over his heart, mocking offense. "Hey, I'll have you know I vacuumed the floor twice a week."

She clapped in slow, silent applause. "And I bet your mom put a gold star sticker on the chore chart for that too."

Wyatt knew she was only teasing him but he didn't want to be made to feel like a boy. Not around her.

"What would one of these vintage housecoats cost, anyway?"

Allie held up the price tag and turned it his way. His eyes grew wide.

"Eighty dollars? That's crazy. I'd do my housework in my pajamas."

"It's not cheap, but they don't make these anymore. They're like, a piece of history."

"So... like an antique. You really need to get your story straight."

For some reason, that joke hit home and Allie dissolved into the kind of uncontrollable laughter that physically hurts. Seeing her in such a predicament made Wyatt join in.

"Hope I'm not breaking up the moment here," Pete said from the entrance.

As Pete stepped inside Allie took a few steps away from Wyatt and their laughter slowed to a halt.

"I never knew ugly, old clothes were so funny. Unless it's something else." He stared down Wyatt. "You putting the move on my girl, kid?"

Wyatt took another sidestep away from her. "No, Pete. We were... We were just--"

Now Pete laughed, but it was a sharp, cold sound. "Don't waste a good lie on this. I'm only fucking with you." He gave Wyatt a playful, but hard, punch in the shoulder. "It's not like you're a threat. Right? Kid?"

Wyatt tried to meet his gaze but failed. "Yeah, well, it's probably time for breakfast."

"Time for breakfast?" Pete mocked him in a falsetto that sounded nothing like Wyatt's own voice. "Don't up and change your plans on my account. Go back to your fun. I'll chaperone, just to make sure you don't get in over your head."

"Pete, it was nothing. Stop."

"No, no. I mean it. You should probably take it easy on the kid though. I mean, how old are you again, Wyatt?"

"Eighteen." Wyatt didn't appreciate being talked down too, especially from a piece of shit like Pete.

"Wow, so you were like thirteen when it all went down? Still a babe. Bet you didn't even have hair on your pubes yet, let alone know how to use 'em."

Wyatt didn't respond. He only stood there, taking the lashes from Pete.

"I mean, and this is just between the three of us, you ever get your dick wet? You can be honest, we won't tell your momma."

"That's enough, Pete," Allie said, moving to him. She grabbed his arm and tried to pull him toward the entrance, but Pete planted his feet.

"Why the hurry? I'm just getting to know the boy." Pete looked back to Wyatt. "You must love having Allie around though. Bet she gives you some juicy material for the spank bank."

He mimed jerking off and that was enough for Wyatt. He pushed by Pete, who was smiling ear to ear, and left the store.

"Don't forget your mutt," Pete said. But he didn't have to. Supper was already on his way.

CHAPTER FORTY-TWO

WYATT BOOTED A ROCK AS HARD AS HE COULD. IT BOUNCED AND skidded along the street before colliding with a wooden post at the far end of town.

He hadn't noticed it upon their arrival and decided to investigate, taking advantage of whatever he could find to get his mind off of Pete's antagonism.

Something was perched atop the post and, when he came within five yards, he realized it was a skeleton. It was far from the first he'd seen and, by this point, the novelty had worn off. Only this one had been posed with its right arm pointing east.

"Well that's weird," he said to himself. Or so he thought.

"That is something, ain't it," River said.

Wyatt flinched and turned. The man was within touching distance. "Shit dude, where the hell did you come from?" He grabbed at his chest, trying to calm his frayed nerves.

River smiled wide. "My friends always say I'm light on my feet. Guess they're correct."

"Yeah, whatever." Wyatt looked up the street and saw his mother and Trooper pushing Seth lazily as they tried to find the best building in which to bed down for the day. Wyatt waved his arms like an air traffic controller until he got their attention. Then he motioned for them to come to him.

Unfortunately, Pete saw his gesticulations too and he and Allie headed his direction.

River leaned into the skeleton and sniffed it. Wyatt tried to remind himself that this odd man was occasionally helpful, or so he said, but he had his doubts. Then River tapped the skeleton's pelvis. "This was a lady. You can tell by the hips. Bigger for birthing."

Wyatt didn't ask why that mattered and remained silent until the others arrived.

"What's going on?" Trooper asked.

"This is a portent," River said. "Means things are going to get worse."

"Is that even possible?" Pete asked.

"It sure is. It sure is. This girl's telling us that there's danger ahead. More cannibals. You know what I mean?"

"Then where the fuck are we supposed to go?" Pete asked. "Allie was such a dumbass, making me come with you retards."

Up until now, he'd only been a whiny presence, a mosquito buzzing in their ears and voicing his dissatisfaction with being there. Now though, he had everyone's attention.

"Son," Trooper said. "If you don't like it, turn yourself around and start walking. No one asked you along."

"Yeah, now that you drug us two thousand miles into the middle of bumfuck nowhere. With man-eating cannibals thrown in for good measure." He stepped into Trooper's personal space. "Maybe no one else has the balls to say it but this plan of yours, marching down to South America, is stupid. There's no happily ever after down there. It's just more of the same shit only warmer."

River nodded his head in agreement. "He ain't wrong you know."

"You're not helping, River," Seth said.

"Never said I was," River said.

Wyatt could feel the tension boiling and as much as he could use a good fight to blow off steam, he knew it was the last thing the group needed.

"River," Wyatt said, his voice commanding. The man and everyone else looked to him. "Is there a way to get to the border that isn't as dangerous?"

"Me thinks so," River said.

"Wonderful. And which way is that?"

River studied the skeleton-like he was an archeologist reading hieroglyphics. He licked his finger, dragged it across the skeleton's pointing arm, then stuck that finger into his mouth and closed his eyes.

"For fucks sake," Seth said.

Wyatt regretted asking the man, the obviously crazy man, for assistance. For putting any semblance of trust in him.

River's eyes popped open. "That way," River said, pointing in the opposite direction of the skeleton.

"Oh, there's a surprise," Seth said.

"River knows his cannibals and River never lets his friends down."

"Aren't all your friends dead?" Seth asked.

River cocked his head. "Perhaps. That is a possibility."

"Fuck it." Pete spun on his heels and grabbed Allie's hand, pulling her back toward town. "We're getting some sleep. Wake us when it's our turn for watch."

"You know, I think I liked it better when he was just bitching about things," Seth said.

Wyatt agreed.

CHAPTER FORTY-THREE

"Do you think I made a mistake?" Barbara watched Trooper who was busying himself with cleaning his .44s.

He glanced her way. "I'm afraid you'll need to be a tad more specific."

"Leaving home. Heading south. Thinking I knew what the hell I was doing. Eating half a can of refried beans that expired eight years ago. Take your pick."

Trooper set the gun he'd been working on aside. "Well, yes to the last one. I told you to throw them out."

She worked up a half-smile, an accomplishment considering how defeated she felt. "You did. And you were right."

"As for the rest of it... Hell, Barb, it's still too early to tell."

She knew pressing the matter would solve nothing, but she wanted, needed, to talk and Trooper was her partner on watch which made him a captive audience. "What if we get all the way to the equator and find out it's just as bad? Will you tell me then that I was wrong?"

He considered it. "Ayuh. But, and this stays between you and me, I haven't felt this alive since I was on the force. This trip of yours, it might be a toll physically but sitting around the house day in day out, each one the same as the last, that wears a man down mentally. If given the choice between the two, I'd rather my body be tired than my mind."

"Do you really mean that or are you placating me?"

He smirked. "Little of both."

She supposed that was fair.

It was near dark and would soon be time to wake the boys. Pete and Allie had taken the previous shift, but rather than going back to sleep, they headed outside and bickered like an old married couple. That had been going on for almost two hours and showed no signs of slowing down.

Barbara watched them through the window. Allie sat on a porch swing, drifting lazily back and forth while Pete paced.

"Those two still at it?" Trooper asked.

"Yeah. It's getting tiresome."

"Stress brings out the worst in folks."

Barbara knew that was true, but also wondered how much good there was in either of them. Pete was more petulant than her teenage sons but twice their age. And Allie, she acted sweet as custard, but the more the woman was around Wyatt, the less Barbara trusted her.

Maybe it took another woman to see it, but Allie was playing Pete and Wyatt against each other. It might not even be intentional, but it was happening. And Barb wished, when they'd told them they could turn around and walk away, the couple would have done just that. Sadly, they seemed to be stuck with them and she could only hope things didn't go bad.

Barb watched Pete grab Allie's arm and the woman jerk it free. She shoved her finger in his face and blathered on about something. Barbara couldn't quite make out the words, but she knew the motions. She'd been married, after all.

In hers, no fists were thrown, but words were sometimes worse. In the end, they always made up, but she knew that was the exception to the rule. And she liked to believe she and her husband were better than Pete and Allie.

She turned her attention from the fighting couple to her sons sleeping on the dusty floor. Wyatt's arm was draped over Supper while Seth was sprawled on his back, mouth agape. She knew Wyatt was falling for the woman and that scared her almost as much as the cannibals.

Most boys - men - his age had experienced heartbreak repeatedly, but Wyatt's emotional growth had been stunted when the attacks happened. He might be eighteen in years but his heart was still that of a thirteen-year-old boy.

Please God, she thought, he's got enough shit to deal with. Don't pile on more.

Outside she heard a raised voice. "Fuck you then!" It was Pete and she watched him storm away from Allie, passing by the doorway to the building in which they'd made camp.

"I need some space," he said to Trooper who sat near the entrance as he stomped by. "I won't wander far."

Trooper nodded. "No hurry."

Barbara watched Allison wipe her face. After a moment she slipped off the swing and came into the building wearing a fake smile, but her red and swollen eyes still betrayed her.

"Can I help make breakfast?" She asked Barb.

"Of course."

Barbara rose from her seat and grabbed some supplies from their stash. She handed them to Allie without a word and began to rekindle the fire.

The woman cocked her head to the side. "Everything alright, Barbara?"

"I was gonna ask you the same thing."

Allie waved her hand, dismissive. "Don't worry about me and Pete. Everything's okay."

"I'm sure it will be. But I'm not worried about your lover's quarrel. I'm worried about Wyatt and where he fits into the mix."

Allie dropped her smile. "That's nothing. We're friends is all."

"Does Wyatt know that? Because he follows you around like a stray cat follows a fisherman and you lap up that attention. Especially when you and Pete are on the outs and you want to make him jealous."

"I didn't mean to--"

"You never mean to. But you do." Barb glanced at Wyatt to ensure he was still sleeping. He was. "He's my son. And it's my job to look out for him. You understand?"

Allie let out a soft laugh. "I get it. And don't worry. I'm not using him to make anyone anything. I like Wyatt. And he's your son, but he's also a man and I'm pretty sure he can make his own decisions."

Allie opened a can of peaches and poured them into a pan. After adding some cinnamon she tore open three sugar packets and dumped that into the mix, then set the pan over the fire. The aroma started Barbara's stomach rumbling.

She knew Allie was right about one thing. Wyatt was old enough to make his own decisions. But he didn't always make the best ones. And she had the scars to prove it.

CHAPTER FORTY-FOUR

ANOTHER WEEK OF NIGHT WALKS AND DAY RESTS SAW THEM make considerable progress and stay safe. A win-win as far as Wyatt was concerned.

After finishing a dinner which consisted of rehydrated beef stroganoff, part of a cache of C-rations they discovered inside an abandoned root cellar, Wyatt was eager to get on the road. However, some of the others were busy savoring one of their few meals which didn't come from a can.

Seth was less than halfway through his meal when he decided to waste more time teasing his brother. "Why such a hurry, Casanova?"

Wyatt couldn't think of a good comeback, and honestly, he wasn't sure it was much of an insult. It made him smile.

"No reason. Just like making good time."

Seth took a bite of food and chewed ever so slow. "Ever hear the saying, stop and smell the roses? You should try that sometime."

"I don't see any roses. Just your ugly face," Wyatt said. "Thank God I already ate or it would have cost me my appetite."

Seth rolled his eyes. "Probably just as well. If there were any roses, I wouldn't be able to smell them over your stanky ass, anyway."

Wyatt wondered if it was just another dig or if there was some truth to it. He tried to discreetly sniff his armpit and recoiled. He was a little ripe but didn't want to let on that Seth was right. "Where's Supper?"

Seth motioned outside the building in which they'd spent the night. "Wandered outside a few minutes ago. I figured he needed to unload some timber."

Wyatt stared at him, baffled.

"Sink the Bismark? Build a log cabin?"

Still nothing.

"How are you so damn clueless, brother? The dog had to go shit. I decided to give him some privacy. Besides, your girl's out there somewhere. Figured she'd watch him."

Wyatt hadn't realized Allie was gone and surveyed the quarters. He saw Pete sucking scraps out from under his fingernails and moved to him. "You seen Allie?"

Pete removed his finger from his mouth. It came out with a pop. "Really? You're gonna ask me that?"

During the night prior the couple had battled through their worst fight yet and, as far as Wyatt knew, Pete and Allie hadn't spoken since it fizzled out. She'd spent the rest of the night walking at Wyatt's side and then took watch with him earlier in the day. Wyatt was thrilled but tried not to let it show. Pete, of course, wasn't enthused.

"I just thought that maybe--"

Pete cut him off. "She ain't mine to babysit anymore, kid. So go ahead, flirt with her. Fuck her. I don't give a shit. Just be aware, that slut's going to take you for all she can get and spit you out like used gum when she gets bored." Pete returned his fingers to his mouth.

"You're a real asshole," Wyatt said.

"I am aware."

Wyatt stood there a moment, but he wasn't sure what he was supposed to do next. He'd expected Pete to throw an insult back and, when that didn't happen, Wyatt was unsure how to respond.

He heard Supper bark outside and took that as his opportunity to exit the awkward encounter.

When he stepped into the diminishing light, he saw Supper's back end disappear into a thicket of dead Texas ash trees that reached skyward like skeletal fingers. He followed.

He pushed through the trees occasionally spotting the dog which drifted in and out of sight before diving through a crop of seven-foot-tall pampas grass.

"Darn dog," Wyatt said as he pushed through the dry grass which slithered along his arms and face. He didn't like going in blind, and he couldn't see four inches in front of his face until he came out on the other side.

What he found there took his breath away.

A beautiful, unsullied lake stretched out ahead of him. The waters weren't blue, but they were clean and clear and looked downright inviting.

Supper had beaten him to the punch. The dog dove and jumped, trying to chomp mouthfuls of water with little success.

Wyatt slipped off his shoes and ran toward the edge of the lake. He kicked a spray of water at the dog which nearly did a somersault in the air trying to catch it. The sight of the gleeful, three-legged mutt got him laughing. Between that and the cool, but delicate touch of the water, he couldn't remember when he'd last felt so good.

He remembered Seth's comment about stinking and decided this was the perfect opportunity to remedy that. It took him under half a minute to strip off the entirety of his wardrobe and even less to plunge headfirst into the lake.

It was cold but incredible. When he bobbed to the surface, he wiped the water from his face, flicked his hair back, and felt cleaner already. Short a washcloth, or even a bar of soap, he used brute force to scrub himself and felt almost guilty about the weeks - maybe months - worth of dirt he was depositing into the lake.

Supper bounced from the water and ran to the shore where he shook himself somewhat dry, then spun around and returned to the wetness. Wyatt thought he looked cleaner too. Less chocolate and more vanilla.

Wyatt dunked himself again giving his legs a good once over before popping back up. Then he heard another, further away splash.

He froze and looked to Supper, making sure he hadn't imagined it. The dog stared in the direction of the noise. It wasn't his imagination.

The sound had come from around a bend in the lake and another patch of pampas grass blocked his view. He waded further into the water and began circling toward it, careful not to make any noise himself, to not alert the splasher to his presence.

Once he was beyond the grass he saw her and the breath was knocked out of him for the second time in just a few minutes.

Allie faced away from him, her dreads soaking wet and hanging halfway down her back. She was only in the water up to her thighs which gave a good - too good - view of her backside. He tried not to stare, aware that sneaking a peek was wrong, but it was a struggle.

Just then Supper bounced through the water, carefree and obnoxiously loud.

Allie spun his way. "Who's there?"

He'd seen her barely there breasts during the encounter behind the bar, but now he saw all of her. His stomach tightened and he felt like his head was floating off his shoulders. He turned away from her, but it was too late.

"Wyatt?"

Oh shit, he thought. He was going to look like a perv. A typical, horny guy who'd followed her there and spied on her. The excitement he'd felt a moment earlier turned to dread.

"How long have you been there?" She asked.

"Not long, but maybe long enough. I'm sorry."

"You shouldn't be. I don't own the lake."

He risked a quick glance back. Allie hadn't moved, hadn't covered herself. He looked away again.

"I'm not an eclipse, Wyatt," she said. "You won't go blind looking at me."

"I didn't know anyone was here. I followed Supper and--"

"Turn around," Allie said.

He did.

Allie stood before him, wearing nothing but the most beautiful smile he'd ever seen. "Come closer." Her voice was soft, maybe even seductive. Or maybe that was his imagination.

He went to her, slow and cautious, like a soldier maneuvering through a field of landmines.

She reached out to him and grabbed her hand, then pulled it to her. She dragged his fingers across her bare waist, then up, closer to her breasts. He looked from them to her face. Her lips were parted, inviting. He leaned into her and took her chin with his free hand. But he hesitated. Is this the right thing to do, he wondered. Is she really over Pete?

But this was what he'd wanted for so long. What he'd dreamed about. How many times in his life was he going to waste the perfect opportunity?

"What are you waiting for?" she asked.

That was when the screaming started.

CHAPTER FORTY-FIVE

Wyatt scrambled out of the water, onto the lakeshore. He grabbed his pants and pulled them on. He was still soaking wet, so that simple act proved more of a challenge than he was used to, but he managed. Then he shoved his feet into his shoes and ran.

The screaming was his mother. It sounded just like that night back in their home. When he failed her. When he wasn't there when she needed him. And here he was, repeating that monumental fuck up.

"Wyatt!" Allie called after him.

He could hear her chasing footsteps but didn't stop. Supper was at his side, galloping on his three legs and keeping pace with Wyatt who was running as fast as his feet could carry him.

Soon he came to the road that led back to the house. Another twenty yards and he was close enough to see, in broad strokes, what was going down.

He froze.

Allie collided with him and they almost fell, but he caught her and regained his balance. She opened her mouth and he knew she was going to ask why he stopped. To prevent her question, he turned her toward the building.

The cannibals, the same group from that earlier night, had arrived. Two of them chased Barbara who pushed Seth in his wheelchair in the opposite direction. But they were faster and closed the gap in seconds.

His mother spun around and Wyatt saw her hand raised. He knew she was holding the .38 and she put it to use. A slug punched a hole in the belly of the cannibal nearest her and he fell into the dirt, holding the bleeding gut shot.

The other cannibal didn't miss a step, kept charging at her. He clutched a machete that was half as long as his body and reared back with it, ready to swing.

Before he could, the left side of his head exploded out in a spray of gore. As the contents rained to the ground Wyatt had a vision of the most disgusting pinata of all time.

Wyatt looked to see who had shot and found Trooper holding his Desert Eagle. Another cannibal was racing at him from the rear, a man with a pair of garden shears.

"Behind you, Trooper!" Wyatt screamed.

Trooper spun around and took aim, plugging the man in the chest. The man dropped to his knees, then face-planted in the soil as he died.

Wyatt turned to Allie. "Stay here and hold on to Supper."

He didn't wait for her response.

As Wyatt ran he saw Red, the big cannibal with the axe, step out of the house where they'd spent the day. He rushed to the second man Trooper had shot.

"Zeke?" Red grabbed a fistful of the man's hair and pulled his face off the ground. When he realized the man was dead his eyes blazed. He eased him back to the dirt and turned to Trooper, axe in hand.

Trooper was too busy fighting off another attacker to see Red's approach. The old man stuck the barrel of his .44s into the man's gut and pulled the trigger, sending a geyser of blood out his back. Trooper shoved him aside and looked for his next opponent.

Wyatt leveled his pistol at Red, not an easy task when running full bore. He aimed for center mass and squeezed the trigger.

The bullet ripped through Red's flank and the big man dropped his axe. His hand went to the wound, but remained upright through it all.

Red turned to face his shooter and witnessed Wyatt's mad dash. Rather than stay put and accept another bullet, he lumbered back into the house, leaving a thin trail of blood behind.

With the big man out of the way, at least temporarily, Wyatt's attention went to his mother and Seth. Two cannibals battled with them. One held a metal pipe and the other a broken baseball bat.

Seth landed a sucker punch to the dick of the man with the bat who fell to his knees in response. Seth grabbed the man's wild hair and yanked his head back and forth, probably giving him whiplash from hell.

As Barb tried to hold off the woman with the pipe, River leaped into the fray and tackled the cannibal to the ground. "Don't you hurt River's woman," he yelled.

The two rolled in the dirt, scratching and clawing at each other like two feral animals, but the woman slipped free and regained her weapon. She popped River in the jaw, smashing in a few of his black teeth, then spun around and swung at Barb.

Wyatt wanted to yell out, but there was no time. The pipe bashed his mother in the temple and she fell in a motionless heap.

"You bitch!" Wyatt screamed as he aimed and shot. The woman who'd struck his mother flew through the air like a figure skater doing a toe loop before hitting the dirt.

"Wyatt, get your brother out of here!" Trooper shouted.

When he looked toward Trooper, Wyatt saw another half dozen cannibals coming in their direction. He wasn't about to tuck tail and run no matter what Trooper told him to do.

Wyatt arrived at his mother's side. Seth was in the midst of

choking the life out of the cannibal who'd once possessed the broken
bat. River was on his knees, holding his hands to his bleeding mouth.

Wyatt pressed the barrel of the pistol at the cannibal Seth had by
the throat and shot. Seth looked to him, wide-eyed.

"Shit, brother, I had that one taken care of. Seems like a waste of
a bullet."

Wyatt didn't respond. He grabbed River by his shirt and dragged
him to his feet. "Take my brother and do what you do best. Run." He
shoved the filthy, bleeding man toward the wheelchair and watched
him grab the handles.

"Fair enough, friend," River said. He pushed the chair as he ran.

He knelt beside his mother and rolled her onto her side. She was
out, but alive and, all things considered, maybe that was for the best.
He turned her face back to the dirt so that a casual observer would
think she was dead and stood. Ready to finish this fight.

"Fucking savage!" Pete's voice was filled with agony. Wyatt
turned toward the noise and discovered that a female cannibal had
just stabbed him in the side. She twisted the knife and Pete yelped, a
miserable sound if Wyatt had ever heard one. The guy might be an
asshole, but Wyatt didn't want him dead.

"Pete!" Allie screamed.

The sound of her voice shocked Wyatt. He'd told her to stay
away, to stay safe, but clearly, she hadn't listened. What good did she
expect to do with no weapon? And where was his dog?

Before the knife-wielding cannibal could finish off Pete, Trooper
dropped her with a gunshot to the hip.

Trooper grabbed Pete and shoved him toward Allie and Wyatt.
"Get everyone out of here," Trooper yelled then turned back to the
wounded cannibal.

He stomped on her wrist, the blow knocking the knife from her
hand. He grabbed it, then with his other hand grabbed a fistful of her
matted hair. She struggled, but he held firm. "You bastards want to
act like monsters? I can play that game too!"

When he put the knife to her throat, the woman began to scream. No words at first, only sounds. Then he started cutting.

"Please!" She yelled. "Please don't!"

Trooper glanced down at her. "You made your bed. Time to lay in it."

He ripped the blade across her neck and hot blood jutted from the wound. He kept cutting, sawing back and forth. Her arms flailed but Trooper held tight and soon she'd bled out.

Shortly after that, Trooper finished cutting. Her body fell to the ground. Her head remained in his hand.

Wyatt thought his old friend had gone mad as he raised the severed head into the air.

"You want to fight? Bring it!" Trooper shouted. He hurled the head across the lawn and it rolled until it collided with the front porch.

About that time, Red emerged from the house. His face was almost as crimson as his hair and Wyatt saw that he'd tied one of their old blankets around the wound in his side. The big man pointed a meaty finger at Trooper.

"Bring me that son of a bitch!" Red's voice boomed like thunder across the prairie. "I want to eat his heart!"

Trooper ran and the cannibals chased.

Red stayed behind and Wyatt watched him go to the headless woman and lift her body off the ground. She looked like a rag doll in his arms.

Part of him believed Trooper could finish them all off on his own, but he wasn't taking any chances. He grabbed his mother's unconscious body and dragged her to Pete and Allie.

"Hide her and hide yourselves." He handed Pete his shirt, which he'd never bothered to put on but had tucked into the waistband of his jeans.

"What's this for?" Pete asked.

"Wrap it around yourself. And try not to die."

He handed Allie his pistol. "Use this if you need to, but make it count." Wyatt turned away from them, but Allie grabbed his wrist.

"Where are you going?"

"To Trooper."

Before she could protest, Wyatt charged toward trouble.

CHAPTER FORTY-SIX

Trooper ran toward the barn he'd seen the night before. It wasn't far, a few hundred yards, but he didn't plan to escape them in a footrace. For one, they were younger and faster than he was. For another, he didn't want to escape them. He only wanted to distract them and draw them away.

He could hear their angry chatter in the near distance and ran faster, pushing his knee to the limit. He felt a pop, but ignored the subsequent pain. He saw the barn ahead, closer now, a football field away and slightly to the east. His knee popped again and that time it was audible, like his body was shouting at him that his running days were soon to be over, probably forever.

He pushed himself to keep going, to not ignore the pain, but to embrace it. To use it as his motivation. As a big fuck you to his past, to the cannibals and to whatever power above - or below - was trying to stop him before he was finished.

A cattle guard and metal fence were ahead. The barn less than twenty yards behind it. When he hopped the fence he landed hard, creating nauseating shock waves of pain that sent him to his knees.

The cannibals were closing in. He could see their ugly, wild faces grinning, thinking they had him. He wouldn't let that happen. He stood up and took his first step, but his knee gave out again.

"Cocksucker," he muttered, trying to pick himself up.

He had to move, but his body was giving out on him. He looked at the cannibals as they came running toward him. The barn was so close. He tried to count how many shots he'd fired and cursed himself for only having the one gun on him. In the haste, he couldn't recall how many bullets he had left, so he dropped the magazine and counted. Three bullets remained.

He looked back to the cannibals who were nearing the gate. His eyes were tired, but he knew there were more than three. Maybe this hadn't been such a grand plan after all.

He shoved the magazine back into the pistol and chambered a round. Then he aimed. But before he could fire, hands grabbed him from behind and dragged him backwards.

"Don't shoot, Trooper."

He looked over his shoulder and realized it was Wyatt.

CHAPTER FORTY-SEVEN

"What the hell are you doing here?" The old man raged at him as they entered the barn. Flecks of spittle flew from his mouth and rained on Wyatt's face.

"That's okay. You don't have to thank me."

"Thank you?" Trooper said. "Damn it, Wyatt, I was drawing 'em away from you. You're supposed to be back there keeping everyone else safe."

"Things are handled there." Wyatt looked out the barn doors. The cannibals hadn't just slowed down, they'd stopped completely. He wondered if there was some chance they hadn't seen the men enter the building.

He took the moment to pull Trooper further inside, depositing him atop a stack of hay bales. Trooper grimaced as he sat, clutching his ruined knee.

"How bad is it?" Wyatt asked.

Trooper met his gaze. "Pretty damned bad."

"And all this time I thought you were indestructible."

"I am. You tell anyone about this and you don't have to worry about the maneaters. I'll kill you myself," Trooper said.

Wyatt smiled. The old man hadn't lost his ego. That made him even more of a badass in Wyatt's eyes. "God, I love you, Troop."

Trooper shook his head. "You're a good kid, but you've got shit taste in people." He peered through the gaps in the wood siding, staring into the field beyond.

"They're coming," Trooper said. "Split off in a few smaller groups. That gives us a chance."

Wyatt didn't like the doubt in Trooper's voice. They needed more than a chance. They needed to win and that's exactly what he planned to do. "How many shots do you have?"

Trooper's eyes told Wyatt everything he needed to know. "Three."

Shit, that was bad.

"You?" Trooper asked.

Wyatt shook his head. "I gave my gun to Allie, to protect mom and Seth."

He saw defeat on the man's face and looked away. This wasn't the Trooper he was used to, the one who thought he could take on the world. This man looked old and hurt and... scared.

No, Wyatt told himself, that was his own doubts clouding his vision. Nothing scared Trooper, especially a bunch of inbred cannibals.

"There's no way he can be far." A man's shadow spilled through the open doors and onto the straw and dirt-covered floor of the barn.

Wyatt tensed, ready to move, but Trooper held his hand steady and shook his head once.

"Get in there and find out!" The voice was familiar, baritone and raw. Wyatt knew it belonged to Red.

Trooper set his pistol on the hay bale and pushed himself into a standing position. He wobbled and Wyatt thought he was going to fall, but he steadied himself and pulled out his hunting knife. You cover me, he mouthed.

As Trooper pressed himself against the barn wall, the cannibal entered. The man was short with a patchy beard and he held a long piece of rebar that had one end sharpened to a point.

The cannibal took one more step, his eyes scanning the sprawling barn. And just as he turned in the direction of Trooper--

Trooper brought his knife up, straight into the soft flesh under the man's jaw. The blade plunged through his mouth and, Wyatt imagined, into his brain. His eyes grew impossibly wide, then fell shut. His body went limp and Trooper managed to hold him upright for a moment before easing the body soundlessly to the floor. Then he ripped his knife free and wiped it clean on his jeans.

Just as Wyatt began to relax, another cannibal, this one a woman with a wild mane of blonde hair, burst through the doors. She wasn't cautious or careful like her friend. She entered with reckless abandon and the suddenness seemed to take Trooper by surprise.

She saw her dead compatriot on the ground, then found Trooper beside the body. She vaulted herself at him, swinging a small hatchet. Trooper jumped backward, escaping her blow but his knee gave way and he fell hard. In an instant, she was atop him.

Wyatt charged forward, slamming the woman into the wall hard enough to knock the breath out of both of them.

Wyatt saw Trooper's gun waiting at the ready, but he knew he couldn't shoot as the sound would draw the lot of them inside. The element of surprise was their only hope. He had to kill the woman but do it quietly.

He thrust his hands into her hair, balling his fists and holding on tight. The woman bucked like a wild bronco and it took everything he had to hang on.

He steered her toward a wooden support beam that must have been ten inches wide and slammed her head into it. She hissed in pain, arms flailing, not about to give up. He hit her again and he heard a muffled sound of something breaking. Still she struggled to break free.

Then, he saw the nail holding a horseshoe fast to the beam. A good three inches of steel extended from the wood and Wyatt thought that was enough.

He lined her head up with the nail and smashed her skull into it. Her body twitched and spasmed and then went limp.

The woman hung there like a discarded Halloween decoration. Wyatt stumbled backward, sick at what he'd just done, but relieved that bout was over.

"That was good, but we need to move," Trooper said.

Now that his heartbeat was slowing down Wyatt could hear the others, their footsteps, their voices. They were at both the main door and the side door. The cannibals had them surrounded.

"Where are we supposed to go?" Wyatt asked.

Trooper grabbed his pistol and pointed to a rope that hung from a crossbeam in the deep recesses of the barn. "Up."

Wyatt followed the rope and found that it lead to a loft twenty feet off the ground. Light dribbled through a dirty window and Wyatt realized that was their escape hatch. They went to it.

"Climb, damn it," Trooper ordered and Wyatt obeyed.

His forearms burned, but he used his thighs and feet to help push himself up. Damn, it was so much harder than climbing the rope in gym class had been, but he was doing it.

Just as he flopped into the loft he realized the footsteps had transitioned from outside the barn to inside.

Wyatt stared down at Trooper. "Come on, Troop!"

Trooper hadn't been watching him. He'd been looking around the barn. Trying to source the footsteps that sounded more like a stampede of animals than people. And they were so close.

"You're gonna have to haul me up." Trooper grabbed his end of the rope. "Untie it from the beam and tie it around your waist."

Wyatt's fingers worked against the bulky knot, undoing it in short order. He grabbed it, looped it around himself, and began to lash it together when--

The rope burned through his hands and disappeared. He stared at his empty palms for a moment, then down to the floor to see what had gone wrong.

Trooper bundled the rope and tossed it behind a pile of moldy feed bags.

"Trooper, what the--"

"There's no time. They would have got us both. This way is better."

"No! You need--"

"Be quiet now and be a man about this."

Wyatt's eyes stung like he'd just caught a face full of saltwater. "But we can't... I can't..."

"Ayuh. You can and you will." Trooper swallowed hard. "You're my best friend, you know that, Wyatt?"

Wyatt thought Trooper might have been crying too, but his bleary vision made it impossible to know for certain.

"Now, keep quiet up there. I won't be going down without a fight, but don't feel obligated to watch." He turned away from him, then shouted. "You keep running, Wyatt! I'll hold them off!"

Trooper hobbled out of sight underneath him, toward the front of the barn. Wyatt saw five cannibals there. Four more came in from the side. All had weapons.

Trooper raised his pistol. He shot three times. He killed three cannibals. Then, he tossed his gun aside and drew his knife.

Red stepped into view. "The boy run off on you, old-timer?"

Trooper shrugged his shoulders. "Can't blame him. I couldn't keep up."

Red nodded. "That's okay. I'll get him, eventually. I'm a patient man."

Trooper took a staggering step toward the de facto leader. "I've taken down bigger men than you. Tell me what makes you so special. You think you're some kind of badasses? You think you're ruthless?"

"No, I don't." Red said. "I think we're hungry."

Two men sprinted at Trooper, but he was ready. He swung at the first, cutting his throat in a spray of blood. The second grabbed

Trooper's arm and yanked it backward, at an angle that hurt just to see. The knife fell from his hand, useless now.

The mob rushed him. All except Red.

Trooper was a hero. But even heroes fall. He threw punch after punch. Then took punch after punch. Then he collapsed to his knees, battered and swollen and bleeding.

"That all you got, you shit heads? One old bastard against the lot of you and that's the best you can do?" Trooper began to climb to his feet, tired, his chest heaving.

"You're one tough son of a bitch, old man," Red said.

"Tell me something I don't know." Trooper spit out a mouthful of blood.

Red swung his ax. It landed in Trooper's neck, above the collar bone. Wyatt choked back a scream. The tears ran down his face, just like the blood continued to run from his friend.

Red jerked the blade free and swung one more time. That separated Trooper's head from his body. The big man stepped to him and picked up Trooper's severed skull with one of his oversized mitts. He passed it off to a woman who accepted it and dropped it into a sack.

"Gut him and bring the meat. The rest of you look for the boy." There was no emotion in his voice. It was just another meal to him.

Wyatt watched them rip off Trooper's shirt, watched them slice open his belly and his steaming intestines spill onto the floor. Then, they each grabbed a limp and carried him away.

No one found him. None of them even took a second look around the barn. Trooper had known exactly what he was doing. He was always right.

CHAPTER FORTY-EIGHT

WYATT WAITED IN THE BARN UNTIL IT WAS BEYOND DARK. HE wanted to ensure the cannibals were gone, but more than that, he needed to cry himself out, alone. He couldn't go back to the others weeping and weak.

He needed to be their strength now, and that meant trying to convince himself that he could step into Trooper's shoes. That he was capable of being their leader. He wasn't quite there, but the tears had ceased and it was time to move on.

Before he could do that he needed to descend from the loft. With no rope to shimmy down, he was left with one option. He stared out the window, to the pile of moldy hay below. The distance wasn't terrible, but he kept wondering if anything might be hidden under the hay. Ancient, rusty farming tools. Something sharp. He had no way of knowing for sure, but there was no other option.

The window was painted shut and it took three hard kicks to break it free. With that done, he slipped through the opening and perched on the window frame. One deep breath and he jumped.

"WE CAN'T SIT AROUND WITH OUR DICKS UP OUR ASS," PETE said. "Those fuckers know we're in here. I'm not trying to be an asshole, I'm just being realistic."

Some of the fear Wyatt had felt on the return trip to the farmhouse dissipated. All the way there he'd worried that the cannibals had returned to the house, had taken - or killed - everyone.

But they were alive. And he breathed a little easier.

"We're not going anywhere," Barbara said. "Not until everyone is back." She stressed the everyone and Wyatt could hear the worry in her voice. He didn't want to break this news, but he also knew to delay it would do no good.

He rapped on the door. "It's Wyatt Let me in."

There came the sound of chairs sliding and footsteps inside. Wyatt heard furniture being moved away from the door and then it opened. As soon as Barb saw him tears burst from her eyes. He would have cried too, he wanted to cry, but his swollen, pained eyes were empty.

"My God, Wyatt. I'm so happy you're back."

She embraced him with such force that he lost his breath. "I thought I lost you. I don't know what I'd--"

"You didn't." He examined her, trying to see how much new damage she'd sustained. He saw the remnants of blood in her hair and a swollen welt near her temple.. "Are you okay?"

She wiped her eyes and nodded. "Allie and Pete brought me in here. I was out for about an hour."

"More like two," Allie said. She'd been standing to the side and Wyatt barely noticed her presence. "I cleaned her up as much as possible."

"Thank you," Wyatt said.

She nodded.

"Where's the old man?" Pete asked, ruining the moment.

This was what Wyatt had been dreading. Throughout the walk back to the farmhouse he'd rehearsed and debated what he'd say but still came up empty. He paused now, trying to find the words, but his hesitation said it all.

"He's dead, isn't he?" Barbara grabbed his forearm and her brief moment of composure vanished. Her happy, relieved tears were replaced with grief. "Oh fuck. Oh fuck! What happened? How?"

Wyatt saw no sense in sharing the gory details. Maybe in time, but he doubted there'd ever be a reason to share what he'd witnessed. No one needed to live with that vision of Trooper except him.

"We were outnumbered and trapped. He blew out his knee and couldn't run anymore." Wyatt forced himself to look each of them in the eyes. "He died saving me."

Barbara stumbled to a hickory rocking chair and collapsed into it. Her body quaked with sobs.

Allie sidled up to him and took his hands in her own. "I'm so sorry, Wyatt."

He wanted to embrace her, to take comfort in her, but this wasn't the time. He nodded.

To his extreme surprise, even Pete came to him and gave him an awkward tap on the shoulder. "Sorry, kid."

Wyatt appreciated their condolences, but didn't feel worthy and their kindness was almost more than he could handle. He had to change the course of the conversation and looked around the room. "Where's Seth?" He asked. "I need to tell him."

He saw Allie's eyes grow wide and began to panic.

"What? Where's my brother?"

Allie reached for him, but he pulled away.

"Stop it. Tell me what's going on." He couldn't lose Seth and Trooper in the same day. Within the same few hours. He couldn't survive that.

"Seth's not here," Allie said. "We haven't seen him since the attack. Him or River."

IT WAS POINTLESS TO SEARCH IN THE DARK, BUT THE NIGHT WAS the longest of Wyatt's life. Between reliving Trooper's death and wondering if his brother had met the same fate, he didn't get a moment of rest, or peace.

He'd never been so anxious for dawn, such that it was.

They searched as a group, not risking anyone breaking off alone. Wyatt had given Supper a good sniff of one of Seth's ripest shirts, but the dog was no search and rescue hound and after three hours they'd found no sign of Seth or River.

Next on the list was the lake. The place where, less than 24 hours earlier, Wyatt had experienced the high point of his life. There, in the water with Allie he felt like he was on the precipice of his greatest dreams coming true. Now his life was in tatters.

They'd made it three quarters around the lake when Wyatt spotted a hedge of pampas grass quivering. The day was windless and there was no reason for the grass to move unless something - or hopefully someone - was within it.

He held his breath as he drew his pistol with one hand and pushed aside the tawny foliage with the other. Please let this be Seth, he thought. Didn't God owe him that much?

As the blades of grass separated he saw not Seth, but River. The man had scooped a shallow trench in the dirt and huddled in it. His entire body shook and his pants were wet around the groin where he'd pissed or shit himself - or both from the smell of it.

"Don't hurt me. River's harmless. He promises." He held his hands in front of his face and kept his eyes pinched shut.

Wyatt grabbed his arm, rougher than he'd intended, and jerked it sideways. "Get up, it's us."

River opened one eye and looked at them. "Are they gone?"

Wyatt dragged him to his feet. "For now. Where's my brother?"

The man squinted in the dim light, his face squinched like it was collapsing inward. "Th-- Th-- They got him, my friend."

Wyatt felt like puking. "What do you mean they got him?"

"The cannibals. They found us just after dark. Five or six of em."

Wyatt grabbed him by the shirt, pulling him close and not even caring about the man's stench. He was on the verge of losing his mind. "What do you mean they found you? I sent you off together, but you're here and Seth isn't so what the fuck is going on?"

"I-- I-- I had to get away, to get safe. River don't fight. River runs, that's what my friends say."

"You don't have any friends, you chickenshit bastard! They're all dead because you left them just like you left my brother!"

He shook the man side to side, sending River's head snapping to and fro. He sobbed and vaguely green snot ran from his nose.

He felt a hand on his arm. It was his mother. "Wyatt, don't. You're making it worse."

Wyatt didn't care. He could snap the coward's scrawny neck for all it mattered. Or he could just shoot him.

He remembered that he was holding the pistol and he pressed the barrel to River's temple hard enough for the gun to sink a quarter-inch into his flesh. He might not have been able to save Trooper or his brother, but he could still get some form of vengeance.

"P-- Please," River pleaded. "I tried pushing him, but that chair don't go through the dirt too good. River did everything he could. Even your brother, he told me to run. So while they were carrying him away I did."

He was less than a second from pulling the trigger when River's words sunk in. "They took him alive?

River nodded several times. "Carried him away in his chair like he was one of those Egyptian queens."

Wyatt removed his finger from the trigger and returned the pistol to its holster. He released River and the man fell backward, looking fearful and grateful at the same time.

As he turned to the others he worked out the plan in his head. It was half-assed but better than nothing. "Go back to the house. All of you. Barricade yourselves inside and load all the guns. If we're not back in two days head south."

"Wyatt what are you--"

Wyatt cut his mother off. "Do it."

She didn't look pleased, but she nodded. Wyatt avoided Allie's pleading gaze and instead focused on River. The squirrelly man quickly bobbed his head in agreement. "I'll go with them. We'll stay inside like you said. Forty-eight hours. River promises."

"River isn't going with them," Wyatt said.

"Why not?"

"Because you're taking me to the cannibal's camp."

CHAPTER FORTY-NINE

Wyatt took his pistol and the .38 his mother typically carried. He also had his knife, but hoped he wouldn't have to use that. Up close battling against these savages was a death sentence, as Trooper had found out the hard way.

He and River had been walking nonstop all day and throughout the night. Part of Wyatt, a big part, understood that River might be full of shit. That he had no way to find his way back to the cannibal's camp. That they might be wandering across these bland, featureless plains for eternity. But if there was one chance in a thousand that he could find his brother, he was going to take it.

A few hours later pinpricks of orange appeared against the black landscape. River pointed as if only he could see and Wyatt had succumbed to hysterical blindness.

"There!" He said. "That's their camp. Right there. River did his job like he promised. Now can he go back?"

Wyatt knew that River was scared. The man had been suffering from full-body tremors for the last several miles. As much as he was annoyed with the man for letting Seth be taken, he had no right to force him to continue.

"Do you have any idea where they might be keeping Seth?"

River nodded. "Yeah, they keep the food - I mean, the people - in cages outside the camp. They say it's so we don't ruin their fun with all our screamin' and beggin', but I think it's so we don't get in their heads." River tapped his own head. "I think they know what they're doing ain't right. And they kept us separate, so we didn't spoil their meal."

Wyatt could see the terror on the man's face. As much as River annoyed him, he couldn't even begin to imagine what the man had endured. And nobody deserved to go through that. He extended his palm. "Thank you, River."

River looked at it then took it in a clumsy handshake. "I hope you make it out. You and your brother."

Wyatt turned back to the fires in the distance. They were brazen, almost cocky. Daring someone to come and find them. And he was ready to do just that.

CHAPTER FIFTY

As SETH CAME TO HE WATCHED RED SPIN THE AXE END FOR end, like a cheerleader twirling a baton during the halftime show. The blade was bloody, dripping crimson. He sat it at the gate to the cage, then flipped open a lock, pulled the door, and joined him inside. That's when Seth remembered what happened and the earlier events crashed into him like a freight train.

He was still bound to the table which wasn't really a table at all. It was a pile of logs arranged into a type of altar. Or, as Seth thought of it, a butcher's block.

Thick belts constrained his arms and head. They hadn't bothered with securing his legs, and he wasn't sure if he should be insulted or grateful. Since he wasn't going anywhere, he supposed it didn't really matter.

What did matter was his agony. His entire body throbbed in pain which ricocheted from one spot to another, like a pinball bouncing off bumpers and shields. His lips betrayed him and allowed a moan to slip free.

Red had been rummaging around in the corner of the cage and

glanced back at him. "Sorry if you're hurting. We're fresh out of ibuprofen."

Seth remembered being taken. Remembered his chair getting stuck in the mud near a lake and River being unable to break him free. Remembered the thundering stampede as the cannibals rushed him and he told River to run.

"My family," Seth said. "Did you get them too?"

Red came to him, having traded in the axe for a well-used chopping knife. "Most of them got away. Left you behind. I can see why."

"What do you mean 'most of them'?"

Red gave what passed for a smile and licked his fingers clean of the blood. "Americans have a stigma against raw beef, but eating it is perfectly normal in many countries."

He reached into a bowl and came out with a chunk about an inch around. "In Korea is called Yukhoe. In Japan Tataki. In France it's Tartare. I bet you can't guess what it's called in Belgium. Try for me."

Seth wanted to remain stoic and silent, but that had never been his bag. "Fucking sick is what I call it."

"Oh, now, don't be so judgemental. I bet the first time someone pulled an overgrown insect with massive claws out of the ocean most people wouldn't have dared eat it. But today everyone loves lobster."

He popped the piece of meat into his mouth. "Toast Cannibal."

Seth stared at him, confused.

"In Belgium, they call it Toast Cannibal. Now, I personally think that's a little too on the nose, but it's damned delicious. They serve it on toast, of course, with shallots and mayonnaise and gherkins and just the right amount of Worcestershire sauce." He made hungry, savory sounds and rubbed his belly.

"What I wouldn't give for some more ingredients though. The meat itself, without anything to dress it up, it gets so routine."

Seth had already decided that he wouldn't beg for his life, that he wouldn't lower himself to that. He was fascinated, in a morbid way, by the man who he'd initially assumed to be a brainless brute who could do nothing but fight, eat, and shit. "So you were always a savage then? Just one with a better cookbook?"

Red laughed, a guttural noise that jiggled his body. "When I was about your age, I was an Eagle Scout. Then I studied abroad. Fell in love with all the different cultures and cuisines of the world."

"And now look at you," Seth said.

Red reached back into the pail and extracted another hunk of meat. He stepped toward him and held it above his face. "How long's it been since you've had meat? Real meat, not something sitting in a can or bag for a decade."

Seth stared up at the moist, raw morsel.

"You have to be craving it. It's only human, after all." Red squeezed the meat and some blood seeped out. A fat drop of it collected on the underside, then rained down.

Seth pinched his lips tight and turned his head sideways. The blood landed on his cheek and dripped across his face and into his ear.

Red laughed again, then popped the bite into his own mouth. "Your loss."

"Fuck you, you Jeffrey Dahmer knock-off. Go ahead and eat me. I hope I give you the shits so bad your asshole prolapses."

Red ran his hands across Seth's chest, which had been stripped bare. He massaged his muscles using blood as a lubricant. "You'll make a fine meal, young man. Good and tender. Unlike your friend over there." He threw a look to the corner where he'd retrieved the knife.

Seth strained to see, to find what - who - the man was talking about. His neck gave an electric shock as he pinched a nerve craning too far. And then he saw the body.

There wasn't much to see. There was no head. It had been stripped of flesh and meat from the chest to the waist. But when he saw the legs, and their loose, black skin, he knew. It was Trooper. This bastard had butchered Trooper and tried to feed him to him.

Seth felt a new pain, this time in his heart, in his soul. It took every bit of emotional strength he possessed not to dissolve into a blubbering mess. "You motherfucker. You better kill me because if I get off this table I'll rip your throat out with my teeth. I promise you that."

"Idle threats," Red said. "You aren't going anywhere. Not in your condition." He motioned downward with his eyes.

Seth peered down at himself. He saw his chest, his waist, his right leg. And nothing more.

His left leg was missing from above the knee. A rope tourniquet was tied tight around his thigh. And there was so much blood.

"What did you do to me?" Seth asked. His breathing quickened and he felt like his body was covered in biting ants.

"Easy now. You weren't using it."

Seth continued to hyperventilate. He felt his thoughts blur, his thinking slow.

"Seriously, boy, calm down. Otherwise, you're just going to pass out and when you come to, I'll have to explain this to you all over again."

"Why'd you kill Trooper and not me?"

"The old guy didn't give us a choice. We had to kill him." He patted Seth's useless, numb right leg. "Because of your... limitations, we can keep you around a while. That way the meat stays fresh."

He grabbed the knife and moved it toward Seth's right leg. "You'll last us a couple of days, maybe even a week if we ration you properly. So, you get to stick around, live a little longer, and we get more pleasing meals. Everybody wins, right?"

Red danced the knife across Seth's leg, toying with him, and Seth couldn't watch it anymore. The man was right, he was teetering on the edge of consciousness and he was about to fall into the abyss.

He looked past the big man, out of the cage, and into the night. Then, he saw a figure silhouetted by the firelight. He knew the shape as well as he knew the sound of his own voice.

It was Wyatt. And he didn't hesitate.

Wyatt swung Red's own ax, raising it over his head and bringing it down on the cannibal. Red crumpled to the ground, motionless.

"Did you kill him?" Seth asked his brother.

"I sure as hell hope so." Wyatt went to quick work on Seth's restraints.

"Trooper's dead," Seth said.

"I know. But we don't have time to talk about that right now." He freed Seth's wrists.

"You're such a fucking idiot for coming after me."

"Your gratitude is overwhelming," Wyatt said while he loosened the strap around his neck. "Where's your chair?"

"How the hell am I supposed to know?"

Seth winced as Wyatt pulled him into a seated position. "Does your leg hurt?"

Seth stared at his stump. It looked like it should, but it was numb as always. The pain that should have been firing there like lightning bolts had redirected itself everywhere else in his body. "Nah."

"It looks so fucking gross," Wyatt said.

"Thanks, brother. I needed that." Seth grinned and Wyatt managed one back.

Then he squatted in front of him. "Hop on."

In any other situation, Seth would have protested, but this was not the time for pride. He did as told and let Wyatt carry him from the cage piggyback style. As they passed Red, Seth saw the axe protruding from his head. He hawked the biggest ball of phlegm and snot he could manage and spat it into the bastard's corpse. "Fuck you, freak."

After escaping, Wyatt galloped away from camp while Seth gawked at their surroundings. He saw another dozen cages, each holding a prisoner, some more than one. He recognized the Captain who had burst into their campsite weeks earlier. The bearded man paced back and forth in his pen like an animal and Seth saw his arms had both been amputated.

Other prisoners were missing legs, like himself. One man was nothing but a head and torso. Each cage brought some new horror and Seth had to look away. "Run, brother."

Wyatt did, but they'd only made it twenty or so yards when the screaming started.

Two cannibals, both smaller than Red, chased after them. One clutched Red's axe which still dripped with his blood. The other held an aluminum baseball bat. As neither was carrying a man on their backs, they quickly closed the distance and within seconds were on their heels.

Seth felt a burst of pain and heard a crack as the bat slammed into his back and a rib snapped. The force of the blow sent them stumbling forward and both Morrill brothers hit the ground.

The cannibal with the bat swung again and Seth got his arms up just in time to save his face. He saw Wyatt draw and aim his pistol at the man with Red's ax. Then the gun went off and that man took three staggering steps backward. A nickel-sized hole in his shoulder oozed blood, but it wasn't enough to put him down. He came at Wyatt again and Wyatt shot again.

Seth didn't get to see what happened because the bastard with the bat was back at work on him. He battered his arms which Seth still used as shields, but he felt like he was on the verge of broken bones.

The man screamed as he raised the bat for another swing.

Before the man could follow through, River exploded from the darkness. He tackled the Babe Ruth wannabe to the ground and wailed on him with furious fists. Punch after punch, landed on the cannibal's face.

"You ate my friends, you did this to me!" River screamed.

The cannibal struggled, but River pulled a rock the size of his hand from his pocket and went to work with it. The first blow shattered the man's nose. The second caved in his right eye socket. The third finished him off.

River bounced to his feet and then he looked to Seth. "You lost a leg, friend."

Seth flashed a wry smile. "Observant as always, River."

"River sees things. River knows things."

Seth noticed things too. He saw Red's discarded axe lying on the ground and grabbed it. Even if he didn't need to put it to use, it would be one hell of a keepsake.

Wyatt grabbed Seth and set him up. River helped him onto Wyatt's back. And then they heard the entire clan of cannibals running their direction.

Seth sighed. Why couldn't any of this be easy?

CHAPTER FIFTY-ONE

"THAT DON'T LOOK GOOD," RIVER SAID. "THAT DON'T LOOK GOOD at all."

"Brother, this is the part where we get the hell out of Dodge," Seth said.

Understatement of the century, Wyatt thought as the horde barrelled down on them.

He spun them away from the coming cannibals, running as fast as his legs would carry them which wasn't nearly as quick as usual with Seth riding shotgun on his back.

"This way." River pointed toward a grouping of rocks that funneled in the land below. He took off in that direction and Wyatt, and Seth by default, followed.

The course through the rocks was maze-like and Wyatt hoped to hell River knew what he was doing. They zigged, zagged, and zigged again and the sounds of the attackers at their rear faded with each turn. Maybe the man wasn't completely crazy after all.

Another series of turns and they broke free of the labyrinth, into open land. And almost ran smack into three cannibals who huddled around a small fire.

They were emaciated and haggard. The runts of the litter, Wyatt thought. They looked like the walking dead and he wondered if they were infected with some disease and sent away to die.

Whatever their malady, their reason for being cast out, they scrambled to their feet when Wyatt and company arrived. Before they could do more than that, River ran straight at them, flailing his arms like he was doing some kind of manic dance move.

He rambled incoherently, making noise and uttering sounds Wyatt couldn't decipher aside from his name - River - dropped in at random intervals. The cannibals stared at him, then gave each other a look that Wyatt read as What the fuck is up with this loon?

And then they charged.

Wyatt felt Seth's hot breath in his ear. "Wyatt, run."

He did as told, breaking past River and toward the two cannibals. Seth swung the axe as if he was a mounted knight riding his steed into battle. He lopped off the head of the nearest man, then pivoted and chopped into the chest of the second. Both fell to the ground, bleeding and motionless. The third man must have seen enough and fled in the opposite direction.

River reached into their fire and pulled out a blazing tree limb. He held it over his head like a torch.

In the distance they could hear the main group of cannibals getting closer. Not within sight, but it wouldn't be long.

River pointed toward a dry creek bed a few hundred yards away. "You go that way. Follow it until you come to the granite rock. It's real big, you can't miss it. Then go east. That'll take you back to where you came from."

"Why are you telling me this? Just come with us." Wyatt said.

River shook his head. "River has some amends to make," he said. "I think my friends would be proud. Even though I don't have any." He threw a wink at Wyatt.

"We're your friends, River. So let's go."

But River scrambled in the opposite direction, casting one last look back at them. "Remember to be like River. Keep runnin'."

The man took off like an Olympic sprinter and soon all they could see of him was the light of his torch.

"No time to be sentimental," Seth said.

He was right. Wyatt ran toward the creek, Seth bouncing along for the ride. When the cannibals broke free of the rocks, the brothers saw them follow River's light into the desert. And Wyatt managed to catch his breath because this battle was finally over.

CHAPTER FIFTY-TWO

WYATT WALKED ALL NIGHT AND FOR SEVERAL HOURS AFTER daybreak. He was exhausted almost to the point of delirium but didn't plan to quit until they got back to the farmhouse. They had to get back before the others left them. Why hadn't he given himself more than 48 hours?

He paused, twisting at the waist to stretch out his aching core. "Dude, you're one heavy motherfucker."

Seth's head rested on his shoulder and Wyatt felt it move.

"You really need to rethink that sentence," Seth said. "That's your mom you're talking about."

"Oh. Yeah." Wyatt sighed and resumed his trek wondering how his brother could always be so sharp. Like he never gave his mind a rest.

"Besides, I should be approximately eleven pounds lighter than I was before."

"Eleven pounds? That's oddly specific. How'd you come up with that?" This wouldn't have been Wyatt's first choice when it came to subject matter, but the conversation was the only thing keeping him from collapsing where he stood.

"I figure I weigh about one-twenty. Maybe less since we hit the road. We're all a bit thin, aren't we? Either way, I was thinking about a pound and a half for the foot. Another four point five for my calf. And five-ish pounds for the chunk of thigh that bastard chopped off." He raised his eyebrows. "Eleven pounds."

"That's fucked up"

"No, it's science."

Wyatt was trying to figure out how Seth came up with those numbers when he saw the lake in the distance. He was so shocked that they'd actually made it that he needed to verify it wasn't all in his head.

"Do you see that?" Wyatt asked. He turned sideways to give Seth a better view.

"A lake."

"Thank God," Wyatt said. "I thought it might be a mirage."

"Not unless we're experiencing group hysteria."

He continued on. It was just a little further. One step at a time. That's what he kept telling himself.

"Hey, brother," Seth said.

"Yeah?"

"Thank you."

"Anytime," Wyatt said. "Anytime."

They fell silent after that, not sharing another word as they circled the lake or pushed through the grass, or even when the farmhouse came into view. And that was okay because everything that needed to be said had been said.

CHAPTER FIFTY-THREE

THE REUNION WENT THE WAY REUNIONS GO. SMILES, TEARS, hugs. Wyatt even got an open-mouthed kiss - from Supper. But as happy as he was to see everyone, what he needed was sleep and that's what he did for the next 30 or so hours.

WHILE HE WAS OUT BARBARA HAD CAUTERIZED SETH'S amputation site. Seth later told him it smelled like barbecue and Wyatt realized that eating from cans wasn't so bad after all. Fresh meat might be ruined for him forever.

BEFORE HITTING THE ROAD AGAIN THEY CONVERTED ONE OF THE shopping carts into a new ride for Seth. He wasn't pleased because it meant he'd need to be pushed all the time now, but Wyatt thought he accepted the inconvenience with more maturity than he'd displayed in the past. He supposed being kidnapped and partially eaten by cannibals was bound to turn a boy into a man.

As they walked, there was occasional small talk and everyone got along fine. Even Pete wasn't being his usual prickish self.

Once in a while, Wyatt held hands with Allie, but it went no further. He was in too much pain of the emotional kind.

They all were. The absence of Trooper weighed heavy.

CHAPTER FIFTY-FOUR

"You guys! Fuck me! You guys!" Pete shouted.

As had become standard he was in the lead. He said he liked the peace and quiet of being up front, not that any of them were chatter-boxes, and Wyatt didn't mind. It seemed like he was always tired these days and having someone else set the pace kept them going.

Pete ran back to them and his expression was so foreign that Wyatt almost didn't recognize him. Pete was smiling.

"What is it, Pete?" Allie asked.

He pointed back the way he'd come. "There's a sign. Del Rio - Five miles."

None of them reacted in the way he'd apparently hoped so he stated the obvious. "That's a border town. We're almost there!"

Wyatt could barely believe his ears. This was what they'd been waiting on for months. And even though they still needed to go through Mexico and Central America to reach the equator, making it this far felt like they'd won the lottery, or landed on the moon, or some other grand achievement. It - almost - made the pain worthwhile.

THEY DRIFTED OFF THE MAIN ROAD, NOT WANTING TO VENTURE into Del Rio itself on the chance that outlaws or cannibals had taken over the city. Going south through the desert added a few miles onto the trip and a few hours, but it seemed a small price for the added safety.

"How will we know when we cross over," Allie asked.

"What do you mean?" Pete said.

"Well, if we're not on a road, how will we know when we actually go over the border? It's not like it's going to look any different."

Wyatt thought that a fair question. One for which he had no answer. It turned out he didn't need one because, after another twenty minutes of walking, the answer appeared to them in the form of a wall.

Steel beams standing thirty feet tall and spaced at six-inch intervals stretched as far as they could see in any given direction. The metal had rusted to a deep orange and was topped with cascading loops of razor wire.

"I thought it would be big and beautiful," Seth said.

"Well, it is big." Wyatt stuck his arm through one of the gaps. There was, of course, no chance of slipping through and unless his brother managed to smuggle an acetylene torch in his shopping cart, there was no going through it.

"I bet I could climb that," Seth said

"The shit you could." Pete rapped the metal with his knuckles.

"I could get further than you, baldy."

Wyatt thought the man might lose his newfound good cheer, but instead, he smirked. "Oh, you got me. I'm gonna need some salve for that burn."

CHAPTER FIFTY-FIVE

With no going through or over the wall, they needed to find an actual border crossing point so Barbara, Seth, and Wyatt walked east while Allie and Pete went west. Whoever found a pass through first was to fire off a shot.

Only it wasn't only one shot Wyatt heard. There was another. And another. And another.

"Oh shit," Seth muttered. Wyatt didn't say it aloud, but he felt the same way. Something was wrong.

He didn't realize how wrong until they saw the cannibals. It seemed like every man and woman who'd been at their camp had made the trek to the border. Wyatt would have been flattered if he wasn't scared shitless.

As he scanned the mass of people for Allie and Pete, he felt Barbara tug on his arm. He looked back at her and saw her holding one of the guns.

"Take it," she said.

He did, but couldn't comprehend her plan. "And do what?"

She handed another of the guns to Seth. "They're never going to give up, Wyatt. That's why we have to kill them. All of them."

Wyatt turned back to the cannibals. They were a hundred yards away and he couldn't get an accurate count but thought there were at least three dozen.

"We need to get closer," he said.

"Then let's go."

They halved the distance and the cannibals still hadn't caught on to their presence. Wyatt thought he might be able to shoot with some accuracy, but knew every yard, every foot, closer they could get would make a huge difference.

At thirty yards he decided to stop pressing their luck.

"Ready?"

Both Barbara and Seth nodded. They aimed their pistols. Wyatt did the same. Then they started shooting.

None of them stopped until their magazines were empty and the surrounding air was filled with acrid, blue smoke. Wyatt tried to peer through the fog, to see what damage they'd done, but all he saw were charging cannibals.

They had back up magazines ready and reloaded. Even though they were in the same place, the cannibals were closer now which made the second volley more accurate, more deadly.

Wyatt watched as blood sprayed, heads exploded, bodies fell. It was like something out of one of the video games he'd played growing up, but he took no satisfaction in doling out real death. Because even if these monsters wanted to kill and eat him and his family, they were human beings. They were people. And he was ending their lives.

By the time they were shot out for the second time only four cannibals continued the forward rush.

Why won't they stop, Wyatt wondered. Why are they making us do this?

They were closer now, too close to switch out magazines, so he grabbed one of the guns from the shopping cart and used it.

As the smoke cleared, he saw the bodies stretched out on the ground ahead of them. And beyond them, at the starting point, he saw another ten figures. He recognized three of them.

Allie.

Pete.

And Red.

"Long time no see!" The big man waved at them with a hand clutching a machete.

"I thought you killed that motherfucker," Seth said.

"So did I."

"Dude's like a fucking cockroach."

Red grabbed a handful of Allie's dreadlocks, pulled them taught, and chopped them off with his blade. Wyatt could hear her sobbing echo across the flat land.

"Send the older boy!" Red beckoned Wyatt with a wave. "No guns though or I'll cut this one's pretty throat while you watch."

Wyatt turned to his family. "Stay here."

Seth shook his head. Barbara grabbed his arm. "No, Wyatt," she said. "Don't you go and try to be a hero."

"It's what Trooper would have done."

"And Trooper's dead." Her eyes welled up when she said that.

"I know because I sat there and watched it happen. I'm not doing that again."

He took a step away from her, but his mother held on tight. He yanked his arm free and ignored her plaintive cries as he left them.

He strode through the field of bodies sidestepping the few who clung to life. As he got closer, he saw that both Allie and Pete had their arms tied behind their backs. Two cannibals who weren't Red held spears to their heads. Red had the upper hand and he was almost certainly walking to his own execution.

Wyatt wondered how Barbara and Seth would survive if he died here. Would they find their way across the border and south or was he sealing their fates too?

That was the question rolling through his head when he reached them. But he still hadn't come up with an answer.

"Brave boy," Red said. "Stupid boy, as well."

"I'm here. No guns." Wyatt held his arms to his side. "Now what?"

"Get on your knees."

"Don't do it, Wyatt!" Allie lunged toward him but the man guarding her held firm. He poked his spear against her cheek and a trickle of blood escaped.

Wyatt knelt before Red.

"Is she your woman or his?" Red tipped his head toward Pete.

"Neither," Wyatt said.

"These are some of your last words. You want them to be lies? How will you explain that to God?"

"You believe in God?"

"I believe in many things. But first and foremost is honor."

Red turned away from him and faced Allie. "Since he won't answer, how about you try? Which of these men do you see when you close your eyes at night? Tell me and I'll spare him. For now."

Allie's gaze fell to the ground and she stayed silent.

"Answer me, girlie or I'll take your hair and your scalp." Red grabbed her dreads again, jerking her sideways.

"I won't!" Allie sobbed.

Red lined the blade of the machete up with her hairline. He began to slice into her flesh, stretching her skin taut.

"Stop it!" Pete yelled.

Everyone looked to him.

His face was crimson with rage. "She's his girl now," Pete said. "So do whatever the fuck you want to me."

Wyatt couldn't believe the man had spoken up, that he'd been honest, because it was going to cost him his life. And it pissed him off that Pete had picked now of all times to be a decent human being.

"Ah, see. Was that so hard? Thank you." Red nodded and the man who was holding Pete rammed the spear under his jaw. It pushed up through his mouth and popped out his left eye which was skewered on the point like a cherry tomato on a shish kebab.

Allie shrieked. One of the other cannibals cut Pete's throat, then tossed his body to the ground.

Wyatt almost jumped to his feet, but Red's eyes were on him again and he stayed put.

"You should have killed me when you had the chance," Red said.

Wyatt nodded. The man was right, after all. He'd had him on the ground and helpless and didn't take the extra second to finish the job.

"I was about to say the same thing," Wyatt said. "Only the other way around."

Red's eyes narrowed. "You're not making any sense. Try again."

"*You* should have killed *me* when you had the chance."

Red grinned, revealing a set of oversized choppers that, although discolored, looked to be strong and healthy. The better to eat you with, Wyatt thought.

"Is that so?" Red asked.

"It is."

Wyatt dove to his left, hitting the dirt and reaching behind his back in one fluid motion. He grabbed the .38 from the small of his back, raised it, and shot. It was a chickenshit move, but he didn't care. There was no room for honor in the world anymore. That was a hard-earned lesson but one he'd finally accepted.

The bullet collided with Red's chin, cleaving his jaw in two and sending bone and teeth out like shrapnel. His tongue fell through the now open chasm and lolled from side to side like the pendulum on a clock.

Wyatt shot again and that one landed square in his chest and brought Red to his knees.

He spun in the dirt, toward Allie and the cannibal holding her, ready to aim and fire when--

"Hit to the ground if you want to live!"

It was a booming, somehow mechanical voice, the omniscient sound of God as heard through a school's PA system. Allie dropped immediately and Wyatt stayed where he was. They were close enough for their fingertips to touch and Wyatt rested his atop hers.

An explosion of gunfire broke out. Not the repetitive *bang, bang, bang* of pistols or rifles. These came in fast-forward, incessant, unrelenting.

The remaining cannibals were shredded by the incoming bullets and a moment later everything went silent.

Finally, a speaker crackled with static and the voice rang out again. "It's all clear. You're safe to get up."

Wyatt grabbed Allie's hand as they climbed to their feet. They turned in unison toward the voice.

What he found surprised him more than anything he'd seen on their journey so far. A group of fifteen or so men and women were grouped beside Barb and Seth. All carried military-style firearms and two others were on the ground with machine guns propped in front of them.

One of the men held a megaphone to his mouth. "Come on over. We don't bite."

Wyatt and Allie ran to them and, as they got closer, Wyatt realized how different these people looked compared to anyone else they'd encountered. They looked healthy and clean and... happy.

The man who'd been barking orders set the megaphone aside and pulled off the baseball cap he'd been wearing. He was tall and athletic with piercing blue eyes. He smashed his blond hair back into place with one hand and extended the other to Wyatt.

"The name's Alexander."

"Wyatt." He shook but felt bad because this man was so clean and he was not. He even smelled the aroma of cologne."Thanks for the help."

"Our pleasure. Those man-munchers don't belong out here. They should know better."

One of the women in the group handed Allie a cloth to wipe the blood from her cheek and brow. Another was busy checking Seth's bandaged leg. More of them passed out bottles of water to share. Wyatt sucked his down in seconds.

He couldn't believe how their luck had changed.

"Can I ask you one question?" Wyatt said.

The man nodded.

"Who the hell are you people? It's like you're angels sent straight from Heaven to save our asses or something."

Alexander laughed, a hearty, friendly sound filled with good cheer. "Or something," he said. "Why don't you come home with us? Get cleaned up. Have a decent meal. Plus, it's safe there and I'd imagine you folks haven't had the luxury of relaxing in a good, long while."

"That's the truth," Barbara said.

Wyatt looked from the new group to his family, to Allie. He saw the relief on their faces, but he realized they were waiting on him to make the decision. It seemed an easy choice.

"We'd like that," Wyatt said. "If you're sure it's not putting you out."

"Not at all," Alexander said. "There's plenty of room in the casino. And I know Papa would love to meet you. Everyone will, actually. It's been a while since we had newbies show up. It'll be good for the community."

That word - community - made Wyatt smile. Maybe his mother wanted to go south for the sun and fresh food, but what he longed for was a place where life could go on. Where people took care of each other.

He wondered if he'd finally found it.

He'd find out soon enough.

AFTERWORD

We hope you enjoyed "The Land Darkened" which is book 1 in the "Cannibal Country" series. Books 2 and 3 will be available in early 2020. And they're going to be freaking insane!

Please take a moment to sign up for our mailing lists where you'll get free stories and novellas and stay on top of all future releases.

Tony Urban's list - http://tonyurbanauthor.com/signup

Drew Strickland's list - https://www. subscribepage.com/u2x7bo_copy_copy

Printed in Great Britain
by Amazon

77695054R00144